GRENADE

Hub City, Lafayette

Doug Hebert

Dugabear Publishing

for my wife Gina

and my parents Shane & Cindy

CHAPTER 1

August 27, 2014

7:04 p.m.

Earlier that evening, long after the job interview concluded, I stumbled drunk and naked into the kitchen of my apartment. I stopped, leaned my head back against the refrigerator, took a long drag from my cigarette, and slowly cast my eyes down to the remnants of the afternoon. Cigarette butts in the ashtray, beer cans on the floor, a pill bottle in the trash, along with thirty-nine pages next to the typewriter. The day had been productive, but it was time to stop picking at that scab. At least for now.

I was in a volatile situation. Numbing myself before scratching open old wounds took a toll. It also took time, another luxury I could no longer afford. I'd cashed insurance policies, hocked guitars; I even sold my car. With the rent due once again and nothing of value to sacrifice, I became desperate.

When my landlord, who doubled as my publisher, had come to collect, my proposal of a novel drew a lukewarm response. With all the income generated from my previous writings long gone, and my current work not capitalizing on that initial success, I offered to find employment while I worked on the proposed novel. This counter would not only cover rent, but also buy time.

My landlord slash publisher smiled with devious intrigue. He knew of a place located a few blocks from the apartment. He would make a phone call on my behalf in the morning.

A squat man nearing sixty, his curly black hair and thick mustache often typecast him as a Colombian drug lord. Instead, he managed an accounting firm for years before becoming a professor at The University of Lafayette.

"One last thing," he said. "If you capitulate to the pressure, don't do it here."

With that, he stepped out into the hallway and closed the door behind him.

A pained laugh echoed about the apartment. In the beginning, there was no struggle. Countless hours spent in various libraries around the Acadiana area ushered in a slew of words akin to learning a new language. Words that were pliable, eager to be molded into story lines. But now they resisted, I no longer had control over them.

And that was what it all boiled down to. Writing afforded control. After witnessing both my father and grandfather consumed by the lack thereof, impressed upon me control meant survival. Yet there I was, willingly sacrificing what I so coveted, knowing damn well once I pulled the pin there would be no going back.

Only till the novel's done, I conceded, but the solace did little to allay my fears.

...nothing like sobering reality in the depths of a drunken stupor...

I felt nauseated. I dropped my cigarette, clutched my gut, and slid down to the floor. It would be yet another difficult night.

CHAPTER 2

August 27, 2014

8:38 a.m.

I staggered downstairs from my apartment on to Buchanan about twenty minutes to nine. The sauna-like humidity stopped me dead in my tracks. As sweat beaded on my shaved head, the Lafayette South Bank time and temperature sign located a block over at Second and Garfield caught my attention. It bore God awful news.

82° 8:38

The impulse came. Though the thought often lurked, the impulse only made the rare appearance. I stepped to the edge of the curb, but there was no traffic. As the impulse faded, the time and temperature sign informed me "Affordable, Flexible, and Innovative Solutions to My Specific Needs Were Available."

Was this divine intervention? My specific needs? All right. After spending twenty-one years with a gig as a shipping clerk, I got canned along with everyone else at the plant in the name of cheap foreign labor. With a couple months of severance before me, a drunken voicemail began a series of events that led me into becoming a writer. Success was immediate but short-lived. I stood there with thirty-nine dollars to my name, three cigarettes in my pocket, two beers in the refrigerator, and a one-month reprieve on the rent. Was there a way out? In less than fifteen minutes, I submit all that remained in one last ditch attempt at the written word. Nothing of any real value. Only mind, body, and soul. So, almighty time and temperature sign, what solutions might you offer?

Right on cue, the sign went dark. I waited out in the heat. The momentum built. I wiped the sweat off my forehead with the back of my hand. Finally, the answer appeared.

82° 8:40

Balls.

I turned to face my apartment. Once an Odell's department store, its insignia still visible on the northeast side of the building, it was home to a dance club before my landlord slash publisher renovated the first floor to include space for retail development. For Lease signs inhabited those spaces for years before a coffee shop moved in later followed by an art gallery. The next phase of the renovation called for turning the upper floor into luxury lofts. In the meantime, my apartment, which covered no more than three hundred square feet of the top floor, provided scant Third World luxuries. The plan was to remain there until I established myself as a writer. That was four years ago.

Hours for the coffee shop were 6-2. I was often in a comatose state till well past the midpoint of the day so this would be my first opportunity to venture inside. I pulled open the door. A short heavy-set woman with numerous tattoos on both arms became animated at my presence.

"He exists!" she boomed with a deep nasal voice.

I laughed.

"I about considered you Cajun folklore," she teased as I walked up to the counter, "like the rougarou."

"Rougarous got more hair."

"Don't know about that. Especially with that beard you got going on."

I smiled.

"Can I get a small coffee to go, please?"

"Of course, sweetie."

She disappeared behind a partition.

I looked around. The place was busy but not overcrowded, many of the tables occupied by college kids staring at laptop screens.

"Mike said to expect you," the woman called out.

"Is that so?"

"Yes. Room for cream?"

"Please."

The woman reappeared. She placed my coffee down on the counter. The name embroidered on her shirt read Nancy.

"So, what roused you early this morning?" she asked.

"Job interview."

"No shit? Where?"

"Thomas, Madison, Smith and Associates."

She arched an eyebrow at me.

"If you say so. No charge for the coffee. Sugar and cream's over by the door. Why don't you come down for some breakfast before you head to that fancy new job of yours?"

"I'll do that."

I prepared my coffee, looked back, and held up the cup.

"Thanks."

"Don't mention it. Best of luck on that interview, Ruston."

I walked back out into the swamp ass Louisiana heat and over to the art gallery. The placard in the window said closed. When it said open, I'd scurry by, unlock the gate that led up to my apartment, and hurry upstairs. But when it was closed, and the lights were off, I sometimes stood out front. Those paintings told stories. They captivated me.

I peered inside for a moment then began the five-block walk down Buchanan for my interview.

CHAPTER 3

August 27, 2014
9:02 a.m.

Thomas, Madison, Smith and Associates, a regional public accounting firm occupying the thirty-ninth floor of a forty-story office building in downtown Lafayette, specialized in tax preparation, financial advisory services, audit reviews, payroll, and basic bookkeeping.

The elevator deposited me there a little after nine. The doors opened to reveal a small reception area offset from an open floor filled with cubicles. To the left, closed door offices. To the right, restrooms, breakroom, and conference room. Immediately before me sat a sofa, coffee table, fake plants, and a woman seated behind a desk piled with papers and folders. She didn't appear too thrilled with her current lot in life or that I would impose upon her time. I walked up to her. She looked at me with indifference. After an awkward moment, I said, "I'm Ruston Delahoussaye. I have an interview with John Breaux at 9:15."

She handed me a clipboard.

"Fill this out," she said.

It was a brief employment application. I took a seat. A phone on the woman's desk rang. She answered.

"GOOD MORNING! Thomas, Madison! How can we help you today?"

I looked at her in disbelief. She continued with orgasmic excitement.

"Oh, yes! YES! Well, we'll put that in the mail first thing this morning! Yes! Oh my God, yes! No, thank YOU! Oh, you're welcome! Uh-huh. Have an AWESOME day!"

After hanging up the phone, she took note of my bewilderment and stared a few daggers in my direction. Impressed, I considered asking what she was doing in a place like this with that kind of ability but instead returned my focus to the task at hand.

The application concerned itself with personal information and prior work history. I filled in my name and address. The shipping clerk gig was the only job I ever held. I started the week after high school graduation and remained until the plant shut down four years ago. I made no mention of being a writer and was not sure how I would account for those missing years if the question arose. Lastly, it asked how I became aware of the job opening. There I wrote in my landlord slash publisher's name, Mike Robicheaux.

The application complete, I placed the clipboard down beside me and flipped my cell phone open to verify it was on silent. I took inventory of the atmosphere. It had a familiarity about it, comparable with the offices at the plant though I spent most of my time on the loading docks. I got on at five dollars an hour while ladies sewing up front swallowed still legal speed pills like candy, made production, and raked in.

Then came NAFTA, followed by chapter eleven bankruptcy. Hours dwindled. Other plants closed. Those with families to support jumped ship. Single, and without kids, I remained aboard the sinking vessel. Under the microscope, everything scrutinized and nitpicked, the managers harped on me constantly. We were the smallest plant still in operation. Accuracy would be key to our survival. Management entrusted me with verifying all loads before they left the yard. No easy feat with multiple shipments loaded simultaneously across several docks over the course of each day.

When the end came, after twenty-one years and a company best load accuracy of 96.3%, my forty-hour pay doubled from two to four hundred, I drove an '85 *Oldsmobile Cutlass Supreme* with a broken muffler and lived in what remained of a 12x50 1964 *Park* mobile home situated on a thumbnail of land behind a gas station on Pellerin Street in Jeanerette.

Ruston Delahoussaye
9403 S Buchanan St
Lafayette, LA 70595

Trudge

Six days a week
For over twenty years
The banal days spun
Relentlessly
Like the needle at the end of a vinyl record.
5:45am, cup of coffee, morning news, breakfast, shit, shower, shave, dress, climb into the car, drive to the plant, lights on, do a full ten rounds, lights off, drive home, supper, evening news, shower, collapse.
Confined to a routine.
Happens to a lot of people
Each day
Same place, same attire, same thing
Hard truth
Confined to a routine
To a jail cell
A coffin
Same place, same attire, same thing

"Mr. Delahoussaye?"

Roused from my funk, I saw a defeated man with sunken eyes before me. We shook. His hand was ice-cold. He introduced himself. John Breaux. He was to be my immediate supervisor.

"This way, please," he said.

I picked up the clipboard and followed. We walked past the elevator towards the row of closed-door offices. The woman behind the desk paid us no mind. We arrived at the third door. He motioned me inside. I entered a stuffy office cluttered with numerous manila folders. The closed blinds denied any chance for sunshine to breathe life into the room. Overall, it held the ambiance of a mausoleum. There was a partially opened door in the corner. Behind it a toilet and sink. A mausoleum with a shitter. Of course.

Breaux glanced over the application. His wrinkled white shirt and frayed tie matched his weary expression. A wooden placard that read John Breaux CPA/CGMA sat at the edge of his desk. The job involved basic bookkeeping duties. From what I could gather, any idiot could do the tasks required. The problem was they continually hired idiots to fill the position. Present candidate included.

Someone entered the room.

"I got it from here, John," a voice from behind said.

With a resigned expression on his face, Breaux rose from his chair and walked out.

"Ruston. Jim Guillory."

His face bloated and red, his belt straining to contain his gut, Guillory, CPA/CGMA, CFE, CGFM appeared to be a man who struggled with everything from walking to breathing. He was the main boss. He greeted me with a limp handshake before rehashing what Breaux previously stated.

"You stay at Mike Robicheaux's place, correct?"

"Yes, sir."

"Took him forever to fill those spaces up. He still talks about turning the upstairs into lofts?"

"He has mentioned that to me."

Guillory half-tossed, half-threw the clipboard off to the side. He leaned back in John Breaux's chair and pointed a pink stubby finger at me.

"Do you know why your rent is three-twelve a month?"

I shook my head.

"Mike told me he had someone lined up to do some work for him and was gonna put them up in his place on Buchanan. It was exactly 3:12 in the afternoon."

With that, Guillory exploded into a coughing and laughing fit, more cough than laughter. His face became even redder. I thought he might burst.

"Good thing we (cough) close at five, or you (cough) might have been paying six, or seven, or eight hundred (cough) a month!"

"Yes, sir."

He now had tears in his eyes.

"Or (cough), or, or if (cough) he had come at ten in the morning (cough), your rent would be (cough) a thousand (cough)!"

I smiled. I had to, I needed the job. Guillory pulled a handkerchief from his back pocket and blew his nose.

"Ruston, we've gone through two people this year. Bookkeeping ain't that difficult! You would be considered a contract worker. You interested?"

All my senses screamed in protest. I calmly nodded my head.

"Yes, sir."

I felt the grip tighten around my throat.

Guillory leaned forward and slapped John Breaux's desk with an open palm.

"All right (cough)."

We walked out to find Breaux.

"Show this man around," Guillory told him.

I spent the next half hour on a tour of the office floor with Breaux. He introduced me to a few people. Each regarded me with disdain.

"You smoke?" Breaux asked.

"Yes, sir. I do."

"We have a designated area behind the manager's parking lot."

Breaux told me the company had multiple locations in the state. But by that point, my interest had waned.

The location of the copy machine and the number to the IT department may have been relevant to some virgin intern with sights set on one day achieving office domination. But I was more interested in the ability to maneuver my way through the jealousies, rumors, and pettiness that often festers inside a competitive workplace environment so I might survive my eight hours a day unscathed and get my novel done.

The last stop on the tour was the cubicle I would be confined to. Isolated from the others, back near the restrooms, it appeared dark, cramped, and bleak. Numerous manila folders, envelopes, and check stubs sat piled high.

As I peered inside, the possibility of perishing within the confines of that dismal space became real. If that would be the summation gathered from my obituary, I just as soon let go now. Whether I remained in that cubicle for the next thirty years or put a gun to my head today, both outcomes would be the same.

The tour complete, and with the understanding I would start the following Tuesday after the Labor Day weekend, Breaux escorted me to the elevator. Just as the doors closed, the woman seated behind the front desk gave me an ominous look.

I headed north on Jefferson and stopped at The Discount Mart on the thruway. I picked up a couple packs of cigarettes and a case of beer. Back at the apartment, I poured a drink, lit a cigarette, chased the last few pills a street hustler named Borel had given me down with a generous swig, and commenced typing.

CHAPTER 4

September 3, 2010
SWLA Free Press
the last stop comes into view
by ruston delahoussaye
Volume 4 Issue 7

An announcement came over the intercom. All shipping personnel report to the conference room. Men sporting expensive suits and shiny shoes greeted us with well-rehearsed looks of concern. They'd flown in that morning from the corporate office. All that was missing were the blindfolds and cigarettes. They informed us the plant was shutting down at the end of the year. They thanked us for our hard work and dedication and said to return to our assigned areas immediately.

Many of my co-workers appeared stunned. Others loudly expressed their anger. At the conclusion of our shift, I saw the men from corporate out in the parking lot taking off their coats and loosening their ties. There was laughter, along with good-natured slaps on the back. I drove off. I needed to go someplace and contemplate what happened. Those with families headed home, contemplating how they would tell their loved ones the news. While the corporate men headed to the casinos, contemplating their luck at the tables before their flight back to company headquarters.

We later learned the decision to close the plant had been made eight months prior to that day. During that time, someone in the receiving department purchased a home. Another acquired land. Major acquisitions made by dedicated hard-working employees confident with their job security. A secretary from payroll bought a brand-new car with a six-year note. A few people went look at it, including a manager, fully aware of the plant's impending fate.

I drove to the city park with a cooler full of beer, walked down to the boat ramp, and sat along the banks of the Bayou Teche. I cracked open a beer and thought of my grandparents. Their house stood not far from the bayou. We spent many weekends there boiling crawfish and barbecuing. During the winter months, grandma would make a seafood gumbo, and we'd crowd around the kitchen table as we ate and played games.

An avid reader and storyteller, my grandfather might have become a writer himself had he not decided on a career in the oilfield following his military service. His retirement was visible on the horizon when the oil boom went bust in the eighties. I dreaded those weekends after he got let go. It was as though attending a wake. Everyone spoke in hushed somber tones with meals nothing more than finger foods.

My grandfather rarely talked after that. He mostly sat and stared off into space. But he did find work, and he and grandma made it through, till he passed from a heart attack a few years later.

Afternoon turned into evening. A motorboat went by.

My dad didn't go out to the oil platforms in the Gulf. Instead, he gained employment with a local hometown bank established at the turn of the century and still going strong some eighty years later. Until new management came to town. Like my grandfather, dad found work. It was when he went in for the physical that they detected the cancer.

My grandfather was let go at 54, my dad at 45. Once proud men who withered away, how much time remained for me at 39? And what would I leave behind? My grandfather had my dad. My dad had my brother and sister and me. The pallets I stacked and shrink-wrapped at the plant were all I had. There might be a wadded-up copy of a bill of lading somewhere with my signature on it. Other than that, the only trace of me would be a headstone at a gravesite no one would visit.

Many beers later, I needed to piss. I stood and took a long one into the bayou. In no shape to drive, I walked home. Once inside, the cooler fell from my grasp. Beer cans rolled out across the floor in all directions. I just about tripped over one and took my bookshelf down with me. Soon came morning. The hangover brutal, I burned some eggs on the stove and washed them down with a can of warm beer before I walked back to the park to retrieve my car.

CHAPTER 5

September 2, 2014

Tuesday morning, I decided to take Nancy up on her offer. After handing the young woman working the register my debit card, I sensed someone sneak up from behind. Two heavily tattooed arms wrapped around me. The woman behind the counter rolled her eyes in disgust.

"GOTCHA!"

It was Nancy.

"I scared you, didn't I?"

"You sure did."

The coffee was hot and the food delicious. Nancy talked my ear off. Born a Resweber in Eunice, she married a Robicheaux from Duson who worked offshore. She did accounts payable for the same company. After she had a premonition the price of oil would drop, she decided to quit and open her own business. Her husband's brother, who happened to be my landlord slash publisher, had a space available.

The young woman came over to refill my coffee. I sensed she would love nothing more than to cut my balls off with the plastic knife I held. Nancy made introductions.

"This is my oldest daughter, Samantha. She's a student at UL. She helps me out sometime."

When I went to leave, Nancy offered a ride. Samantha voiced her disapproval. They made a scene. Samantha got in her mom's face.

"Mom! I will bring him!"

She pulled into an open parking space near the corner of Buchanan and Convent. She was the spitting image of her mom. Dirty blonde hair, blue eyes, tats on both arms.

"Mom gets bored with dad gone all the time. Just so you know, I've about had enough of assholes taking advantage of her."

"Samantha, I'm not interested in your mom."

She looked at me. I felt she wanted to believe me.

I reached for the door.

"Thanks for the ride."

I took the elevator up to the thirty-ninth floor. Breaux escorted me to my cubicle and gave me a crash course in bookkeeping. He said if I got stuck to DILLY, Do It Like Last Year. I took a seat and grabbed a stack of check stubs. I struggled mightily. My first bank reconciliation was off over $10,000. An hour passed before I got it to balance. No fireworks went off. I placed all paperwork in their appropriate folders. Now what? I was to grab the next stack and continue. I needed a cigarette.

The smoking area was right where Breaux said it would be. A few stood taking puffs and scrolling on their phones. A tall guy with long dreadlocks walked up.

"What's up, bruh?"

"How you doing?"

"You new here?"

"First day."

He laughed.

"Who you with?"

"Thomas, Madison on thirty-nine."

He raised a closed fist to his mouth.

"Oh damn! Ya'll some high rollers up on that floor."

"You know it. What about you?"

"Judice Real Estate on twenty-two."

He gave me a firm handshake.

"Winslow."

"Ruston. How long have you been in real estate, Winslow?"

He took a long drag from his cigarette and blew smoke out as he talked.

"Three years. Fuckin' love it, bruh. You just happened to catch me here today. I rarely come to the office. I can work anywhere there is Wi-Fi."

"I'm envious, man."

"Hell yeah, bruh."

He handed me his business card.

"You ever in need of a new spread, give me a holla."

I finished my cigarette and headed back up. A cup of coffee from the breakroom sounded nice. A couple women were in there sitting at a table. They abruptly cut short a devilish laugh they were having and stared at me. This would not be good.

"Well, *hello*," the brunette on the left said.

"How ya'll doing?"

"Tell me; is it Rusty, or Russell?"

A blonde on the right snickered.

"Actually," I said, "it's Ruston."

"Ooh," the blonde said, "sexy."

"Sure, whatever," said the brunette. "So, tell me, *Ruston*, is it true you don't have a car?"

Last week, Breaux made me aware of the need of a parking permit if I were to utilize the employee parking lot. This woman was responsible for doling out said permits.

"Yes. That's true."

"How can you not have a car? How do you get to work?"

"I walk. I only live a few blocks away."

"What if it rains?"

"I own an umbrella."

"What if you go across town?"

"The bus. Or a cab."

Her voice grew frustrated.

"What about out of town?"

"I would rent one."

She huffed in disgust. The blonde chimed in.

"What if you take a woman out on a date?"

"Let me guess," the brunette said. "You would rent a car and a cab driver would chauffeur you around. How wonderful. I'm sure the three of you will have an amazing time. Don't forget your umbrella."

With that, they all exploded into laughter. That was my cue. I turned and walked out. I sure could have used that coffee.

Back at my cubicle, the next month of bank reconciliations only took thirty minutes to complete, and by the following month, I had gotten the hang of it. As long as I entered the correct amounts in their corresponding boxes, the bookwork program did the rest. There was no thinking involved, and that was the idea when I sold it to Robicheaux last week.

By day, I'd put in my eight hours. By night, the typewriter would snap to life. In no time, the novel would be complete. I would then turn in my resignation at Thomas, Madison, Smith and Associates, or just stop coming all together. It might take a few weeks, maybe a couple months, but I was determined to write my way out of this. There was no other option. In the meantime, I grabbed another stack of check stubs and continued.

At five, I logged off the computer and took the elevator down. I exited the building, walked behind the Buford Monument, crossed Lee Street, and made my way to The Bistro. I took a seat near the cash register. Harleigh Hebert, a waitress there and a friend, turned and saw me. I met Harleigh the day I moved to Lafayette. She even saved my life that day.

"Well, look who decided to show his face," she said in her hoarse cracked voice.

"Take it easy, Rosceaux. I had a rough day at the office."

"Yeah right."

She pulled her orange hair back into a ponytail, then paused and dropped both arms to her sides.

"Wait. What the fuck did you do?"

"I got a job."

"A job? What about the novel?"

"I'm going to work this job as I write the novel."

She folded her arms across her chest.

"Look, I had to do something," I continued. "The money's gone and the rent's due."

"I guess. Where are you working?"

"Thomas, Madison, Smith and Associates."

"Jesus Christ! So what, now you're one of those conservative corporate cocksuckers?"

"Precisely. And tomorrow we begin taking away guns and handing out free abortion vouchers."

Harleigh grinned and slid me a beer.

"Bastard."

I tilted the bottle back. It went down easy.

A few hours later, I headed to my apartment. When I made the corner from Congress on to Buchanan, something red in the distance caught my attention. Shoes. Bright red shoes worn by a young lady sitting on the bench in front of the art gallery. She seemed to be expecting me. Middle twenties, slender, cute, with strawberry blonde hair, green eyes, and a turned-up nose. She was magic.

"Hello Ruston," she said with a mischievous grin and heavy Texas accent. "I heard you were on the loose."

She held out her hand.

"I'm Evangelina."

We shook. Electricity shot all through me.

"Nancy told me you got a job."

"Did she?"

"Indeed. Mr. Robicheaux once told me you were a writer."

"Yes, I was once."

She flashed her mischievous grin.

"You didn't say anything about my new car."

She motioned toward a light blue *Volkswagen* parked nearby.

"I would have thought red might be your color," I said.

She glanced down at her shoes and smiled as she tucked a loose strand of hair behind her ear.

"They called it red. Sorry, that was burgundy. I know my colors. But this is a pleasing one, don't you think?"

With that, she stood and walked around to the driver's side of the pleasing light blue colored Volks, leaving an intoxicating trail of strawberry scented perfume in her wake. Her arm brushed against mine. Zap!

"By the way, if you see anything in the gallery you like, come inside *when I'm open*. Don't just stand out here like a lost puppy when I'm closed."

I looked at her.

She laughed.

"There's a room in the back. I sometime spend the night."

The Volks started right on cue. She gave a wave then took a left on Garfield.

I stood for a moment breathing in the lingering effects of her scent, then checked the mail, unlocked the gate, and went upstairs. Later, I undressed and climbed in bed. Next thing I knew my phone read 3:30. It had been quite some time since I had fallen asleep without some sort of chemical or pharmaceutical assistance. I lit a cigarette, took a seat before the typewriter, and stared at the blank page. About a quarter to seven, I headed to the office. The page was still blank.

CHAPTER 6

September 4, 2014

About mid-morning on my third day, I heard a woman scream something about a gun from across the office floor. I jumped from my chair, expecting to find a chaotic scene unfolding before me. Instead, I only saw the others peeking timidly above the walls of their cubicles. I did not see a gun or anyone with a gun.

The prospect of dying in an office shooting never occurred to me. I imagined the news blurb.

> *Ruston Delahoussaye, 43, of Lafayette, was only employed with the firm for three days. He leaves behind a mother, two siblings, and a half ass attempt at an unfinished novel.*

There was no mad scramble for the exits. Instead, everyone stood frozen, faced in the direction of a danger unbeknownst to me. Were we being held hostage? Was it a displeased client? A domestic situation? Maybe even a disgruntled former employee? With no idea of what was going on, I remained in my cubicle.

Ten minutes passed. Nothing happened. Then the elevator doors opened, and a casually dressed woman emerged. Instead of warning her of imminent danger, everyone watched in silence as she turned left and sashayed her way out of my view.

Another ten minutes went by. Just as I was about to lose interest, I saw the woman making her way back to the elevator. Behind her, with a defeated expression on his face, walked Mike Touchet, CPA. When they arrived at the elevator, the woman's eyes met mine. The look of bewilderment on my face seemed to amuse her. I still didn't see a gun.

The sequence of events that transpired quickly spread across the office floor but due to my rank and file no one informed me as to what had occurred. As far as I can piece the story together, Glenn Richard, CPA, CFE, was with Touchet when a discussion grew heated. A shoving match ensued. Richard threw Touchet to the ground. Touchet drew a pocket pistol from somewhere off his person. A secretary screamed.

The woman from the elevator was Touchet's wife. She worked nearby in the downtown area. The secretary that screamed called her rather than 911. She walked into her husband's office and berated him until he put the weapon down. Astonishingly, no one took the incident seriously.

I saw Richard later that day. Someone commended him on his composure. Another called him a hero for not allowing the situation to escalate out of control. I happened to notice the jogging pants he wore. No mention was made of the composed hero shitting himself.

The remainder of the day went by without another weapon drawn. That evening, I sat before the typewriter and pounded out fifty-two hundred words regarding the lone survivor of an office shooting. I wrote how law enforcement was struck by the man's composure; his face unmoved as he described the sequence of events as they unfolded. Though seemingly truthful and forthcoming, the man withholds a crucial detail: The pocket pistol concealed inside his blazer. He had not resorted to using it, only because someone had beaten him to it.

The next morning, I leaned against the kitchen counter and read over what I wrote. After I was done, I threw the pages in the garbage and headed for the office.

CHAPTER 7

September 5, 2014

The phone in my cubicle rang.

"Hello?"

"Ruston?"

"Yes?"

"This is Darby."

"Yes?"

"Can you come help me?"

"Sure."

"Thanks!"

I hung up and rose from the chair.

Who was Darby?

I walked across the office floor. The blonde from the breakroom smiled and waved me over. The other day, she dressed modestly in bland office attire. Today, she sported bright red lipstick, matching acrylic nails, tight tan pants, and a snug white blouse. The purpose of her outfit I gathered to send someone a message.

"Thank you so much! I'm Mr. Breaux's secretary. He told me to call you."

Three boxes needed to go down to the file room on the twenty-eighth floor. Darby provided a dolly, a list of bin numbers, and the door code. I was in the process of placing the second box in its appropriate bin when I heard the code being inputted and the door open. Darby walked in.

"Hey!"

"Hey."

"No problems?"

"No."

"I want to apologize for the other day."

"Don't worry about it."

"I looked for you on Facebook."

"I'm not on Facebook."

"Why not? I found you on Wikipedia."

"Wiki what?"

"Ha! Wikipedia. I guess you could say it's an online encyclopedia. It said you're a writer. Are you working here for a story?"

"I guess you could say that."

Her fascination with me was a little disconcerting. Darby Naquin, in her early thirties, had married at seventeen. Her husband, the 2013 Lafayette Businessman of the Year, was twenty years her senior. I gave my full attention but felt uncomfortable alone with her on this isolated floor. Sure enough, suspicious eyes greeted us on our return to thirty-nine.

Non-tax season hours on Fridays were 8-12. I left the office at noon, headed to the cafe near my apartment, and got a plate lunch of fried catfish, smothered okra, roasted potatoes, and a small piece of pecan pie. I walked down to Girard Park, found a shady tree, ate, and dozed off. A familiar voice awakened me.

"Well, I'll be damned."

I opened my eyes. It was Harleigh. She stood next to her bike.

"Must be nice," she said.

"The work bored me, Rosceaux."

She rolled her eyes, put the kickstand down, and took her place beside me.

Harleigh Hebert was originally from Winnfield. The birthplace of Louisiana politics I once heard. She'd been born a blonde, evidenced by old, cracked *Polaroid* pictures she showed me not long after we first met. After a semester at Northwestern State, she transferred to UL. She wanted to become a teacher. Then she met Randall Desormeaux on the McKinley Strip one weekend. Randall, from Denham Springs, attended LSU for medicine. She told him she was a virgin. He said he respected that. She swooned.

The first time he cheated on her, he apologized profusely. Cried real tears, said he could not exist without her. The second time he blamed her. Said she wasn't attending to his needs as a man. He labeled the third time a mistake. Then he proposed.

On their wedding night, he basically raped her. She was hesitant. He was persistent. He said he waited long enough. She confided in her mom. Her mom told her a good Catholic woman submits to her husband.

Randall continued to cheat on her. One day she walked in on him with another woman in their downstairs bathroom. Harleigh said it was over and started packing her belongings. Randall placed a gun to the back of her head. She attempted to run but tripped just as he fired. The bullet missed, but her head hit the corner of a glass table. There was a lot of blood. Randall apparently thought he killed her and walked out of the house. Police located his body the following morning in a sugar cane field a few blocks away.

A couple years later, some friends introduced her to Randy. She worked on the south side. He managed a store at the mall. They urged her to give him a call. The time had come to move on, they said. She walked in on him with one of those friends one afternoon. Harleigh threw the woman out of a second-floor window then beat Randy senseless. She was subsequently arrested, given probation, and issued a restraining order.

My first day in town, a food truck parked near The Tongue sculpture by the library. As I waited for my order, Harleigh, sporting blue hair and numerous piercings, rode by and saw my profile. Randy also shaved his head and sported a beard. There was a strong resemblance. She threw her bike down and lunged forward. I turned just in time. She looked up at me with rage and confusion.

"Can I buy you a waffle?" I asked.

I got the attention of the lady at the window.

"Add another Rosceaux to my order, please."

After we finished our buttermilk fried chicken and hot honey waffle sandwiches, we shared fries and war stories.

"Be glad you turned around when you did," she said. "Or I would have beaten you to a bloody pulp."

"You saved my life. Thank you, I appreciate that."

She laughed.

We sat this afternoon in silence up against a tree under a bright blue sky observing the goings-on in Girard Park. We saw runners, walkers, and disc golf enthusiasts. There were intense pick-up games played on the basketball courts for money and bragging rights while kids nearby made a raucous on the enclosed playground.

Around five, we made our way to Parc International for the first Downtown Alive of the season. We cut through the campus and followed University to Lee. Harleigh, her orange hair blowing wildly in the wind, walked her bike alongside me. Many assumed we were a couple which was only to her advantage. She developed a tough outer shell that warded off potential suitors. The remainder eliminated by the belief she was in a relationship. The simple truth was we trusted one another, and that meant a lot in the world today.

After the music stopped, we went to The Bistro. Harleigh locked her bike outside to the yellow lattice fence. She took off her jacket and hung it on the back of a chair while I bought the first round. We threw our cigarettes and lighters on the table and settled in. Karen, the owner and Harleigh's boss, came sit with us.

When Harleigh first introduced me to Karen Migues, she hugged me like a long-lost friend. A nurturer of local artists and musicians, she turned a dilapidated old house into one of the most adored live music venues and galleries in the area. Though legally classified as a restaurant, the business routinely met resistance for selling more alcohol than food. Karen's efforts to amend this staunched because of a moratorium on new downtown bars. She resorted to buying food herself and donating it to local charities.

As she talked to us, equal parts stress and frustration began to swell in her eyes.

"Is there anything we can do?" I asked.

"Order some food!" she cried as she ran her fingers under her eyes, wiping away the tears and smeared makeup.

"We can certainly do that," I said.

Harleigh wanted a chicken salad. I got a burger plus another round of drinks. Harleigh's roommate Theresa joined us.

Standing over six-four, with hair down to her ass, Theresa Elias made her living as a PG rated cam girl. She had gained a substantial online following doing nothing more than folding clothes, vacuuming, watching television, and exercising all while clad in only bra and panties. Subscribers paid a monthly fee. She auctioned her undergarments off to the highest bidder at the conclusion of each performance. She once offered me a complementary pair of undies after a particularly sweaty workout. I politely declined.

Seeing her duck her head as she entered The Bistro always got a chuckle out of me and Harleigh. Once, at Girard Park, an errant throw from a nearby baseball game headed in our direction.

"Theresa!" Harleigh yelled out.

Instinctively, I ducked. We both laughed on that for a good while.

Later, the crowd thinned, and we called it a night. I watched Harleigh water a small bamboo plant she kept behind the lattice fence. She then got on her bike and headed south on Johnston. I walked back to my apartment.

CHAPTER 8

Darby happened to mention the IT department placed previously abused laptops up for sale. One morning an email indicated just that. The inclination to trade in my typewriter was something I'd been considering. Not that it would matter much. I had not put anything down on paper concerning the novel in over a week.

The email said to ask for someone named Barry on the twenty-fourth floor. A pale thin guy wearing glasses and sporting a puberty mustache sat at a tall table covered with computer parts.

"Can I help you?"

"Yes sir, I'm looking for Barry."

"You got a warrant?"

I gave a confused look.

"You found him, bub," he said.

"I'm Ruston Delahoussaye. I'm here about the laptop."

"Ah, yes. Follow me."

In another room were laptops adorned with yellow post-it notes. He passed a few before he settled on one. The asking price of $250 outmatched the fourteen dollars I had on me. Barry informed me payroll could deduct it from my paycheck.

"They can do that?"

"Darn tootin' fig newton."

He placed a phone call to the payroll department. A woman answered.

"Hello."

"Ah, Diane."

"Yeah."

"Barry."

"Yeah."

"Mr. Ruston Delahoussaye is here with me. He's decided to take the laptop for two fifty. He has a commune in Gueydan and blogs about potted meat sandwiches."

There was silence on the other end. Barry winked at me.

"Can I speak to Mr. Delahoussaye?" Diane asked.

I spoke up.

"I'm here."

I agreed to knock twenty-five dollars off my debt over the coming weeks. Diane questioned if there was anything else. Barry leaned forward.

"HOW 'BOUT 'DEM COWBOYS?"

She hung up.

He burst into laughter.

"I always mess with her."

Barry retrieved a canvas bag with a shoulder strap and placed my new purchase inside. The next morning, I went down to the coffee shop and met Nancy's husband Dean. Dean listened to pop country, wore a backwards ball cap, drove a lifted truck, and designated me a pussy with the revelation I did not hunt and fish. My lack of tattoos also soured him on the authenticity of my manhood. He lifted his sleeve to show me his latest addition. An eagle with its talons extended.

"You talked to Evangelina?" asked Nancy.

"Not for a while now," I said.

"She's having a showing Friday night. She invited us, but we're going muddin' up in Colfax. Samantha's going to open up the shop while we're gone."

Over the course of conversation, I mentioned my laptop purchase.

"Send me a friend request," Nancy said.

"A what?"

"On Facebook."

"I don't have a Facebook."

"I met Dean on there. Well, actually it was on Myspace."

Dean put his arm around her.

"Yep. She messaged me, O-M-G I'm so bored, only she typed b-o-a-r-d instead of b-o-r-e-d. So, I respond, what a coincidence, you gave me wood."

Nancy giggled.

"She starts telling me she's a foodie. So, I go all out and buy her one of them seven course meals. You know, a six-pack of beer and a link of boudin. And let me tell you what podnuh, the next morning I had me one happy beer belching boudin farting girl cuddled up next to me."

Nancy turned red as a crawfish as Dean howled with laughter. I mentioned I had no internet.

"Oh, you're welcome to use our Wi-Fi," Nancy said.

She got up from the table and returned with the password written on a piece of paper. I glanced at it, then stuck it in my pocket and headed to the office.

Later that morning, Darby came by my cubicle. She'd taken a real interest in me. It was flattering but she was a married woman. She asked if I was enjoying my new laptop.

"I haven't touched it. I don't know how to get on the internet."

"I can help. What are you doing this weekend?"

I told her I planned to head to the pub Saturday for Vinyl Brunch. She thought that was a wonderful idea. She insisted I bring the laptop and would meet me there.

On my lunch break, I went back to my apartment to catch up with Evangelina. When I arrived, the doors to the gallery were wide open. She sat on a stool working on a painting while classical music played. I stroked my beard as I took it all in. She turned her head.

"Ruston! What a surprise!"

She took off her smock, walked over, and embraced me. I breathed in her scent.

"I wanted to talk to you," she said. "I'm having a showing tomorrow evening and I would love if you could attend."

"Of course. Do you need help setting up?"

She placed both hands over her heart.

"Are you serious?"

She fanned her face.

"You made me tear up. Thank you, Ruston. I would appreciate it."

The next afternoon, there was a small delivery truck parked outside. I unlatched the door, unloaded the tables and chairs out on to the sidewalk, and brought everything inside. Evangelina marveled at me.

"You've done this before."

"I worked in a warehouse for twenty years."

"I did not know that."

We were done setting up by four. She headed home to get ready. I waited upstairs for her to return.

At seven, she threw open the doors. She hired someone to play acoustic guitar and another to serve drinks. I pitched in where needed. She had a decent turnout. At eleven, she shut it down. I stayed to help clean up.

About one that morning it was just the two of us. We sat on the floor with our backs against the wall. We both had quite a lot to drink. She told me about a road trip from her hometown of Pasadena, Texas over to New Orleans with a stopover in Lafayette. She wanted to open her own gallery and happened to see the For Lease sign in the window with Robicheaux's number at the bottom. She then grew quiet and stared at the empty wine glass in her hand.

She tried to stand. It took some effort.

"If you don't mind," she said, "I'm exhausted."

I walked out. She locked the door behind me.

It was almost noon when I awoke. I wasn't in the mood to meet Darby, but I didn't want to stand her up. She was the only one in the office who showed me any courtesy. I took a shower, shaved, and went downstairs. Through the front window of the gallery, I saw the wine glass on the floor where Evangelina had sat. I walked around to the parking lot. The Volks was not there.

Darby was waiting at the pub when I arrived.

"Where's the laptop?"

"Aw, shit."

"No problem. Don't you live close by? We can go to your place. Are you okay? Is something wrong?"

"I'm just hungry."

"Well, let's eat. The Creole omelet sounds delicious."

Later, I led Darby to my apartment. She had done herself up real nice. I especially enjoyed watching her walk up the stairs before me. I took two beers out of the refrigerator and handed her one. She sipped as she glanced around.

"This is just how I pictured your place," she said.

"Is that so?"

I didn't quite know how to take that. My apartment had a seventies style vinyl floor with large chunks of it missing. The living area consisted of a beat-up leather sofa, thirty-two inch fat back television, and a bookshelf made of cinder blocks and six pine boards. Two mismatched chairs sat near the door underneath a cream-colored Formica kitchen table while my bed was nothing more than a mattress on a box spring with two milk crates stacked atop one another acting as a bedside table.

"Are you divorced?" she asked.

"Never married."

"Kids?"

"No."

"How come?"

"Never happened."

"What about your parents?"

"Mom lives in Jeanerette. Dad died a few years back."

"Any brothers or sisters?"

"One each."

"Where are they?"

"My brother's in and out of jail. My sister lives with my mom."

"Do you keep in touch with them?"

"We have not spoken in four years."

Darby fondled the bottle in her hand.

"You're not like other guys," she said.

"What's your husband like?"

"Herman? He says I can have anything I want."

"What is something you want?"

"Another kid."

"*Another* kid? You never told me you had kids."

"I have just one. A boy. I want a little girl with blue eyes. That's why I got my nipples pierced. I have inverted nipples."

"I never heard of that."

Darby lifted her blouse and her bra.

"It's when the nipple is turned inward," she said.

She squeezed her breasts.

"Poor little David had a terrible time latching on to me when I tried to breastfeed him."

She made sure I got a good look. Her breasts were beautiful. And she knew it. They got a rise out of me. She knew that too. She pulled her bra and blouse back down and opened the laptop.

"Do you have Wi-Fi?"

I found the paper Nancy had given me and read the password out loud.

"Swingerz!!69."

Darby looked at me.

I shrugged my shoulders.

I finished my beer and grabbed another. Darby pointed her phone at me.

"Don't move."

She took my picture.

"What's that for?" I asked.

"Your Facebook page."

"Jesus Christ!"

"Oh, come on."

"Fine."

I sat next to her as she created a Facebook page for me. When she was done, she sent a friend request. I protested.

"Don't accept it. She looks like some inverted nipple freak."

Darby gave me the finger then clicked confirm.

"There. Aw, poor baby. You only have one friend. You should try being nicer to people."

"How many do you have?"

"Over fifteen hundred."

"Do you know them all personally?"

"Not even."

"So, what's the point?"

"You follow people and see what they're doing. It's interesting."

"If you say so."

"You can get Facebook notifications sent to your phone, but you'll need to upgrade from the one you have."

"I'll look into that."

She noticed the time.

"I better get going."

I walked her to her car. She warmly kissed my neck before she climbed in and drove off. Back at the apartment, I saw Samantha's car parked out front. I glanced inside the coffee shop but did not see her. Later, I was a couple bottles in when it hit. Something felt off. My focus settled on Darby's half empty bottle of beer on the kitchen table.

Up until that moment, my apartment had been my refuge from the outside world. That isolation gave me comfort. That comfort was now gone.

CHAPTER 9

With tax season fast approaching, there was now sudden interest in the accuracy of my work. Guillory and Breaux harped on me constantly. It was all too familiar. As a shipping clerk, I was the last line of defense before the product left the yard. Now I was the opening salvo. Individuals showed up at my cubicle to audit my bank reconciliations. There was no intention of sabotage on my part no matter how much I loathed the place. I would grab my lighter and cigarettes and wait downstairs.

The smoking area was partially enclosed with three adjacent parking spots next to it. At any given time, someone would back their car in and sit with the engine idling, a remarkable feat with the price of gas hovering above four dollars a gallon.

Darby occasionally accompanied me although she herself did not smoke. She was slowly becoming more flirtatious with me. I did my best not to react, but my indifference only made her more daring. It was uncomfortable. Still, she was my lone ally in the office. I played the part and jerked out my frustrations a few times each week.

After one of those smoke breaks, Darby and I shared an elevator with one Mrs. Wilhelmina Aguillard. Halfway up, Mrs. Aguillard looked at us with absolute disgust. She found the smell of cigarettes and car exhaust on our clothing offensive, and thus renewed previous efforts of hers to ban smoking from the property.

Darby told me Mrs. Aguillard came from privilege. She managed an investment firm on the top floor and thought her shit didn't stink. From what I could gather, her husband was a working stiff. Unfortunately, the same couldn't be said of his cock. So, with her nether regions numbed from too many battery powered orgasms, she resorted to other means of getting herself off. Darby clued me in on some.

In '99, she lobbied against a hardcore metal/rap outfit set to perform in town. She distributed flyers, met with church officials, even visited local media outlets with the assertion the performance, billed under the moniker "Family Values", did not in fact bear any resemblance with the traditional, conservative, wholesome values of southwest Louisiana.

Another time, she personally had NO THRU TRAFFIC signs erected along Farmington Drive near her home. Drivers used the neighborhood as a shortcut to Ambassador to avoid backup on Robley. The city removed the signs and replaced them with speed bumps. One could only imagine the thrill she got when she passed over one.

That night, Harleigh and I had a drinking bout up in my apartment. I told her about the events of the last few days. She listened in silence, then picked up her glass and spun the ice.

"So, what do you think about her?"

"Who?"

"Darby. Sounds like she's into you."

"It's awkward when she flirts with me."

"She's gonna keep messing with you if you don't do something."

"I should tell her I'm gay."

"That would only piss off the pussy liberals in your office when they find out it's not true. Don't you have enough people against you already?"

I tipped my chair on its back legs.

"Shit."

Harleigh knocked the ashes from her cigarette.

"What kind of piercings did she have?"

"Huh?"

"Straight barbell, curved barbell, CBR?"

"Uh, straight barbell, I guess."

"She really showed you her tits?"

"Yes."

Harleigh shook her head.

"It doesn't make any sense."

"That's exactly what Robicheaux said about the last short story I submitted him."

Harleigh smiled. I let the front legs of my chair come down on the floor.

"Maybe the 2013 Lafayette Businessman of the Year ain't taking care of business at home," I said.

Harleigh lifted her glass. She stopped just as it touched her lips.

"Wait. That's who she's married to?"

"You know him?"

"Do I know him? Are you fucking kidding me? Herman Naquin. He owns all those dollar stores and fast-food places in town. I worked for him before. He's a grade A douchebag."

"Serious?"

"Fuck yeah. He has these franchises that pay only minimum wage with part-time hours and no health insurance while they live in a six thousand square foot mansion in McMillan Branch. Businessman of the Year? They can kiss my ass."

She downed what remained of her drink. I poured her another.

"So, what do I do?"

"Write. Get away from there as soon as possible."

Mrs. Aguillard's efforts proved unsuccessful, though by the end of the week, two huge blowers mounted on the ceiling at opposite ends of the smoking area offered welcome relief on a warm day. Also, cars were no longer allowed access to the nearby parking spots as two trash dumpsters were now parked permanently in their place.

Friday afternoon, I met Robicheaux near the water fountains in Parc Sans Souci. I handed him two months' rent. He licked his thumb and counted the wad of bills before stuffing them into his breast pocket. He asked how the novel was progressing. I grimaced. He lit a cigarette.

"You know, Ruston," he said, "you had momentum. I truly believed that screenplay would lead to bigger and better things for you."

That screenplay, written when my writing was pulling in more income than a forty-hour work week at the plant, was Robicheaux's suggestion. He wanted to bankroll a small independent film shot somewhere around the area. He even promised Harleigh he'd campaign for her to play a part in it.

"Now look at you. You lost all that momentum."

"I don't know what to write about."

"You could always write a resume and go back to being a shipping clerk. Not that there is anything wrong with that. I mean, that was what you did before, right?"

He drew on his cigarette.

"You may want to contemplate it, because no one's anticipating a novel from Ruston Delahoussaye."

With that, he mashed his cigarette into the ground and headed east on Vermillion.

I flipped my cell phone open and called a cab. One arrived within ten minutes.

"Well, shit," the driver said, "I always gotta be driving your ass somewhere."

It was Samantha.

"What's the deal?" I asked.

"Making some extra bucks."

"I never got picked up by a female cab driver before."

"Well, I guess you can scratch that off your bucket list. Get in."

I climbed in. She pulled from the curb.

"Where to?"

"Congress and Bertrand. I'm going get a new cell phone."

I held up my current one to show her.

"Wow. A flip-phone. Mister cutting edge technology right here."

She laughed and slapped the steering wheel.

"How's your mom and dad?" I asked.

"Their cruise is coming up in November. They go every year. It's all they're concerned with right now."

She dropped me off in front of the phone store. I walked inside. A young woman with an attitude came up to me. I showed her my phone.

"I'm here for an upgrade."

"My grandpa has a phone like this. Do you have an account with us?"

"Yes."

"What's the name?"

"Ruston Delahoussaye."

"Have a seat."

She went and showed a couple of her co-workers my relic. Truth was I didn't need a new phone. The one they took turns mocking worked fine. Yet there I was.

The woman returned.

"So, Mr. Delahoussaye, what can I interest you in today?"

She ended up sweet-talking me into a smartphone that cost more than my rent. I regretted it immediately. Compared to my old phone, this one felt like a brick in my hand. It also fit awkwardly in my pocket. In addition, my monthly bill about doubled. The young woman explained how to text, email, pull up YouTube videos, stream music, and update my Facebook page. The thing even made phone calls.

I walked over to Harleigh and Theresa's place on Carl Street, but neither were home. I took a bus back to Parc Sans Souci. Downtown Alive was underway. I got a burger from a food truck parked nearby. A gentleman came up to me.

"Good evening, sir," he said.

"How you doing?"

"Jay."

"Ruston."

He gave me a firm handshake.

"Mr. Ruston, would you be interested in donating to Faith Haven Trust today?"

He motioned to a brand-new car near the stage. The rear seat was filled with numerous stuffed animals of various shapes and sizes.

"For a donation of one dollar, you'll have a chance to guess how many are in there. The closest will get the opportunity to win this car during the last Downtown Alive of the season. All proceeds go to Faith Haven Trust, a crisis center and shelter for victims of domestic violence. Are you aware that an average of three women are killed by a current or former partner each day and Louisiana ranks in the top five in homicides related to domestic abuse?"

I dug a dollar out of my pocket.

"Yes. A good friend is a survivor."

Jay nodded his head.

I bent over and looked at the stuffed animals in the back of the car. I gave Jay the dollar and had him put me down for the area code. The number announced was 389. The winner had 381.

I left and walked to The Bistro. Harleigh motioned me over near the kitchen and handed me a beer.

"Can you stick around? Karen wants to talk to you."

"Sure."

"Theresa's outside. You can sit with her if you want."

I didn't but I did anyway. Theresa wasn't much of a friend, only an acquaintance. I felt as though I could never really trust her. She sat at a table with four other people and made introductions.

"So, Ruston, what do you do?" one of them eagerly asked.

"Ruston is a writer," Theresa responded from the rafters.

"Who does he write for?"

"The SWLA Free Press."

One never heard of it, two were indifferent, and the other feigned interest.

"He also wrote a screenplay. He's currently working on a novel."

They quickly became disinterested. Theresa might make for a decent literary agent one day if she so desired.

The night went on and attendance diminished. Soon I was the only one left at the table. I began to play around with my new phone. I logged on to Facebook and found a couple people from the office had sent friend requests.

Harleigh came out to join me. Karen followed soon after with a letter in her hand from The Louisiana Office of Alcohol and Tobacco Control. It stated that Karen's personal money could not go toward the food sale requirement needed to maintain the restaurant permit. Without that input, sales would drop below the minimum required amount. It also informed her that an independent auditor was being retained in the matter. The accounting firm of Thomas, Madison, Smith and Associates.

There was genuine concern on both their faces. I handed the letter back to Karen.

"Make a copy and I'll see what I can do."

CHAPTER 10

I got off the elevator at a quarter after seven and walked to my cubicle. The bullshit crew had already taken their positions. That was the name I had given a select group of office personnel who gathered every morning around the breakroom to loudly expound views on race, politics, officer involved shootings, and tan suits.

As I sat listening to them complain about black women who pat their heads, my phone rang. It was Darby.

"Good morning! How was your weekend?"

"All right."

"What's wrong?"

"I need your help with something."

"I'm kinda swamped this morning. How about we meet for lunch?"

"Sounds good."

I got up and made my way to the breakroom. Usually, I waited for the bullshit crew to disperse, but I was in serious need of a cup of coffee.

"I tell you what," I overheard one of them say, "I sure as hell would never buy a house from a black guy with dreadlocks."

Sure enough, Winslow was in the smoking area later that morning. I noticed money pinned to his shirt.

"What's the deal?" I hollered over the roar of the blowers.

"It's my birthday."

"Well, shit. Happy Birthday, man."

"Thanks, bruh. You gotta come help me get rid of the cake they got me. Whatever's left, I gotta take home."

We took the elevator up. I cut myself a slice and leaned against a refrigerator adorned with pictures of an office Christmas party. Two ladies walked in. Winslow made introductions. Jackie and Rosalyn. An elderly but spry looking woman followed.

"Ruston," Winslow said, "this is my manager, Mrs. Callie Savoy. Mrs. Cal, this is Ruston Delahoussaye from Thomas, Madison on thirty-nine."

Mrs. Cal proceeded to tell me when she first heard a young man with dreadlocks was coming work for her, she responded, "Oh no he's not." She then laughed and said not only was she glad to have him, but proud of what he'd accomplished with the company thus far.

Winslow walked me to the elevator. I wished him well on his day and headed back to thirty-nine.

At noon, Darby and I walked to the corner of Convent and Jefferson for a poboy. We sat at the parklet across the street. I handed her a copy of the letter from Karen. She glanced over it.

"What do you want to know?"

"I don't know exactly."

"Well, give me some time and I can find out who is involved with this. We can go from there!"

"Thank you. I appreciate it."

She smiled.

"Ruston, are you Catholic? I'm just curious."

"No, I'm not Catholic."

"Do you go to church?"

"No."

"We attend Holy Cathedral in Scott. You should come sometime."

I told her I would consider it.

The next night, I saw Evangelina standing barefoot in the gallery wearing a rose-colored sundress. I knocked on the front window. She broke into a huge grin and opened the door.

"Hey you!"

"How's it going?"

"I'm good, I'm good. Come in."

I walked in. She closed the door and locked it. She held a glass of wine in her hand.

"Hey! What are you doing Friday?"

"I work till noon."

She looked at me with her mischievous grin.

"Any chance you can skip?"

"What for?"

She twirled around with her arms outstretched.

"It's going to be a beautiful day. I want to go for a drive! Full blast and top down!"

She giggled then snorted.

"Where to?" I asked.

"You tell me. Show me some sights, man!"

She bit her lip as she waited my response.

"I guess I can take a day off for that," I said.

She let out a squeal of excitement and gleefully jumped up and down. Some of the wine in her glass spilled to the floor. She took my hand.

"I want to show you something."

On an easel sat the painting she worked on the other day. It seemed to be a simple image of a young girl on a swing, but I knew there was more to the story.

"What do you see?" she whispered.

"I see a little girl sitting on a swing focused on something in the distance. There's a walking cane with a red kerchief tied around it against the door of the old house behind her."

I turned to her.

"Who does the cane and kerchief belong to?"

"They belonged to my grandmother. Those last few months she could hardly walk. All her hair had fallen out. I would spend every summer with her. She was a painter. We'd paint just about every day, then go out about an hour or so before sunset and walk around the farm. She'd push me on that swing as the sun set. I always thought if I went high enough, I would see my future over the horizon."

She sipped from her glass.

"Would you like some wine?"

"I would love some."

Truth be told, I hated wine, but if I mentioned that, or made a quick trip up to my apartment to grab a beer, all momentum might be lost. She poured us each a glass. We walked around the gallery. She shared more about her grandmother. I told her about my grandfather and what a proficient storyteller he was.

She poured two more glasses of wine.

We talked about the many avenues of storytelling. I put mine on paper, she used canvas. I sang her rough versions of songs I wrote on guitar years ago. She acted out scenes from plays she did back in high school.

She poured another two glasses of wine.

Funny thing, I had no interest in talking to other writers. Buk described them as flies on the same turd. I met my fair share when I moved to Lafayette and found refuge at The Bistro. Karen went out of her way to feature creators of all sorts. She adorned the walls with paintings, photography, and metalwork created by local talent. Those were the types of people I had interest in, and now one had interest in me.

We both needed to piss. She went first.

The back of the gallery had a bed, desk, stove, and refrigerator. In a separate room was a toilet and shower. When Evangelina came out, the strap of her sundress had fallen off one shoulder. She walked over and embraced me. I put my hands on her hips. We kissed. She briefly slid her tongue into my mouth before she pushed me away.

"Go before you pee your pants," she said. "Hurry up!"

I tried but pissing with a hard-on takes time and effort.

When I walked out, Evangelina was lying face down on the bed passed out. Her purse and a set of keys were on the desk in the corner. I left a note telling her I let myself out and that I'd leave her keys in my unlocked mailbox. Upstairs, I checked the time on my phone. It was a quarter after midnight. I rubbed one out, took a shower, and climbed in bed.

The next morning, the keys were gone. In their place was the note I left with a note of her own written on the back.

"Thanks! I'll pick you up Friday at 9am!"

CHAPTER 11

Darby came by my cubicle. She had yet to turn up anything concerning the audit, but claimed she had a connection.

"You know the tall redhead in payroll?"

"Diane?"

"No, she's the brunette from Dallas. The redhead is Debbie."

"Oh yeah," I lied.

"She gives me the scoop on a lot of stuff. The audit hasn't been assigned yet. Don't worry, she'll keep me posted."

"Thank you for doing this."

"Oh, you're welcome."

"Another thing. Who do I let know when I need to take a day off?"

"Just shoot Mr. Breaux an email. What you got going on like that?"

"Oh, just boring personal stuff."

I emailed Breaux. I told him I needed to tend to a personal matter Friday. He replied that was fine.

After work, I met up with Harleigh for Fish Taco Wednesday at the pub. I told her I enlisted Darby to help find out what was going on with The Bistro audit.

"Did you have to get on your knees and blow her?"

"No, but I may have to get on my knees at her church."

"Watch out, she may offer you as a sacrifice for her sins."

A petite woman with long raven black hair walked up.

"Excuse me," she said. "But aren't you Ruston Delahoussaye?"

"Yes, I am."

"I knew it was you! I'm Jaime. I have all the issues of the SWLA Free Press you're in. I love your stuff."

"Thank you. I appreciate that."

"How come I don't see you in it anymore?"

"Well, I'm currently working on a novel."

Harleigh snorted.

"Holy shit!" Jaime said. "That is so awesome! Can't wait to read it. It sure was a pleasure meeting you."

I stroked my beard as she walked away in her tight jeans.

"Hold up swole up," Harleigh said. "She's way too fast for you."

"You know her?"

"I know of her. You can't keep up with that. What about your office wife? What's her name again? Dorothy?"

"Darby."

"Right, Darby. Darby would be highly upset if she saw you stroking your beard and drooling over that girl's ass."

"She would be more upset if she found out I kissed someone last night."

"Excuse me."

"I kinda made out with the girl from the art gallery."

"I see. And how far did you get?"

"I got her in bed."

Harleigh arched her eyebrows at me.

"She passed out," I said.

"Quite the lover, ain't ya?"

"Darn tootin fig newton."

My phone began to aggravate me. I took it out of my pocket and placed it on the table. Harleigh looked down at it.

"Let me guess, someone in your harem told you to upgrade your phone. First the laptop, now this. Who are you trying to impress? I told you to write and get away from that place."

"I don't know what to write about."

"Write about it all."

"About it all?"

Harleigh put the back of her hand to her forehead in feigned despair.

"Oh, how will you ever manage when I'm gone?"

"Gone? Yeah, right. You've been talking about leaving Lafayette since the day I met you."

"You're my inspiration. They haven't found you yet."

"That's because no one's looking."

"All right, wise ass. You'll see. One day you'll wake up and I'll be gone. What are you gonna do then?"

I thought for a moment.

"I'll probably end up with someone like Jaime."

Harleigh shook her head.

"Unfortunately, I think you're correct."

Friday morning, I went downstairs for a cup of coffee. Nancy was cleaning up by the door. She gave me an uncomfortable hug then hollered to a young girl behind the counter to bring over a small coffee to go.

"What are you up to this morning?"

"Evangelina and I are going for a drive."

"Dean and I are going on our cruise next month. I can't wait!"

"Sounds like fun."

"Sure is. We leave the Saturday before Thanksgiving. Couples only."

The girl came with the coffee. Nancy said no charge. I prepared it and walked outside. Evangelina drove up a short time later with the top down on the Volks. She wore a low-cut red sun dress and a pair of huge black sunglasses. She pushed them on top of her head. Her green eyes were alive and hungry.

"Hey there you!"

I raised the cup in my hand.

"Want a coffee?"

She held up one of her own from the center console.

"Aw, thanks sweetheart, but I picked something up on the way. Climb in."

I got in and put my seat belt on. Evangelina reached down between her legs and produced a cell phone.

"First, let's take a selfie."

I leaned towards her and smiled. She put the phone back between her legs.

"Where to?"

I pointed ahead.

"Go to the thruway and take a right."

We headed for St. Martinville. Down by the Evangeline Oak, we found a place to park.

"Hey!" Evangelina said. "My grandmother brought me here when I was small!"

After reading the historical marker, she twirled around to face me.

"Did you know my real name is Evangeline?"

"Seriously?"

"No, I'm just messing with you. Ha-ha!"

After she snapped a few pictures, we got back in the Volks and took Highway 31 into New Iberia. We stopped at The Shadows on the Teche, a historic home built in the late 1800s for a sugar planter and his wife. In 1922, a great grandson, who happened to be an accomplished artist, took up residence in the home. We stood in a room the guide referred to as his art studio. The grandson would invite many famous people of the day into his home. Many left signatures on his door. I glanced over at Evangelina. She stood mesmerized.

After the tour, we went to the city park. We parked under a huge moss draped oak tree. Evangelina took pictures of the Navy jet plane near the Veterans building, the ducks around Devil's Pond, a sun dial behind the pool, and what we believed was an alligator on the far side of the bayou.

We both made a visit to the restroom. The bottom of the door to the men's room had been kicked in and would not close properly. I knocked twice. There was no one inside. I was about finished my business when the door burst open and a young boy, maybe ten years old, rushed in. He saw me and froze. I smiled.

"Be done in a minute, sir."

He turned and ran out.

When I opened the door, I saw a woman approaching fast, the boy clinging to her with all he had. She looked none too pleased.

"What were you doing in there?" she asked.

I pointed to the door.

"I don't think it will close all the way. Might be a good idea to keep an eye on him while he's in there."

I failed to convince her. Her mind was already made up about me. The young boy kept his face pressed against her side.

Evangelina walked up. I took her by the arm.

"Are you ready?"

She looked back at the woman and child as I led her away.

"What's going on?"

"It's nothing."

Evangelina steered the Volks east on 87 towards Jeanerette. We arrived at the coffee shop on Cooper Street and ordered bacon and egg biscuits with tea and coffee. Evangelina marveled over the beautiful interior of exposed brick and rustic wood while a few patrons cast curious glances our way.

When Evangelina went grab honey for her tea, a woman I didn't recognize walked by.

"You got some nerve showing your face around here," she said.

I didn't bother to ask who she was.

The owners of the business graciously put our free refills into to-go cups. Back in the Volks, we stopped in front of the bakery on Main Street to pick up a French bread. The red light was on. Evangelina stared at it and didn't move.

"I just had a déjà vu moment. I think I've been here before."

"With your grandmother?"

She nodded her head.

"Had to be. This is so weird."

We stepped inside. Evangelina froze. An older gentleman, dressed all in white and covered with powder, looked at her, then at me.

"She's having a moment," I said.

Evangelina put her hands to her face.

"I have been here! I have been here before!"

The man smiled.

"When might that have been, darlin'?"

"Oh, I was young. I think it may have been around 1998."

"Mais cher, I thought you looked familiar."

When we got back in the car, Evangelina kissed me on the cheek.

"I'm having so much fun."

"I'm glad."

"What are we going to do with our French bread?"

"Any ideas?"

Her eyes widened.

"Can we get some boudin?"

"Sure."

"Also, is there a beach somewhere?"

"Yes."

We went back to New Iberia and stopped at the boucherie on Jefferson Terrace. Mr. Tony came out from behind the counter. He and my dad were good friends and grew up together.

"How you doing, Mr. Tony?"

"Can't complain. What about yourself?"

"I'm good, living in Lafayette now."

"Your sister was here the other day. She told me you were homeless."

I laughed.

"Well, you know how those Jeanerette people like to make up stories."

He smiled and put a hand on my shoulder.

"You take care, Ruston."

With French bread and boudin in tow, we headed south on 83 toward Cypremort Point Beach. Evangelina, looking radiant in her red sun dress, happily sang along with the radio while I watched the sugarcane fields and marshlands go by.

She veered left near Weeks Island and turned the Volks on to 319. The huge Louisa Bridge came into view. She slammed on the brakes.

"What's the matter?" I asked.

"Tell me we're not going over that."

"We're not going over that."

"We're not?"

"We are."

She shook her head.

"Oh no, no way."

"Wait a second. What about the I-10 Bridge?"

"The what bridge?"

"The pistol bridge in Lake Charles."

"Uh, nope. I take 210."

"This isn't much different from 210."

"This is a lot different from 210."

"You can do this."

She began to fidget and hum. I shifted the car into neutral and put the hazard lights on. A truck pulling a boat came up behind us. I motioned for the driver to go around. His passenger side window came down.

"Ya'll all right?"

I smiled and pointed to Evangelina.

"She's afraid of heights."

The man laughed and passed us by. I opened the driver's side door, pried her hands from the steering wheel, and walked her around to the other side of the car. After I buckled her in, I climbed into the driver's seat and sat on her phone. She snatched it from my hand and placed it back between her legs.

I inched the Volks forward. Evangelina covered her eyes and stomped the floorboard. I eased the car along as gently as I could. Being that the bridge was over seventy feet high and seven hundred feet long it took a little time to cross. Luckily no other cars came to hurry us along.

At the top, I glanced at the Intercoastal Waterway down below, then over at Evangelina as we began making our descent. The bottom of her dress had slid up her thighs. I put my hand on her leg. Her skin was smooth and cool to the touch.

"You did it."

She spread her fingers apart.

"Oh, Jesus! Oh, God! That was horrible! I need a drink."

We bought beverages from The Marina then made our way down to the beach.

We parked the Volks, sat underneath a pavilion, ate, and had a drink. There were several people fishing on the other end. We walked over just as someone reeled in a black drum. Another caught a four-foot garfish. The men held up their catches and posed for pictures. Evangelina snapped a few of her own.

Just then, we heard a splash and saw a fishing pole out in the water. Unfazed, one of the men calmly picked up another and cast it into the bay. We watched him slowly reel in the lost rod along with a twenty-five-inch red he'd been tussling with. Evangelina grabbed my arm.

"Oh wow! Did you see that?"

We went back to the pavilion. Evangelina took off her sandals and stuck her feet in the sand. I lit a cigarette. Pelicans in the distance dove into the water.

"Ruston, why did those people at the coffee shop react to you the way they did? They kept staring at us. I heard what that woman told you."

"They didn't appreciate something I wrote."

"The whole town?"

"No, a vocal minority who grumble about anything and everything."

"What was it you wrote?"

"A story about the racially segregated proms we had in high school."

"When you say story, you mean news article?"

"No, a short story Robicheaux published."

"Tell me about it."

"It's senior year. We're preparing for prom. A fellow student approaches with a convincing argument. Our class had just spent twelve years together. Why then were the white kids still planning to hold their prom separate from the black kids?"

I took a drag off my cigarette.

"I told her that's just the way it is."

Evangelina remained silent.

"Years later, I read an article about her in the local paper. She had recently been appointed principal of a high school in Texas. She'd been an educator for over seventeen years by that time, and held a bachelor's degree in history, and master's in education leadership. The interviewer asked what she drew inspiration from. She mentioned her faith, her family, and her diligent commitment to combating the detrimental absurdity of ignorant individuals still clinging to the closed-minded irrationality of 'that's just the way it is.'"

"Oh wow."

"Yes ma'am."

A boat-tailed grackle landed nearby. I took a piece of boudin and threw it near him. He caught it in midair.

"Why did people get angry?"

"First, they claimed the story was a complete fabrication. That what the white kids attended was a private event, not a prom. Then they said, yeah, okay, there were two proms, but all the white kids went to the same one as the black kids."

"What did you say to that?"

I flicked the ash off my cigarette.

"I said look at the pictures."

Evangelina nodded her head.

After the sun sank into the bay, we went back to Lafayette. Evangelina slouched in the passenger seat and was asleep before we crossed the Louisa Bridge. She didn't wake until we passed the Lafayette airport. She was hungry. So was I. We parked near the Buford Monument and walked to The Bistro.

Harleigh waited on us. I made introductions. We ordered sliders for an appetizer and shared a pizza. Harleigh and Evangelina hit it off about as well as they could. Harleigh knew her way around the drunken college girl type. I told Evangelina how I gave Harleigh the nickname Rosceaux. She enjoyed that. She began to address Harleigh as Rosceaux. Harleigh was more amused than annoyed as this was the person I romanced into a coma the other night.

After several drinks, Evangelina began fading fast. I had to practically drag her back to the Volks. Several people stopped to stare. With no idea of where she lived, and no intention of digging into her purse for her driver's license, I drove her back to the gallery. After I carried her inside and placed her on the bed in the back room, I put her phone up to my nose. It only smelled like a phone. I locked up and left her keys in my mailbox.

CHAPTER 12

October 8, 2010
SWLA Free Press
blood relation
by ruston delahoussaye
Volume 5 Issue 1

I reluctantly agreed to meet my sister Rebecca for lunch at the seafood and steakhouse in town. I got a beer and ordered the fried catfish with fries while she contemplated another trip to the buffet.

"The plant is closing," I told her as the waitress set my beer on the table.

"Um, yeah I know."

"I should be able to find another warehouse job. I have more than enough experience."

"So, that 'I'm going to take this opportunity to become a writer' crap was bullshit?"

I looked at her.

"You don't even remember," she said.

I made a face and shook my head.

Rebecca reached for her cell phone. She pressed a button then laid it down on the table.

"You have one saved message," an automated voice said. "First saved message."

The voicemail was incoherent at first. The person speaking obviously intoxicated. It took a few seconds before I recognized my own voice. I stared at my sister's phone in disbelief as I pieced together the disjointed ramble of slurred words.

"The plant's closing, I'm losing my job. Remember what happened to dad and grandpa? I have, at most, ten years. What am I supposed to do in the meantime? Pace my trailer and mark the days off with a piece of chalk while I wait for the inevitable?"

I wondered aloud how it would play out. Car accident? West Nile?

"No," I said. "I'm not going out that way."

Then, after a long pause, came one final statement.

"I'm going to take this opportunity to become a writer."

And with that, mercifully, the call ended.

"When was that?" I asked.

"Labor Day Weekend. You remember now?"

"Kinda sorta."

She made a second trip to the buffet. My food came but I lost my appetite. I got another beer. Rebecca sat back down.

"Rory's getting out next summer," she said.

"Thanks for the heads up."

"He's gonna need a place to stay."

"That's his problem."

"Mom doesn't want him at the house."

"Good for her. Now if she could just get rid of you, she'd be doing all right."

"You know what? Fuck you, Ruston! When was the last time I asked you for anything?"

"Fourth of July weekend. You asked me for fifty bucks."

Rebecca became infuriated. I was well accustomed to that shade of color in her face.

"I'm sorry but Rory is your brother! What is he supposed to do when he gets out?"

"Not my problem. I'm about to lose my job. I have my own shit to deal with."

Our raised voices quieted down the restaurant. Even the people in the buffet line strayed from near our table. Our waitress gently walked up.

"Can I get ya'll anything else?"

My sister stood and slammed her chair against the table.

"Yeah. My bill."

She paid and stormed out. I got another beer and a to-go box.

After she graduated from Jeanerette High, Rebecca attended the technical college in New Iberia for billing and coding before she got on at the hospital across the bayou. She had a daughter and was doing quite well for herself, until she rubbed off three consecutive dollar signs on a scratch-off with her house key and took home just under $70,000.

It went as easy as it came. There was the sizable down-payment on a beautiful home, the brand-new car, a couple luxury cruises, and numerous handouts. With the money gone, her meager salary barely covered her mortgage. After budget cuts eliminated her job, she got on at a small grocery store in town and moved in with our mom.

Back at the trailer, I took a seat in the kitchen and overthought my situation. Hours at the plant had been reduced to thirty-two a week with layoffs set to begin at the end of the month. I imagined my brother moving in with me. The last time I saw him, he showed up unannounced, smoked six cigarettes, drank five beers, and helped himself to the forty dollars on my dresser. His existence had been one misstep after another, yet he survived. He clearly had been spared the job malady that inflicted our family as holding one was of little importance to him. He'd likely die shriveled and senseless well into his nineties.

I climbed in bed and turned out the light. There wasn't much recollection of the voicemail on my sister's phone, or the potential life altering decision I made that night, but there was money in my account, and forty weeks of severance upcoming.

CHAPTER 13

Tuesday night, I sat on the sofa with a beer in my hand and my feet up on the coffee table. My phone chimed with yet another Facebook notification. I was being bombarded with friend requests from old classmates and former co-workers. I imagined the sudden popularity nothing but a vain attempt at inflating egotistical social media statistics.

One of the requests though was from Evangelina. I had not seen her since Friday. The pictures she'd taken of us were on her Facebook page. I grabbed the laptop for a better look. They came out quite well. One might even get the impression I was a joy to be around.

She looked to be spending time back in Texas. I scrolled through her pictures, many of them intimate peeks into her life. There she was gazing seductively into the camera, blowing kisses and sticking out her tongue. More than a few were revealing images of her glistening flat stomach, bikini bottoms, tan thighs, and red toenails. I did not put the laptop down until early the next morning.

After I dozed off for an hour or two, I got dressed and went downstairs. I had neither showered nor shaved. I saw Dean's truck, now outfitted with two huge Confederate flags, parked out front. Inside the coffee shop, Nancy hollered at me as soon as I walked in.

"Hey! You didn't shave!"

She rubbed the top of my head.

"Ooh, that's just how my tootie cat feels when I don't shave her."

"Mom!" Samantha yelled from behind the partition. "Please don't."

Nancy laughed.

"What? I'm just saying."

Nancy sat with me while I ate. My phone chimed with another friend request on Facebook.

"You got a text."

"No, it's a Facebook notification," I said as I took my phone out of my pocket. "I was playing with it the other night…"

"You were playing with it? I could help with that. Oh, you meant your phone. I thought you didn't have a Facebook."

"I do now."

"I'm going to have to send you a friend request."

"Awesome. How do I turn off these notifications first?"

"Give me your phone."

She swiped and tapped the screen a few times.

"You're boring. You don't take any pictures."

"Did you fix it, nosey?"

"Yeah, you're good."

Later at the office, Darby came by my cubicle. She brought up The Bistro audit.

"Why are you interested in this?" she asked.

"When the owner found out I was a writer, she got in touch with my publisher and her place became a distribution point for his magazine. I'd only been in town a week. How many people go out of their way to help someone like that?"

"All this because of one person."

"How do you mean?"

"Someone went before the city council and complained downtown was going to turn into another Bourbon Street if they didn't start limiting the number of bars in the area."

"Oh yeah. I did hear something to that effect."

"Do you happen to know who it was?"

"No. It doesn't matter. At least I don't think it does."

"Ruston, we'll figure this out."

I felt she genuinely wanted to help, and I appreciated that. After all, how much could I accomplish on my own? I was merely a contract worker earning enough to make rent while I supposedly wrote a novel.

She called after lunch.

"You know what I would really like right now?"

I hesitated to ask but I did.

"Gelato," she answered.

"Gelato?"

"Yes!"

"Right now?"

"Right now! You're due for a smoke break, aren't you?"

"I guess."

"Go downstairs. I'll meet you in five."

She appeared in ten. We walked across Convent to the gelato place on the corner. After tinkering on the piano out front, I got a small cup of stracciatella while she chose salted caramel. We took a seat outside.

"I never did this before," she said.

"Eat gelato?"

"No, silly. Sneak out of the office."

"Can we get in trouble?"

"Nah."

She spooned a heaping mound of salted caramel gelato into her mouth and grinned.

"So, what are you doing this weekend?"

"I'm going to Festival Acadiens."

"We're having a special service at church Sunday I think you might be interested in. You should come."

"Sure."

"You promise?"

"Yes, I promise."

She handed me a spoonful of salted caramel to try. It was delicious.

CHAPTER 14

I squirmed uneasily in my chair as I checked the time on the computer. 9:15 a.m. I got antsy. My plan was to leave as Darby and I had done the other day, only I had no intention of coming back to the office for the remainder of the morning. It was festival weekend, and I was anxious to get on with it. In the meantime, I continued to work as normal.

At 10:45, I shut my computer down and made my way to the elevator. The woman at the front desk paid me no mind. With cigarettes and lighter in hand, I pushed the button and waited. I thought if I made no sudden moves, Darby would not spot me. She came by twice that morning. I did not mention my plans to her.

After arriving on the first floor, I walked through the smoking area and exited the gate. Once in front of the South Buchanan Parking Garage, I stopped, shook a cigarette out the pack, and looked back. I don't know what I expected to see but I felt completely ridiculous. I headed for Parc Sans Souci.

Bach Lunch, a lunchtime concert series with proceeds earmarked for the downtown science museum, was underway. I purchased a smoked sausage poboy and found a shady area to sit. The musicians on stage cranked out one feisty Cajun tune after another to the delight of the small but dedicated cluster of dancers. A few took brief respites from the noontime sun to fan themselves and wipe the sweat from their faces and neck. It all ended way too soon. I watched the park empty out before being reclaimed by the homeless. I then stood and went to my apartment.

The weekend of Festival Acadiens et Creoles was something I looked forward to each year. Taking place in Girard Park, it offered Cajun and Zydeco music, arts and crafts, and Cajun and Creole cooking. Many events held in conjunction with festival occurred throughout the area, including The Bistro. Harleigh would work multiple shifts over the course of the entire weekend. Our plan, as always, was to catch up with one another Sunday morning during festival brunch.

I left my apartment around five, headed down Jefferson, took a right at McKinley, passed through the strip, crossed St. Mary, and entered the park at the Scene Ma Louisiane stage near Earl K. Long gym and the Alumni Center. The official cutting of the boudin ceremony had begun. Festival goers crowded around two brown folding tables. The local news broadcast live as the emcee of the event welcomed everyone to the fortieth anniversary of the festival.

Drinks flowed in anticipation of the five-foot-long ribbon of spicy boudin about to be sliced up and divided into three red and white crawfish emblazoned platters. Soon the tables would be cleared away, and the Friday night fais do-do would commence. The city mayor/parish president took hold of a pair of black and green scissors, and with one snip, festival was underway. A woman wearing a *Wanna Be Loved Bayou* t-shirt handed me a piece. It was delicious.

Over the last four years, I met the best of mankind at the various festivals and events held around the area. Lafayette had recently been named Happiest City in America. These people didn't get into scuffles on Black Friday, cut people off in traffic, or insult others over differing political viewpoints. Rather, they danced and sang to the heavens. Their cars started on the first crank, their internet didn't lag, their checking accounts had generous bounce protection, and when their time came, they went peacefully in their sleep. Theirs was an existence unknown to me.

I spent the next day crisscrossing the park between the five music venues catching multiple performances while stuffing myself on crawfish spinach boats, chicken and sausage jambalaya, shrimp on a stick, kettle corn, fried frog legs, and countless servings of festival punch. I didn't return to my apartment till well after midnight. Pleasantly buzzed and fully anticipating the final day of festival, I remembered the promise I made Darby.

The following morning, I went downstairs for a cup of coffee. The coffee shop was busy with the extra business brought on by festival. Samantha and the young girl from the day Evangelina and I drove down to the beach manned the counter. Both looked stressed. Samantha greeted me curtly. As the two of them scrambled to fill orders, it occurred to me that they might be sisters. Nancy had introduced Samantha to me as her oldest daughter.

A cab dropped me in front of Darby's church half an hour later. Inside, a man and woman warmly greeted all who entered. I took a seat up in the risers. Darby was nowhere in sight though I sensed she was somewhere among the flock watching my every move. Even so, I decided to check in on Facebook as proof of my attendance.

The lights dimmed. My phone vibrated with a text from Harleigh.

where r u?

At church

I added a smiley face emoji. She responded with one throwing up green vomit.

The congregation rose to its feet as the worship band took the stage. There were no flowing robes, stained-glass windows, or need to suppress an echoing cough. The music was thunderous. I'd been to shows downtown where it took an overflow of alcohol and the lateness of the hour for the crowd to come alive. Here, everyone was dry and eager to get their praise on.

The pastor came out dressed in jeans, sneakers, and a long-sleeved button down. Members of the prayer team took positions near the stage and at the base of the risers. If we had a need, we were encouraged to find someone who would agree with us in prayer.

As the band played a more subdued number, I stepped out from my seat and sought someone to pray over me. A soft-spoken gentleman gave a firm handshake. He asked if I had a need.

"I'm a wannabe writer struggling for inspiration."

He smiled.

"Well, you're here on a good day. Today's message should greatly inspire you."

He asked if he could pray over me. I agreed.

He prayed over me in such a whisper I could not make out one word he said. But as he did, a convincing feeling of warmth came over me. I thanked him and returned to my seat.

The pastor then introduced a guest speaker. A writer, it turned out. We rose to our feet and gave a warm welcome. The man had written numerous books, several of which were available for sale out in the front lobby. It was then it hit me why Darby insisted I attend. I guessed she figured I would appreciate listening to a fellow writer.

What I appreciated was that this guy had it made. Open a Bible, quote a few verses, discuss those verses, put a spin on one or two, hold at least one bumper sticker or Twitter worthy original statement at the ready, hit print, and hello church circuit. Beat the nightclubs, especially if you'd sworn off drinking and were allergic to cigarette smoke and temptation.

The speaker's message concerned creative worship and nothing about writing. At its conclusion, the pastor came back out on to the stage. He asked everyone to close their eyes and bow their heads.

"If you've been running from God and not living life like you should, here's your chance to receive God as your personal Lord and savior. Please stand and raise your hand to acknowledge you need a savior."

I rose from my seat.

"Don't be embarrassed or ashamed," the pastor continued. "Christ died for you, the least you can do is stand for Him."

I stood there with my head down, my eyes closed, and my hand raised high. Supposedly I was saying yes to God's grace and no to the sin separating me from Him. The truth was I stood to remain in Darby's graces and for her continued help with The Bistro audit.

After service, I had a cab drop me off at the corner of Girard Park Circle and Lewis. A couple hours later, I sat near the Scene Mon Heritage stage enjoying my third serving of festival punch of the afternoon when I spotted familiar dreadlocks heading my way. I stood with both arms raised.

"Twenty-two Winslow!"

"Thirty-nine Ruston!"

We hugged. Winslow carried a case in his hand.

"What's that?" I asked.

"My fiddle. We're playing at 4:30."

"Playing?"

"Yeah, bruh. I never told you?"

"No, you never told me."

"Well, shit. Come listen then. We'll be at the Atelier tent."

His group, Bayou La Chute, played traditional Cajun music. After their set, Winslow introduced me to the band. He said they were playing at The Silo on Garfield later. I told him I would be there.

Back at Scene Ma Louisiane, dancers had worn the grass in front of the stage down to dirt. A man appeared with a water hose. He fell in line with the others, one hand holding the hose up high, the other pinned to his side, as he sprayed water to tame the clouds of dust still being kicked up late into the evening.

After festival ended, I went back to my apartment, grabbed a few dollars and another pack of cigarettes, and walked the three blocks over to The Silo. I got a beer and found a place to sit. The area filled quick. Theresa appeared, towering above everyone. She walked up to me and laughed just as someone slapped me on the back of the head. It was Harleigh.

"What the actual fuck, dude?"

"What?"

"What are you doing here? Shouldn't you be sacrificing a calf while praying fourteen Hail Marys or something?"

"Already prayed and done, Rosceaux. How did you know I was here?"

"I didn't. After you stood me up this morning, Theresa and I planned to meet here after work."

She sat down beside me. Theresa went for drinks and asked if I needed one. I shook the bottle in my hand, downed what remained, and said yes.

"So," Harleigh said as I pulled two cigarettes from my pack, "how did Darby take to her lover sitting in a church pew?"

"I never saw her. It was a waste of time."

Harleigh lit her cigarette and took a drag. She turned her head and blew smoke out the side of her mouth.

"Serves you right. Karen's been asking if you heard anything. So, have you?"

She handed me her lighter.

"No. She said it takes time."

"I think she's full of shit. I don't trust her."

I conceded she may be right. Theresa returned with our drinks. The three of us sat there surrounded by a sea of smiling faces as Winslow and his bandmates began to play. It was a Sunday evening, and for all things considered, I felt decent for a change. Maybe those prayers from this morning's service had an effect on me.

Ruston Delahoussaye
9403 S Buchanan St
Lafayette, LA 70595

SNIA

To repeat the days with the others
Like the others
Endlessly empty
VOID
Nothing to do but kill time
Nothing to do
Sunday night in America
Complaining about the Mondays
A given
But no one mentions the terror of the night before
The worry that festers in the pit of a nervous stomach over the upcoming week
Jobs
Appointments
Deadlines
Diagnoses
Perhaps it's just too painful to mention
Changing channels
The leggy blonde struts across the screen
While men in turn collectively mount their wives
Red faced
Sweating buckshot
Furiously pumping with half hard-ons
Sunday night in America
She glances over at the time
As he struggles to come

The next morning, rain poured outside, and I couldn't find my umbrella. I went into the coffee shop, got a small coffee, and initiated a conversation with Nancy in hopes she'd offer a ride to work. The young girl was behind the counter with her. She wore a Catholic school uniform. I asked Nancy if she was her daughter. Indeed, she was. Her name was Sheila. She was a junior at St. Thurman. The conversation stalled.

I asked the young girl how many weeks until their cruise. I faked interest. I only wanted a ride.

"I told you," Nancy said, "it's adults only."

She did tell me that. I just needed a ride.

Nancy put both hands on her stomach.

"I wish I could lose a few pounds before though."

"What for?"

She looked at me.

"You like big girls?"

"You bet."

A normal person would just ask for a ride.

She asked Sheila to fetch something from the back. After the girl left, Nancy turned around, raised her shirt, and revealed a fresh tattoo on the small of her back. Done in such an extravagant font, I had trouble making out what it read.

"That's me, baby," she said.

"Oh, that's you all right."

I could be at work by now and not in this awkward hole I was digging for myself.

"Sexy bitch, that's me," Nancy said.

Sexy bitch? I guessed sixty inch.

It was 6:52. I told her I best be getting on my way. It was then she offered a ride.

We both ran in the rain out to her car. She pulled into the manager's parking lot, stopped in front of the trash dumpsters, then reached over and put a hand on my knee.

"Ruston, can I ask you something?"

"Sure."

"Are you gay?"

I considered it. A lie would just be an added burden.

"No, I'm not."

She put her meaty hand further up my leg.

"Are you seeing anyone?"

"No."

She leaned over. We kissed. She tasted of mayonnaise and pickles.

"Let's exchange numbers. You know, if you ever need a ride, or just want to get together and talk. Dean won't mind."

I gave her my number.

The first thing I saw when I got to my cubicle was my umbrella. I went into the breakroom for a cup of coffee. The bullshit crew stood discussing the current unemployment rate. I got back to my cubicle, sat down, picked up the umbrella, and promptly knocked my coffee over. I retrieved a wad of paper towels from the breakroom. The phone rang. It was Guillory. He told me to come to Breaux's office immediately. I hastily wiped up the spilled coffee and headed over.

Guillory was red-faced and pissed. Breaux wore his usual resigned expression.

"Ruston, why has there been no activity on Martin's Grocery?" Guillory asked.

"Martin's Grocery?"

"Yes, Martin's Grocery."

"That is not a name I'm familiar with, sir."

"What do you mean that is not a name I'm familiar with, sir," he repeated, mocking me.

"Sir, Martin's Grocery is not on the Master List."

"Impossible," Breaux said.

Not only possible, but true. The Master List had accounts listed in alphabetical order. Mac's Meat Market. Merlin's Car Wash. No Martin's Grocery.

"That bitch," I heard Guillory say under his breath.

Martin's Grocery was a grocery store, a huge one at that. Most of the bookwork I did thus far had contained, at most, one to two hundred checks a month. Martins wrote well over a thousand each and every month. Nothing difficult, just time-consuming. Most bookwork arrived in envelopes. Martins came in boxes. Those boxes took up space. It had been decided that those boxes were to be placed in the supply room.

The person who held this position before me only reconciled the first month of the year, then apparently said the hell with it, deleted the name from the Master List, and didn't bother. The boxes piled up. No one noticed or cared. I certainly had no clue. Martin's Grocery made a phone call to the office last week. Decisions were about to be made concerning Christmas bonuses. How were the numbers looking? There were no numbers. Thus, the consequences of someone else's actions were about to fall into my lap, or better put, on my head. To catch up on the eight months of neglected bookwork, Guillory increased my hours from seven-to-seven Monday through Thursday, in addition to seven to five on Fridays and eight to twelve on Saturdays.

And that was that. I would get no help. I happened to see Darby sitting at her desk when I went to retrieve the boxes from the supply room. She refused to look at me. I placed the boxes of bookwork in and around my cubicle. Some of the coffee that hadn't been sopped up with the paper towels had dripped to the floor. Meanwhile, three members of the bullshit crew still harked on those unemployment numbers.

"Hillary said Bill created a hundred times more jobs than Reagan."

"Well, that may be true, but what about Benghazi?"

"Right, can't forget Benghazi."

"Somehow it all comes back to Benghazi."

I leaned forward and placed my head in my hands.

CHAPTER 15

October 14-17, 2014

I worked my share of long hours during busy seasons at the plant. Christmas, Black Friday, back to school; it got intense. Two huge differences between an office and a warehouse. First was space. The plant covered over 200,000 square feet. My cubicle, already cramped, tightened its grip. Some businesses had only begun to drop off their bookwork for the year. More boxes piled up. Over time, my cubicle resembled a sixth-floor book depository sniper's nest.

The other difference was the unsettling silence the office took on after everyone left for the day. While the warehouse was a constant barrage of commotion spread out over multiple shifts, the daily sounds of the office were nothing in comparison.

There was the steady murmur of voices both near and far, with intermittent bursts of laughter and phones that rang constantly. Then something would fall to the floor. CRASH. The elevator doors opened. WHOOSH. A soda can barreled down the vending machine. THUMP, THUMP, THUMP. Someone flushed a toilet. SPLOOSH. The hand dryer went VROOM. The copy machine spit out four copies. SHA-SHUK, SHA-SHUK, SHA-SHUK, SHA-SHUK, while the overhead fluorescent lights BZZ.

But after five, only silence. Occasionally, there would be some odd noise and I would think only one thing. Darby. Even though she had not spoken to me all week, I feared she would appear in nothing but a long trench coat. Or worse, Nancy would show up.

"The guard downstairs told me where to find you," she'd say. "Need a ride? Dean won't mind."

I wondered if I should attempt to locate Touchet's gun.

At seven, I would shut my computer down and turn out the lights. There were other people in the building. I sometimes rode the elevator down with them. I got to know a few of the guards. The conversation would come around to me being a writer. One or two were familiar with Robicheaux's magazine but my name didn't ring any bells. The sun having already set, I walked to my apartment in the dark.

One morning, Darby called.

"I'll have a box ready for the file room in twenty minutes."

Twenty minutes later, I went to her desk. She was nowhere in sight. I found the box with a bin number written on top. I placed it on a dolly and made my way to the elevator. That was it. She was done with me. My fake performance at church Sunday ruined everything. Who would help with The Bistro audit now?

Down in the file room, I had trouble finding the bin. I did find a whole other area further back I didn't realize existed. There was a light switch. It didn't help much. Deep into the bowels of the building, everything covered in dust and cobwebs, I finally located the bin. As I reached for the box, I felt a presence.

"Bloody hell!" I cried out.

It was Darby. She studied me with an amused expression on her face, then put her arms around me and slid her tongue in my ear. I got hard. She giggled before walking away. I heard the door close. I had to wait a few minutes before I went back up to thirty-nine.

The day got better.

Breaux called. I needed to go to his office immediately. He stood outside the door and motioned me inside. Two detectives with the Lafayette Police Department greeted me.

"Mr. Delahoussaye, I'm Detective Landry. This is Detective Wilson. May we have a word with you?"

Detective Landry possessed a rather huge nose. The sort of nose where if people didn't know you by your name, they knew you by your nose. Detective Wilson stood off to the side. His laser focus burned through me like a magnifying glass in the sun. Breaux entered the room and left the door partially open. The detectives asked about an incident that occurred on the third of October at the city park in New Iberia.

"Were you there on the day in question?" asked Detective Landry.

"Yes, sir."

It was the day I requested off from Breaux. I hoped he wouldn't make the connection.

"Anything unusual happen?"

"Unusual?"

"Out of the ordinary."

I thought for a moment.

"Well, some woman freaked out because her kid ran into the restroom while I did my business."

"Tell us exactly what happened."

"The door to the men's room wouldn't close. This kid comes barging in. I guess his mom thought I was up to no good."

"What did you tell her?"

"I told her about the door."

"Then what?"

"My friend came out of the women's restroom, and we left."

"Mr. Delahoussaye, the Iberia Parish Sheriff's Department received a report about a possible attempted child abduction."

"Possible attempted child abduction?"

"Yes."

"Seriously?"

"Yes."

I rubbed my forehead.

"Wait. How did they determine it was me?"

"The mother of the child got the license plate number of the vehicle you rode in."

"Jesus. And you're just coming talk to me about this now?"

The detectives glanced at one another.

"The mother is…," Detective Landry hesitated. "Let's just say all the local agencies are familiar with her. She is notorious for calling 911 and having emergency services dispatched based on false reports."

The detectives mentioned Iberia Parish talked to Evangelina by phone and went to the park to see the door for themselves. They also got a statement from an elderly woman who witnessed the whole thing. They had not bothered to come all this way and had Lafayette Parish go through the motions. I had nothing to be concerned about. What I didn't know was word got around the office about me being in a park restroom with a young child.

That night, I pulled the pages I typed the day of my interview down from the closet and thought about Borel. A reader of the SWLA Free Press, I first met Borel Jeffery in front of the closed down barber shop near the underpass on Jefferson. Unkempt, with a scraggly gray beard, he stood about Harleigh's height and weighed well over two hundred and fifty pounds. He inquired as to why Robicheaux no longer printed my work. I confessed my struggles to him. He reached into his tattered backpack and produced a small plastic pill bottle.

"These babies will get you focused," he said. "You'll break barriers."

I went for the bottle. He quickly pulled it away.

"Hey. They ain't free, you know."

He followed me up to my apartment. I handed him a beer as he looked around. His focus settled on the guitar I had leaning up against the sofa.

"That's a real nice guitar you got there," he said.

The plan was to sell that guitar to cover rent for the remainder of the year. I finished the bottle the morning of my interview. That afternoon, thirty-nine pages sat next to the typewriter.

After I was done reading, I tore the pages in half and tossed them in the garbage. Over ten thousand words, and there was nothing there. I tapped out, then drank myself unconscious.

Sometime later, the sound of gunshots awakened me. I walked over to the window and looked out over Buchanan. The only movement was the stoplight at Second and Garfield. The Lafayette South Bank time and temperature sign read 2:37. It had been quite some time since I heard gunshots in the area. Borel told me that two o'clock was when the roaches came out. Robicheaux mentioned the same thing. When he first purchased the building, he had the gate installed at the top of the stairs. But after he continuously found trash, needles, blood, urine, feces, and the occasional overdose on the stairwell, he relocated it to the bottom. I adored that gate. It prevented thugs, coffee shop owners, and administrative assistants from coming up to my door.

At daylight, I went down to the coffee shop. Nancy showed me no interest. Dean told me about the commotion last night.

"Drug deal gone wrong," he said. "Three people shot, one critical."

"Damn. Where?"

"By the underpass."

"Shit."

"You got a gun?"

"No."

"We all have one. Don't play that neighborhood watch bullshit. We take aim and shoot. Don't we, babe?"

He turned to Nancy who was busy behind the counter.

"Yep," she said.

"All right, I'm heading to Rachel's."

He stood and gave me a fist bump before he left.

"Who's Rachel?" I asked Nancy.

"It's a tanning salon."

"A tanning salon?"

"Yep. He's getting a tan before the cruise."

I headed to the office. Just as I sat down the phone rang. It was Darby.

"What did you do?"

"What?"

"Why were the police here talking to you?"

"Darby, they…"

She laughed.

"Ben told me all about it."

"Who?"

"Ben, Ben Landry, the detective. I've known him since high school."

"Oh. Well, that was kind of him."

"That lady was a nut."

"I guess so."

"Just want to warn you, people are saying stuff about you."

"I can about imagine."

"They think you and I are messing around."

I didn't respond. She laughed.

"Someone also complained about your clothes."

"My clothes? What's wrong with what I wear?"

"It doesn't follow the dress code."

"We have a dress code?"

"We do. Not you. You're a contract worker."

While the other men in the office sported ties, slacks, and dress shoes, I wore my standard issue long sleeve button downs, vests, boot cut jeans, and *Chelsea* boots.

"Keep wearing your jeans. They fit you snug."

After a horrendous start, I got a handle on the bookwork for Martin's Grocery. The person in this position before me apparently plugged a number somewhere in January's reconciliation and that threw February's numbers off. I got it corrected and got a good rhythm going just as the people who'd come by to audit my work made another appearance. I went down for a smoke break. Darby accompanied me. She wore ferociously high heels that clicked loudly as she walked.

"Sorry I didn't say hello to you in church Sunday," she said.

"I didn't see you."

"Herman and I were in the sound booth."

"Okay."

"What did Mr. Leo tell you?"

"Who?"

"He prayed over you."

"Honestly, I couldn't understand a word he said."

"He doesn't talk, he whispers."

"Sounds about right."

"It was wonderful when you stood and raised your hand."

I smiled weakly.

When I arrived back at my cubicle, the auditors were nowhere in sight. I continued unscathed while the inside of my head crackled and spit.

About a quarter to twelve, Darby's heels approached fast. She exploded into my cubicle with eyes wide.

"Guess what?"

"What?"

"The Bistro audit's delayed."

"Delayed?"

"Until May."

"What does that mean?"

"It means they don't have to worry about the food sale numbers for now."

Darby beamed. She was mighty proud of herself. She told me she would find something out about the audit and that she did. It was more than I had done. At least I now had news to share, though the thought of still sitting here seven months from now about made me sick to my stomach.

By noon, everyone left. I made a pot of coffee. The breakroom sat in its usual disarray. Housekeeping was pretty much nonexistent. The men's room would get downright atrocious at times. Urine on the floor, butt crack residue on the toilet seat. Even Darby complained of how appalling the women's restroom fared. It seemed quite a few of the ladies preferred to squat and splatter rather than sit and piss.

At five, I went to The Bistro and saw Karen. I shared the news Darby had given me. Turned out the decision to delay the audit had been made Monday. Not only was she aware of it, but she was there when they rendered the verdict.

I headed to my apartment. There was a line of cars parked along Buchanan. A sign out front of the gallery read CLOSED FOR PRIVATE FUNCTION. Through the window on the front door, I saw Evangelina standing among a crowd of people. She wore a tight black V-neck evening gown. A clean-shaven young man with a chiseled jaw line handed her a glass of wine and whispered something in her ear. Evangelina blushed, covered her mouth, looked around cautiously, then grabbed his arm and laughed, as though what he told her was inappropriate but later possible.

"Excuse me, are you going in?"

I stood blocking the door. I apologized, unlocked the gate, and went upstairs. The music blared from down below for hours. I paced the apartment, lighting one cigarette after another, getting more uneasy as the time went by. I downed a couple beers to take the edge off then went piss. The toilet wouldn't flush. When I removed the lid, the music stopped.

I pictured Evangelina passed out on the bed in the back room. Would Mr. Chiseled Jaw be a gentleman, or take advantage of the opportunity before him?

CHAPTER 16

In the morning, the inside of the gallery sat in disarray. The Volks remained in the parking lot next to a red *Corvette* parked a few spots over. I went to the office for my eight to twelve shift. I made a pot of coffee and checked out Evangelina's Facebook page.

The event from the previous night turned out to be a fundraiser for a local charity. Evangelina tagged herself in numerous pictures, several of which featured Mr. Chiseled Jaw. Underneath one, a woman asked his name.

"Hunter," Evangelina responded. "Isn't he handsome?"

"Dayum!" the woman declared. "You go girl!"

Hunter Hilliard, a pediatric anesthesiologist at the Children's Hospital, was also a world traveler. His Facebook showed him in various places around the globe. The United Kingdom, South Africa, Japan, and Mamou, where he seemed to be from. I left the office at a quarter to twelve. When I got to the gallery, the parking lot was empty. I spent the remainder of the weekend holed up inside my apartment.

Monday morning, I was to meet Robicheaux to pay my rent. I walked to the ATM across the street, put in my debit card, and waited for the machine to stick its cash green tongue out at me. No accountants or bank reconciliations needed for my finances. ATM slips were more than sufficient to deliver the grim news. On this occasion though, something odd occurred. Even after I withdrew over three hundred dollars, I still had a decent amount remaining in my account.

Robicheaux came out of the coffee shop. I walked over, counted the money, and handed it over. He snatched it out of my hand.

"When I say I'm coming for the rent, I expect you to have it on time."

I didn't reply.

"What the hell did you do for detectives to show up anyway?"

I remained silent.

"You better watch yourself. Fuck this up and I'm not helping you land another job."

After he stormed off, I went into the coffee shop. Nancy stood behind the counter. She looked pissed.

"Mike was looking for you," she said.

"I just talked to him."

"Asshole wants to catch an attitude with me. We've never been late with the rent before. Fuck him."

I got a small coffee and headed for the office. Two individuals were having a heated dispute out in the parking lot. Winslow stood in the smoking area with a grin on his face. He motioned toward the chaos with the lit cigarette in his hand.

"That is some funny shit, bruh," he hollered to me over the roar of the blowers.

"What's going on?"

"Ya boy took home girl's parking spot."

Danny, one of the security guards, walked past us with a disconsolate expression on his face. Danny made minimum wage, yet there he was, about to referee two adults bitterly fighting over a parking spot when as many as a dozen sat empty nearby.

Up on thirty-nine, Darby came by.

"You saw that out there?" she asked.

"Yeah."

"That's so stupid. Each one tries to get here before the other for that spot. Why do you get a coffee before work? There's coffee in the breakroom."

"The crowd in there takes a while to clear out."

Darby giggled loud enough for the bullshit crew to hear then walked away.

She wasn't giggling a few days later though when the office got a handsome young man named Julian as an intern. Every one of the ladies, ladies who sat in sterile cubicles all day long only to go home to husbands who didn't possess the capability of satisfying them sexually, only sporadically, were goo-goo eyed over him.

Darby hated his guts, as she was now required to call on him when something needed to go down to the file room. For that reason, I was goo-goo eyed over him as well. He and I would talk occasionally. He knew all there was to know about Saints football.

"Hey!" he'd say. "Do you happen to know who their first quarterback was?"

I gladly tolerated his useless sports trivia as his presence prevented Darby from violating me in the file room.

Friday at five, I made my way to my apartment. As I checked the mail, Samantha walked out of the coffee shop.

"What's up?" I asked.

"Nothing," she said unconvincingly.

I unlocked the gate.

"Look," she said, "you didn't see me here. All right?"

"Sure."

"Fuck. First Evangelina, now you."

"Evangelina?"

"She just left with some guy in a red 'vette."

I went upstairs, took a shower, and had a pizza delivered. After I ate, I went on Facebook and saw Evangelina had checked in at The Blue Pooch with Hunter. She posted a picture of the two of them having drinks along with a message for all her friends.

"Single ladies: be patient. He's out there."

It had already garnered fifty-seven likes.

I grabbed a beer then searched the name of the last woman I got myself involved with. Lauren Gonsoulin moved to Lydia from Harahan a few days before Hurricane Lili came through. Tall and thin with blonde hair black at the roots, she fought many a demon. She got on at the plant and moved in with me soon after. Our relationship, fraught with turmoil, revolved around tension and drunken sex. On our last morning together, she threw a bottle at me from across the room.

I came across a familiar face. Lauren Gonsoulin Suire had married, moved to Baton Rouge, and colored her hair some weird burgundy color. I looked through her pictures and discovered one I took myself of her and her three sisters. The description below said #TBT 2004. There was a long scroll of comments underneath. Most concerned clothing and hairstyles, sprinkled with a couple OMGs and LOLs, in addition to this exchange.

"Who took this?"

"I think his name was Russell. Right, Lauren?"

"Something like that."

"I don't remember him."

"I do. Lauren, just think if you had married him."

"Yeah, you could still be living in a trailer behind a gas station LMAO."

"I know right LOL."

"Bahahaha talk about living the life."

I closed the laptop and stared at the wall till morning.

CHAPTER 17

Final Week of October 2014

Monday morning, I received an email from someone named Bridgett Laviolette. It concerned my attendance at a seminar to be held Wednesday at The Oaks on Kaliste Saloom. I forwarded it to Darby. She told me the program I entered the bookwork into was being discontinued. The purpose of the seminar was to introduce a new program to the company.

"Who's Bridgett Laviolette?" I asked.

"Glenn Richard's secretary. She also handles the parking permits, among other things."

Great.

"Mr. Guillory isn't too happy."

"About what?"

"The new program. It's faster and likely to reduce billable hours. You won't be here till seven each night, that's for sure."

Bridgett showed her face in my cubicle later that day.

"You have a problem with attending the seminar Wednesday?" she asked.

"No, I don't have a problem with attending the seminar Wednesday. I just wanted to know what was going on. This is the first I hear of this."

"Mr. Breaux never told you?"

"No."

She let out a sinister laugh.

"I realize you don't have a car or anything, but it is kinda mandatory you attend."

"No, it's not. I'm a contract worker."

I waited for her to say something. She turned and walked away.

I briefly considered giving Nancy a call to ask for a ride to the seminar, but the thought of mayonnaise and pickles persuaded me to get a cab instead. When I got there Wednesday, the seminar, led by a fiery redhead named Melanie Stokowski, was about to start. Individual round tables with placards on top sat near a projection screen. Each placard indicated an office location. Lafayette, Baton Rouge, Lake Charles, Opelousas, Morgan City, and Metairie. The table for the Lafayette office had four chairs. Occupying them were Breaux, Bridgett, and the two who'd come by to audit my work. Bridgett saw me and turned her head. I sat in the back by myself.

Miss Stokowski wore a long-sleeved green dress that struggled to contain her. She worked the audience like a seasoned pro. Every so often, she'd purposely bend over and expose just enough cleavage to wake any men who happened to doze off on her. She then sweet talked the ladies. "Oh, girl," she declared with a wave of her hand. "How I just love those earrings." She would then feign a brief mental lapse, and pause long enough to allow someone to come to her rescue. "Oh my, thank you so much for that! I don't know where my head is at today."

After two hours of a presentation that went straight over my head, we took a break. I found a restroom then got a cup of coffee. As I headed back to my seat, Melanie stopped me. She held out her hand.

"I don't believe we've met. I'm Melanie."

"Ruston."

We shook. Her hand was warm and inviting.

"What office are you with?" she asked.

"Lafayette."

"Oh yes, Mrs. Bridgett informed me of the backlog of bookwork you guys have. Don't worry. This program is user-friendly. I guarantee you won't have any of the issues like the ones you're facing now."

She was under the impression the backlog was due more to my ignorance than to the fact eight months of bookwork had been stashed in the supply room without my knowledge. I took a sip of the coffee. It was horrible.

After another two hours, a lunch of burgers and fries was served in brown paper bags. I grabbed one and went outside. A few others made their way out there to smoke and talk on their phones. I ate, lit a cigarette, and watched the planes take off and land at Lafayette Regional. Someone stuck their head out the door.

"Hey everyone! We start back up in ten minutes."

I finished my cigarette and went back in. Bridgett walked up.

"So, what do you think?" she asked.

"The coffee sucks but that burger was good."

"I meant about the program, wise ass."

"What about it? All I need to know is where to input the numbers."

"I don't appreciate your attitude."

"I don't appreciate you failing to tell Miss Stokowski about the eight months of bookwork placed in the supply room and deleted off the Master List."

Before she could respond, Melanie walked by and asked if everyone was ready to get started. Bridgett returned to her seat while everything in me screamed to leave. But I didn't. I couldn't. I had no choice.

After the seminar, I had a cab drop me off at The Bistro. I caught Harleigh up on the goings-on over the last few weeks. She listened with amusement as I told her of mayonnaise kisses, file room hard-ons, twelve-hour shifts, and visits from detectives. She shared news of her own.

"I met your office wife," she said.

"Where?"

"I ran into them at The Supercenter. Herman remembered my face but not my name. I told him it was Sheryl. He didn't even bother to introduce us. She looked so uncomfortable. Don't worry, I didn't say anything about you."

"I appreciate that."

"She's got a nice ass. I see why you got a thing for her."

"It's all a show. She gets a kick out of people talking about us."

"So, she's using you for attention like you're using her for week old information about the audit. Tell me, are you letting that coffee shop woman kiss on you for free Wi-Fi?"

I frowned.

"What about the one from the gallery? Evelyn."

"Evangelina. She got herself some stud. A doctor who travels the world."

"You still talk to her?"

"No, I just stalk her on Facebook."

"You creeper, you."

Friday was Halloween. The bullshit crew were in an especially raucous mood. It seemed in years past they took offense to people from other areas trick or treating in their respective neighborhoods. Together they collectively decided to hand out candy the night before. They found it hilarious parents would bring their kids only to find every light off and door closed.

"Serves them right. Go buy your own candy instead of taking it from hard-working families."

"Watch, they gonna start protesting."

"They only come to scope out the neighborhoods. Someone had a four-wheeler stolen last Halloween."

"That's all it's good for."

When I went in the breakroom for a coffee, they fell silent.

"Look, it's the molester," one said in a low voice.

I pretended not to hear.

"Hey Chester! Oops, my bad, thinking of someone else. Hey Ruston! Been in any good park restrooms lately?"

A few of them laughed. Another chimed in.

"What are you dressing up as for Halloween, Ruston?"

I turned to face them.

"I'm going as Father John Bergeron."

Their faces dropped. I stirred my coffee and walked out.

Father John Bergeron, an infamous name in south Louisiana, was a Catholic priest in the early eighties. He allegedly abused over fifty young boys before the diocese transferred him to another area with no charges filed. Years later, they welcomed him back, all sins forgiven, only for police to catch him in a park restroom with a young boy.

Five o'clock came. When I rounded the corner from Congress on to Buchanan, it was déjà vu. Up ahead, on the bench in front of the gallery wearing her red shoes sat Evangelina. Only this time she was not magic. Looking weathered and defeated, she saw me coming and stood. She wore no makeup and had pouches under her eyes. She mustered a smile.

"Hey," she said. "Long time no see."

She gave me a feeble hug. I smelled body odor on her.

"Yes, it's been a while."

"What are you up to?"

"Trick or treating."

She gave a laugh.

"No, I'm going check out Downtown Alive. They're giving away a car."

"Can I come with?"

"Sure."

We walked the two blocks down Garfield to Parc International. Many in the crowd wore costumes, children as well as adults. Someone rolled a tumbler filled with index cards on stage, another gave it a whirl and plunged a hand inside. Even though I had no chance to win, my heart did jump a little when they slowly called out the name Russell Armentor.

Later, we climbed into the Volks and hit a drive-thru for some fried chicken. Back at the apartment, she grabbed a bottle of wine from the gallery and followed me upstairs. We took a seat in the kitchen. In no time, she scarfed down two wings and a leg. She stopped to sip from her diet cola.

"Have I ever told you I'm a vegetarian?"

"No, you haven't."

She smiled a greasy fried chicken encrusted smile back at me.

"How about that phone call from those detectives?" I asked.

"Oh God. Let me tell you. I had my mom in the car with me. She doesn't like anyone to talk on the phone when they're driving, so I just let it ring. They left a voicemail. Call back at your convenience. I thought something happened here at the gallery. They start asking me questions. About you, about the park. It took a while before they finally got to the point."

"They paid me a visit at work."

"They didn't?"

"They did. Some of my co-workers now think I'm a pedophile or something."

She gave me a serious look.

"You're one of the most trusting individuals I know."

We moved from the table to the sofa. Evangelina finished her bottle of wine then gave me her keys to go downstairs for another. I grabbed two. She told me how she met Hunter. She was in the gallery, doors open, classical music playing, when in walks this handsome guy wearing khaki pants and a light-colored pink shirt. He said he worked at a local hospital, was president of a non-profit, and was scouting the area for a location to hold their yearly fundraiser. He claimed he'd passed by and gotten intrigued by the paintings he saw through the window.

At first, he was overly kind and polite. But she soon learned of his anger issues. She homed in on last Friday night.

"A car cut us off and he got enraged. I was so petrified. When we caught up to them, Hunter told the guy he'd kill him and his b-i-t-c-h."

She paused.

"He couldn't let it go and starts taking it out on our waitress. I was so embarrassed. Someone told him to shut up. Hunter says, 'Mind your own f-ing business.' I thought they were going to fight."

I noticed her hands shaking.

"He drives me home, parks in front of my house, and pulls his thing out. He grabs me by the back of my head and takes out his phone. He said it would be something for him to watch later."

She put her face into her hands and started sobbing. I didn't know what to say. A part of me wanted to question why she made him out to be God's gift to women on Facebook with all that going on. Instead, I remained silent.

Well into her second bottle of wine, she randomly asked if I knew of Bernie Sanders. I shook my head no. She then needed to use the restroom. I helped her get there, then carried her back to the sofa and covered her with a blanket after she dozed off.

I climbed in bed. When I woke up a few hours later, she was already awake. Though drowsy and a bit hungover, she seemed to be in better spirits. She took my keys and went downstairs to get us coffee at Nancy's.

I showered and dressed. When I was done, I found her in the kitchen running a finger through the layer of dust on my typewriter.

"I could never be with a writer," she said.

"Why is that?"

"Words are intimate, more intimate than a picture. Someone describing in detail…"

She trailed off.

"You work today?"
"Yes."
"I can drive you there if you want."
She pulled the Volks into the parking lot at the office.
"What time you knock off?"
"Noon."
"Give me your phone."
She tapped in her number.
"Text me. I'll come pick you up."

She came for me about twenty minutes after twelve. She wore a long gray skirt that flowed down to her sandals and tastefully hugged her hips. Her scent as strong as ever, she looked more like herself than she did yesterday, but with a hint of sadness in her eyes.

We spent the afternoon at her place in Duson. She stayed in a small two-bedroom house cluttered with paintings. She made lunch, then showed me a piano that was there when she moved in. She opened a few windows and sat down to play. I took a seat across from her in a ridiculously comfortable chair. I didn't understand why I was there, but it beat sitting alone in my apartment. Afternoon turned into evening. I pulled her panties down and buried my face between her legs, nuzzling my nose through her dark mound of pubic hair. At first, she struggled to break free. I grabbed her wrists and pinned them down to her sides. Her breathing deepened. She then tensed up and arched her back, tightening her body in one final clinch. I felt her give and let out a long sigh. I climbed up, wiped her wetness off my face, and slid inside of her. She turned her head to the side. I was just about there.

"Am I boring you?"
"What?" I said, looking around.
She had gotten up from the piano and stood over me.
"You dozed off. I must be boring you."
"Oh no, I'm sorry. This chair is so comfortable."
She laughed.
"I never had anyone play the piano for me before. You're good. I enjoyed that."
"Thanks. My grandmother had one. Would you like to have dinner with me tonight?"
She took me to an intimate little pizza place on Ambassador. We settled in a booth near the back.
"Ruston, can I ask you something?"
"Sure."
"Are you surviving off your writing?"

"I was, at one time."

"Is that why you have that job?"

"Yes."

Our waitress took our drink order. Evangelina wanted a half sweet half unsweet tea with extra ice. She then confided she was having a difficult time trying to make it off her paintings.

"My parents are giving me a hard time. They want me to move back to Texas. I'm not making any money. They're paying all my bills, plus everything for the gallery. I still have over two years left on my lease."

The waitress returned with our drinks.

"Please don't be mad," Evangelina continued, "but have you ever considered that maybe you're not good enough?"

"Only with every word I currently write," I blurted out.

Evangelina frowned.

"It wasn't always like that," I said. "There was a time when ideas just flowed. It was effortless. Robicheaux published everything I sent him."

"How did you meet Mr. Robicheaux?"

"I came across his magazine and submitted a couple stories."

"Do you think becoming a writer turned out to be a good idea?"

"Some people asked what I would do after the plant shut down. When I told them I was going to be a writer, they said I was only gonna dig a hole for myself, and when it got too deep, I would take anything that came along to climb out of it."

Someone who worked with Hunter recognized Evangelina and came over. They glowed in their admiration of him.

"Where is Mr. Wonderful, anyway?" I asked after the person returned to their table.

"At a training seminar in Memphis."

She grew quiet. We ate in silence.

After I paid the bill, she drove me back to my apartment.

"See ya," she said.

I grabbed a beer from the refrigerator, sat on the sofa, and lit a cigarette. Her musky scent remained on the blanket I covered her with. She never did explain the reason for the state she was in yesterday.

My phone chimed. She had sent me a text.

    Thank U 4 being there 4 me

I took a sniff of the blanket, leaned my head back, and closed my eyes.

CHAPTER 18

I awoke Monday morning to daylight coming in through the window. I jumped from the sofa and checked my phone. It read 6:25 but that couldn't be right. Sunrise was not until at least a quarter after seven. I hurried and got dressed. Halfway down the stairs, I realized I forgot my cigarettes. I went back up, grabbed them off the counter, and stopped cold. It was the third of November. Saturday had been the last day of daylight savings time. How I had no clue was beyond me, yet there I was. I shook a cigarette out of the pack, lit it, drew my head back, and blew smoke straight up into the air. It was official. Thomas, Madison, Smith and Associates had me by the balls.

I arrived at the office and found people huddled inside my cubicle. I stood nearby not quite sure of what to do. I couldn't help but overhear them.

"Bet he downloads kiddie porn."

"Something smells."

"He probably jerks off in here."

"EW."

The bullshit crew occupied the breakroom, so I went find Darby. She told me about some commotion that happened in her neighborhood Friday that I only halfway paid attention to. Julian came by. He asked if I watched the Saints play Thursday night. He said they broke a seven-game road losing streak, though he didn't think they would make the playoffs. Bridgett walked up.

"There you are. Look, we put the new program on your computer, but don't open it. All right? Don't open it. It's not ready. IT has to see about something first. Okay? Don't open it."

Jesus.

After the bullshit crew vacated the breakroom, I went in for a coffee. I noticed a bag of chips on the table along with an open jar of salsa. I got my coffee and headed to my cubicle. Later, I went piss. Multiple cups of coffee fueled multiple restroom breaks which prevented my ass from taking root in my chair. I walked in on someone attempting to fumigate the men's room with a can of disinfectant. I held my breath, assumed my position before the urinal, and heard the toilet flush. I observed the culprit exit the stall and walk out of the restroom without washing his hands. After I completed my business, I washed and dried mine, as any civilized man would do, and used the wadded-up paper towel to open the door. I went into the breakroom for another coffee. There I encountered the fumigating offender rifling through the open bag of chips with the hand he more than likely just wiped his ass with. After finding one that was suitable, he dipped it into the jar of salsa, crammed it into his mouth, and walked out.

A few days later, I ran into Winslow downstairs in the smoking area. He told me his band had a gig at the pub Saturday and said to bring a friend. I planned to ask Harleigh, but that was before I received an unexpected text from Evangelina. I texted her back. It was generic back and forth at first: hey, how you doing, how you been. Then I went for it. I told her about Winslow's gig that weekend.

"Sounds wonderful," she wrote back.

We made plans.

"Yay! That'll be fun," she added.

Saturday evening, I led her to a table up front, helped her take off her coat, and hung it on the back of the chair for her. I placed my cigarettes and lighter on the table then ordered us a round of drinks. Winslow came over. I made introductions. The place filled and the band started. Evangelina leaned over to me.

"I'm thinking of doing another showing," she said. "Do you think I could get them to play?"

"We can ask."

"Okay. I'll let you know. Maybe some time before the end of the year."

I smiled and sipped from my drink.

Later, the band took a break. Evangelina excused herself to go to the restroom. When she returned, I asked about the question she posed last week.

"Hey, why did you ask if I knew who the chicken guy was?"

She climbed back in her seat.

"Chicken guy?"

"Yeah, you asked if I had ever heard of Admiral Sanders."

"Admiral Sanders?"

"That wasn't his name?"

She gave a confused look. Then her eyes got wide. She covered her mouth with her left hand as she slapped the table with her right. She almost knocked my beer over.

"OH. MY. GOD. Admiral Sanders. Really? Wasn't it Bernie Sanders?"

I grabbed my beer and pointed it at her.

"Yeah, that's him."

Evangelina was in hysterics. She wiped the tears from her eyes with the heel of her palm.

"Why did you think it was Admiral Sanders?"

"I don't know," I said feeling foolish. "We were eating fried chicken."

"That's not the right name for that either."

"Darn."

She rubbed her arms and reached back for her coat.

"What exactly did I say?"

"You just asked if I had heard of him. That's all."

She grew silent. There was a pained expression on her face.

"Look," I said. "I'm sorry I brought it up."

"No, Ruston. I must tell you something. I haven't told anyone this."

She contemplated for a moment what she was about to say then inched closer to me. This would not be good.

"Mr. Sanders is a Senator from Vermont. He's going to be our next President. You wait and see. I had his bumper sticker on my car. My other car. I had another little car. Well, I'm at a red light, and there's this tall truck behind me with tinted windows. I couldn't see who was inside. They began blowing their horn, and when the light turned green, they passed me and blew out all this black smoke. Not long after, someone keyed my car. They also scraped off my Bernie Sander's sticker. I figured whoever was in that truck was responsible."

The band started back up. Evangelina leaned in closer. I listened as best I could. She said her landlord owned an auto salvage yard. She asked if he could repair the damage to her car once she had enough money saved. Turned out the blue Volks was not hers as she had led me to believe but was in fact a loaner.

She told me what happened to her the day before Halloween. She was at Hunter's place in McMillan Branch. He videoed her doing humiliating things she refused to go into detail about. After he fell asleep, she grabbed his phone and locked herself in the bathroom, intent on deleting anything and everything that contained her likeness. In doing so, she discovered similar pictures and videos he had taken of other women.

She then came across several dark and grainy images. She enlarged one with her thumb and index finger. In it, she made out the license plate number of her car along with the remnants of her Bernie Sander's bumper sticker. She got sick to her stomach. His phone fell to the floor. The screen shattered.

Right then Theresa appeared at our table. She gave me a bored "Hey Ruston," then turned all her attention to Evangelina, raving about a painting she purchased from her. Evangelina smiled and was polite and appreciative. There was another piece Theresa had interest in. She peppered Evangelina with questions about it.

As soon as Winslow's band finished their set, Evangelina was ready to leave. She barely touched the drink I bought her. I walked her to her car. She gave a quick hug then drove off.

The following Tuesday, she called.

"Hey, Admiral Sanders, you hungry?"

"Why yes, I am."

"Where are you?"

"Still at work. Where are you?"

"In the drive-thru. What you want?"

"Three piece, white, spicy, with dressing."

"Meet me at the gallery. Later, alligator."

She was at the door when I arrived. We sat in the back room and ate. Instead of the sundresses and long flowing skirts she usually wore, she was in a tight gray tank top with a pair of black yoga pants.

"Look at this," she said.

She slid a piece of paper towards me. It was a restraining order.

"That's going to be difficult to adhere to with my apartment being right upstairs," I joked.

She didn't laugh. I looked closer. It had Hunter's name on it.

"And check this out."

She picked up her purse and flashed a small handgun concealed inside.

"I say Miss Connor, what have you been up to?"

"I got tired of being fucked with," she said.

I looked at her.

"You know how I said Hunter was the one who vandalized my car?"

She only alluded to it, but I nodded anyhow.

"Well, after I came across those pictures on his phone, I realized he was the one in the truck that day. I think he happened to find me and did that to my car. When he saw his phone, he went crazy. He kept saying, 'You fuckin' libtard. You fuckin' libtard bitch.'"

"Libtard?"

"It's a word they use to describe a liberal. I'm not even liberal. I'm progressive."

I had no idea what that meant. I picked up a spoon and dug into my rice dressing.

"He wouldn't let me leave," Evangelina continued. "He talked about a race war and how the blacks were gonna get their asses handed to them. He went on and on. I locked myself in the downstairs bathroom and climbed out the window. His roommates showed up. They had to restrain him. One of them walked me to my car. He told me not to bother reporting any of this as

Hunter was currently at a training seminar in Memphis and no one would believe me. I drove to the gallery. Then you came."

"A training seminar in Memphis?"

"Yeah. I assumed it was his alibi. But who knows? And guess what? As I'm driving away, I happened to see that truck that blew the exhaust out at me parked nearby."

She put her purse back down on the floor.

"Anyway, none of it happened because he was at a training seminar in Memphis."

When she said training seminar, she made quotation marks in the air with her fingers.

"I couldn't defend myself. But I tell you what. If he ever comes near me again, he better pray I shoot his ass because if I get my hands on him, I'm gonna seriously fuck him up."

For someone who'd never used profanity in front of me before, that was her second f-bomb in less than five minutes.

"Well, I think you came out of all that pretty good."

"I joined a gym."

She raised both arms and struck a double biceps pose.

"And I haven't been drinking as much."

"I'm a bad influence."

"Ha! No. I have a problem. Here's the thing, though. A lot of guys have taken advantage of me. You never did. You always look out for me."

She smiled. She obviously had no recollection of the kiss we shared the last time we were in this room together.

"You don't paw at me or try to put your hands all over me. One time I mentioned you to Hunter. He said you either liked dudes or were too old to get it up."

I laughed.

"Even my trainer tries to cop a feel on me. One day, I'm gonna kick his balls straight up into his throat."

"So, you're hitting the gym, you got a trainer, you're not drinking anymore, yet here we are eating fried chicken. Again."

She flashed her mischievous grin.

"It's my cheat day."

After we ate, Evangelina sat cross-legged on a stool sucking on a thirty-ounce bottle of water. She talked about her workouts and the diet she followed. Around nine, she headed home to do some yoga. I walked her to her car. There was no hug.

She kept in touch. I heard all about the meals she cooked and how much she benched. One afternoon she called to tell me she deadlifted twice her bodyweight. I bumped into her a few times after work leaving the gallery with a towel draped around her neck. She did look good, though I preferred her soft and delectable over cut and defined.

Saturday after work I stopped at the pub during Vinyl Brunch for a Cuban sandwich and a couple beers. When I got to the apartment, Evangelina was out front with a water bottle in one hand and a half-eaten protein bar in the other. Her bright yellow yoga pants elegantly highlighted every delicious curve below her waist. We sat on the bench.

"You're just getting off work?"

"Yeah," I lied.

"How's it going?"

I mumbled something in response. I did not want to go there with her. Harleigh was the only person I vented to. She in turn offered sarcasm over sympathy.

"You know what you need? A change of scenery."

She checked the time on her phone.

"Oh, shit. I gotta go. I took my preworkout like an hour ago. After while, crocodile."

The next afternoon, she called while I was at the laundromat.

"What's up?" she asked.

"Not much."

"What?"

"I said not much."

"I can't hear you."

"I'm at the laundromat. Hang on."

I walked outside.

"You still there?"

"Yes, I'm here. Are you writing?"

"Writing? No, I'm washing clothes."

"Ruston, you're not knee-deep in the Vermillion River beating them against a rock now, are you?"

"No."

"Then you could be sitting with your laptop hammering something out."

"I know."

"Have you tried getting someone else to publish your work?"

"Yes."

"Who?"

"A publishing company here in Lafayette."

"What happened?"

"They wanted to know if I had anything published before. I showed them Robicheaux's magazine. They laughed. They told me writing should evoke the elegance of a ballroom dance and that my writing was like a bare-knuckled fistfight between crackheads on a dead-end dirt road strewn with overgrown weeds and discarded diapers."

"Jeez."

"They said I looked like a shipping clerk and I better go back to that before I hurt myself."

"Do you agree with Mr. Robicheaux not printing anything you've written lately?"

"Well, he's trying to maintain what little credibility I have."

"What are you doing for Thanksgiving?"

"Thanksgiving? Uh, nothing."

"What about your family?"

"We don't get together."

"Aw, that is so sad."

"Wasn't always like that. Things changed after my dad and grandparents passed away."

"Do you ever talk to your mom?"

"Not in years."

"So, you're just going to sit alone in your apartment?"

"Looks like it."

"Why don't you come take a ride with me."

"Where?"

"I'm going see my parents. They would freak if I brought you home, but I can drop you somewhere and pick you up on the way back. Any place you want. Lake Charles, Beaumont, Houston."

She gasped.

"Ooh, Discovery Green!"

"What's that?"

"A beautiful park in downtown Houston. You'd love it. Go online and book a room nearby."

"I'll think about it."

"I'm leaving the Tuesday."

"I work that day."

"Just think about it and let me know."

A couple days later, I got to the office, shook the computer awake, and typed in my password. It didn't take. I tried a second time. Same result. The phone rang. It was Darby.

"Were you able to log in?" she asked.

"No. I tried twice already."

"We got a virus. Someone opened an email and it spread. Let's go take a smoke."

We went downstairs. I asked about the work schedule the following week. She said Thursday and Friday were paid holidays, and most everyone scheduled vacation Monday through Wednesday. Including herself, as her birthday always fell on or around Thanksgiving.

When we got back up to thirty-nine, I got a coffee then went to my cubicle. Darby called about ten minutes later and said we had to reset our passwords. She gave me the steps to follow. I got to where it asked to input a new one.

I tried my old one first, "70595rcd".

It couldn't be the same as my previous password.

I tried "70544rcd".

It couldn't be like my previous password.

I put in "ruston".

It needed to be at least ten characters.

I tried "ruston43!!"

No special symbols.

How about "rustonchristopher"?

At least one capital letter.

Frustrated, I typed "thisissomestupidfuckinSHIT111".

That took. I jotted it down on a yellow sticky tab.

Bridgett walked up.

"Why didn't you sign on to the new program?"

"You told me not to."

"Well, I need you to do it like right now."

I double-clicked the icon while Bridgett moved in uncomfortably close. She barked out orders as I maneuvered the mouse around. I got this sickening image of her doing the same to her husband as he tried to get her off.

"What are you doing? Right there. Wait, that's not it. Ooh, right there. Keep it right there. Don't move. That's it. Go down. Down! Faster!"

She put her hand on top of mine. I had no idea what she wanted me to do. I assumed it was routine for her to guide a man's hand on the proper way to handle her business.

The program said to restart my computer. When I logged back in, I accidentally typed in my old password. When it didn't take, I tried my new one and got that wrong as well. I referred to my yellow sticky tab.

"You don't even know your own password?"

After I put it in, she said, "Let me do it. I can do it faster myself anyhow."

"I'm sure you can."

I grabbed my lighter and cigarettes and walked to the elevator. When I got to the smoking area, I took out my phone and texted Evangelina.

Hey. Is offer still good?

Yes!

Count me in.

YAY!!!

Departure time Tuesday 9 SHARP!

BE READY FREDDY.

I finished my cigarette and went back up. Bridgette was nowhere to be found. I took a seat and began scouting hotel rooms around the downtown Houston area.

CHAPTER 19

November 25 – December 1, 2014

Tuesday morning, I went downstairs to the coffee shop with my duffel bag. A crudely written sign taped to the front door read "drink orders only." Sheila stood behind the counter sporting cut-off jeans and a white halter top. She wasted no time in asserting her sixteen-year-old independence from her parents while they were away on their cruise. I saw them off Saturday before I headed to the office. Nancy gave me a tender peck on the cheek. Dean followed with a bro hug. He told me to keep an eye on the place. I didn't mention Houston.

As Sheila poured my coffee, I asked how her parents were doing.

"Mom's probably swinging on a dick while dad is knee deep in poontang."

I gave her a confused look.

"Ruston, my parents are swingers. They're on a swinger's cruise."

"Swingers?"

"Jesus. I knew you were too dense to figure it out. They're always talking about you. You didn't know about Miss Rachel?"

"Tanning salon Rachel?"

"Yep. That's who my dad is porking."

"Wait. Why were they talking about me?"

"Mom wanted you, but you wouldn't play along. Too bad, I could have helped you out. I know what she likes. Their bedroom is right next to mine. I hear all the gore."

She put my coffee down on the counter.

"Although, I don't get it. You're so ugly. That whole beard thing is a major turn off. Plus, mom said you probably have a small wiener."

She grinned. I hadn't had a teenage girl try to humiliate me like that since high school. I prepared my coffee and got out of there.

I didn't notify anyone at the office I wouldn't be going in that day. Or tomorrow for that matter. Darby was correct when she said hardly anyone would be there. I emailed my timesheet to payroll before I left. Being that I was only a contract worker, I was not in position to receive any vacation or holiday pay. Even so, after I made rent and paid for the hotel in Houston, my account remained in the black. In addition, payroll deducted the last twenty-five dollars for the laptop the previous week.

Evangelina drove up. She wore faded jeans, a tucked in white button down, and a navy-blue blazer. I tossed my duffel bag in the backseat and off we went. She reached over and fumbled with the radio as we conversed back and forth. In no time, we passed the frog capital of the world and settled in with the I-10 traffic headed west. At mile marker seventy-two, near the adult superstore, she playfully slapped me on the leg.

"I have an idea," she said.

Her idea was to paint portraits of local musicians inside various music venues around the Acadiana area. She wanted to begin with Winslow's band at the pub and asked if I would write something to accompany each piece. She said publicity generated could spark interest in both our respective ventures. It was a fine idea and I said as much. She smiled. We would begin as soon as we got back to Lafayette.

She took the 210 exit into Lake Charles and asked if I was hungry. I was. I planned to eat at the coffee shop but Sheila was only serving up drinks and humiliation. We stopped at a sports bar off College. It took a few minutes before a table opened. There were napkins piled on it almost a foot high. Evangelina suggested I get a shrimp poboy. When the waitress asked if I wanted jalapeno mayo on it, Evangelina responded for me.

"Yes, he does."

It was one of the best poboys I ever had. I made use of about a third of those napkins on the table. I had the goodness of my poboy in my beard, running down my arms, even on my shirt. Evangelina laughed.

"You're making a mess!"

"Hey, when it's this good, you eat some and you wear some."

Two hours later we were in front of my hotel on Bell Street. Evangelina said she'd call when she got to her parents' place. I checked in then ventured over to Discovery Green. The first thing I encountered there was a bronze statue of a naked anatomically correct male sporting wings and a bird mask crouched low on a sphere. He seemed ready to take flight at any moment. Behind him, a pair of round limestone structures sat roughly seventy feet apart. The concave interiors focused sound waves, an inscription read, allowing one to speak very softly in one vessel and be heard clearly in the other. I had to take their word for it.

I continued along and came across a restaurant. Since I was still wearing some of my poboy from earlier, I did not go inside. Next to the restaurant was an outdoor ice-skating rink. I explored the park for another hour or so before coming back to the rink and taking a seat. My phone rang. It was Evangelina. She was in good spirits. I told her where I was.

"Oh, how fun! Are they ice skating?"

"Yes," I said. "I'm watching them now."

"I love to ice skate. My parents would take me to the Galleria when I was young. You should see me. Although, I know you would enjoy that. You like watching me, don't you? I catch you looking. You think I don't notice but I do."

I was not expecting that. She continued.

"Go walk around tomorrow. The architecture is breathtaking. Who knows? Maybe it'll inspire you. Maybe you'll write about what you're doing right this moment. Maybe you'll even write about me. Wouldn't that be something? How would you describe me? Wait, don't tell me. God, I don't know if I'd even be able to read it. Well, gotta go. Talk to ya later. Miss ya. Bye!"

I hung up and looked around. The park was aglow in beautiful light. Holiday music played. All around me were laughter and smiling faces. In a city of four million people, I suddenly felt alone. I stood and went back to the hotel.

The next day, I took Evangelina's advice and went walk around the city. Along Jefferson Street, I spotted a sleek eye-catching building with black reflective paneling. As I stood across from it, captured in its reflection, I considered if working in an attractive building such as this one had the ability to make any job less nauseous. I decided no and moved on.

The war-torn building two streets up stood in stark contrast to the one I just admired. Standing thirty stories tall, it looked to be an old, abandoned hotel. Many of its windows were either missing, broken, or covered in graffiti splashed plywood. I imagined it known for being a public eyesore than for any glamour once attached to it.

Halfway up, something caught my eye. At first, I thought it was a ball perched up against one of the broken windows. Or maybe a balloon? Or a head? It was a head. Someone was sitting with their arms folded on the windowsill. From this distance and through a dirty discolored window, the head looked the color of three-day old piss in an unflushed toilet. I stood transfixed as this individual raised a hand and scratched underneath its nose while it looked out over the city.

At the next block, I turned right on Louisiana Street. I was awestruck. These buildings of glass and steel were works of art. I imagined walking hand in hand with Evangelina as she gave me the detailed architectural history of each one's exterior. I took a right on Congress. Up ahead, a short Mexican guy with a cigarette dangling from his mouth fumbled about for a lighter. I pulled mine from my pocket and walked over. He cupped a nervous hand over the flame.

"Gracias," he said.

I smiled and lit one of my own. After a couple quick drags, he looked up at me.

"It's no good," he said in broken English. "They lie."

He looked back down at the ground.

"No good," he repeated.

Someone hollered something to him from across the street. His name apparently. I didn't catch it. Two men in business suits stood near a sign that read Harris County Family Law Center. One motioned with his hand. My friend took one last drag, stomped out his cigarette, and jaywalked in their direction.

After I finished my cigarette, I came up to a Catholic Church on Crawford across from Minute Maid Park. An afternoon wedding had just concluded. Family, friends, and well-wishers were lined up underneath a maroon canopy. I watched as the blushing bride climbed into a horse drawn carriage and scooched over. The look of trepidation on my face seemed to cause her pause. To smooth her concern, I waved and mouthed "congratulations." She smiled the biggest smile.

My stink eye was not meant to cause harm. I simply was not sure as to what degree of expertise her new husband happened to be behind the reins. I pictured the news crawl.

Cajun crushed after carriage careens out of control on Crawford

The lucky groom climbed in, gave a tug, and off they went clopping down Texas Avenue.

A vigorous cold front pushed through Thanksgiving Day. I ate breakfast at the hotel and had a pizza delivered. I logged on to Facebook and saw Evangelina had posted pictures of her family. So had Darby. Nancy shared a few from the cruise. There was no hint of swinger activity. Harleigh called. I told her where I was.

"You went all that way just to have her dump you off while she goes spend time with her family?"

"I had no interest in meeting them anyway."

"I figured you would say that."

I told her about the portraits Evangelina wanted to do and the stories I would write to go along with them.

"That's cool, but this whole thing is weird."

"What's so weird about it?"

"You have a hard-on for her. How would you feel if some guy twenty years younger than me got me all worked up?"

"Well, figuring that would make the guy a teenager, I'd think you were sick."

"There you go."

"She's twenty-six."

"So?"

"She's not a teenager."

"She's still a lot younger than you, dude."

We went back and forth like that. After we hung up, I drank myself unconscious.

The next day, I emerged from the hotel and walked over to Discovery Green. The weather was crisp, about fifty degrees, with a strong north wind and abundant blue skies. I got a small coffee then took a seat and watched a couple ice-skate. An older man approached and sat next to me. He wore a vintage newsboy's cap, round wire rim glasses, and carried a cane.

A few minutes went by. Without looking at me, he said, "Nice weather out."

"Yes, sir. It is."

"That accent. Where is it you're from?"

"South Louisiana."

"Ah, yes. South Louisiana. There is a Cajun restaurant over on Richmond. Has a crawfish on the roof, it does. What is it you do in Louisiana?"

"I'm a writer moonlighting as a bookkeeper."

"A writer. I see. Name's Gustav."

"Ruston."

"What you got there in your hand, Ruston?"

"Coffee."

"Ah, yes. Coffee. Know what warms my bones on a cold day like today?"

"What's that?"

"A hot toddy."

"I've never had one."

"I'll make you one."

"Where?"

"My place."

He stood and pointed with his cane to a tall building next to the park.

"Come, now. I want to hear more about this writing you do."

I hesitated. One of two things could happen. One, he might be someone who could help me. Two, he may murder me. Figuring either way I had nothing to lose, I got up from the bench and followed.

We entered the building underneath a huge Texas state flag and took the elevator up to the twenty-fifth floor. He led me into a warm sun-lit apartment with a study. There might have been a hundred books along its walls. Gustav left me while he went into the kitchen. I heard glasses tinkering and spoons stirring. He returned with a glass in each hand, the crook of his cane draped over his forearm. He handed me my drink then motioned with his toward a section of ten or so books.

"Those are mine."

"You're a published author?"

"That I am. Come. Follow me."

He led me out onto the balcony. The view over the park was spectacular. I sipped from my drink.

"Mm, good. Thank you."

"That it is. You're welcome."

We sat in silence. Then it came. I knew it would.

"Ruston, I'm a lonely man. I need someone to take care of me and my needs as a man. Being that you're a man yourself, you know what it is I'm referring to. You're a writer. You can write here. I can get you published. You're moonlighting as a bookkeeper. That tells me things are not going well for you. I have connections that can make things happen."

He took some of his drink.

"The fact you have that beard is a bonus. I had a bearded fellow once. It tickled when he tongued my ass."

"Sorry, Gustav. Not my thing."

"Won't you at least consider it?"

"Sorry."

He nodded his head and turned away from me.

"I understand. You can see yourself out."

Back outside, I looked up at the building and counted the floors up. There he was. Legs crossed; his face faced upwards absorbing the warmth of the sun. If he was a she, I would still be up there. I would text Evangelina not to bother coming for me. Speaking of which, the last I talked with her was Tuesday.

She texted the following day. She would be at the hotel around ten Sunday morning. She drove up at 10:45 in a rotten mood. When I asked how it went with her family, she only shrugged. I figured some drama went down and was glad not to have been a part of it.

We stopped in Lake Charles for gas. I went in for a pack of cigarettes. When I walked out, she was arguing with someone on her phone. We drove the remainder of the way in silence. Outside of the apartment, I got out and grabbed my duffel bag.

"Thanks," I said.

"Uh-huh."

She sped off.

I checked the mail, unlocked the gate, and climbed the steps. Once inside, I lay on the sofa and fell fast asleep.

The next morning, I went downstairs and found the windows of the art gallery covered in newspaper. I knocked lightly and tried the door. It was locked. I walked around to the parking lot. The Volks was not there. Evangelina had apparently returned at some point. I decided that if she was not there when I got back that night, I'd give her a call.

When I got to the office, the bullshit crew stood around the breakroom discussing the runoff election between Bill Cassidy and Mary Landrieu set for Saturday. Darby came by. She snuck a kiss on my cheek and told me all about her birthday slash Thanksgiving weekend. Bridgett appeared. She pestered me about the new program and said Breaux would soon show me how it worked. The auditors arrived. On my way to the elevator, Guillory cornered me. He said all bookwork needed to be done by the first of February. A way out of this mess did exist.

Gustav's ass.

I continued with the bank reconciliations.

At seven, I headed to the apartment. When I got there, I saw that the newspapers that covered the windows of the gallery this morning were gone. And so was everything else. The place was empty. Not a painting or an easel. Not even a paintbrush. I stared in disbelief. In the corner of the window was a For Lease sign with Robicheaux's number at the bottom. I considered the logistics. She had gotten the place cleared out in less than twelve hours. Unless she had help, and a head start. The newspapers in the window concealed that possibility to me.

I went upstairs and checked Facebook. I couldn't find her page. I sent Harleigh a text.

> Hey. you busy

Whats up

> Can you look for someone on Facebook for me

Perv. Now U want me to stalk your bitches 4 U

Who?

> Evangelina Davis

The girl from the gallery?

> Yes

> She's gone

What?

I'm calling you

"What do you mean she's gone?"

"The gallery is empty. There were newspapers covering the windows this morning."

"Weren't you with her yesterday?"

"Yeah, but she didn't say anything."

"Theresa bought some paintings from her today."

"Really? Did Evangelina tell her she was leaving?"

"Not that I know of."

"Is Theresa there now?"

"No. She's not coming back till late."

"Damn!"

"Dude, chill. I'll ask her about it in the morning, okay? I'm looking for your girl now. I think I remember what she looked like."

She pecked on her computer.

"I think this is her. Evangelina Davis. Pasadena, Texas?"

"Yes."

"Her page is set to private. There is nothing to see besides her profile picture."

"Why can't I get to it?"

"She must had blocked you, dude."

"Blocked me?"

"You sure nothing happened?"

"She barely said five words yesterday."

"What about before that?"

"The last thing she told me Tuesday was she missed me."

"I don't know what to tell you. When Theresa gets back, I'll talk to her."

"Thanks, Rosceaux."

CHAPTER 20

I began the year determined to get back on track. Twelve months later and that optimism eroded completely. Any thought the novel would be my salvation was gone. I found myself in the clutches of dreaded familiarity, back within the confines of a routine. My thoughts now consumed with the approach of the February bookwork deadline imposed upon me. I convinced myself that if I did not complete the bank reconciliations in time, I would be let go.

In addition to my imagined termination, thoughts of Evangelina weighed on my mind. She told Theresa she met someone online and was going back to Texas to be with them. There were two moving trucks parked out front when Theresa arrived Monday morning. Evangelina's parents were there as well. Theresa purchased several paintings at a discounted price and left soon after. Nancy and Dean, back from their cruise, also mentioned the trucks along with Evangelina's parents. Evangelina told them she couldn't pay her bills.

"Big surprise," Dean added. "Nobody earns a living painting pictures. She needs a real job. These libtards just want everything handed to them. I told my brother leasing her that space was a bad idea."

Dean's comments made me suspicious. Could Hunter Hilliard be responsible for Evangelina leaving so abruptly? His Facebook provided no clues. Meanwhile, I took to searching Evangelina's name at least once a day in the hope she unblocked me. Harleigh mentioned she more than likely blocked my number as well so any calls or texts would go unanswered.

During a drinking bout up in my apartment, I asked to borrow her phone. I figured Evangelina would not answer a number she didn't recognize so the plan was to call and leave a voicemail. I had no idea what I would say. It was just one of those moments. Harleigh looked me square in the eye.

"Dude, I know it sucks but you need to let it go. I told you she was too young for you. Though I think something forced her hand. She didn't have a choice. Be glad it ended this way. It didn't get messy. She doesn't want anything to do with you anymore. Okay? Just let it go."

I was thankful for Harleigh in moments like that.

On the fourteenth, I met up with Robicheaux near the 9/11 Memorial in Parc San Souci to pay my rent. He confided Evangelina's parents cut a check for the remainder of her lease with no explanation given. We noticed construction over by the water fountains. A friend of his with the Downtown Association walked up and showed us a sketch of the area with Lafayette, minus the Y, spelled out in huge six-foot tall concrete letters. I asked about the missing Y. The woman took a step back, cocked her hip to one side, and raised her arms high.

"So people can stand and fill it in themselves," she said. "We're asking everyone to share their pictures online with the hashtag Y Lafayette."

I had no clue what that meant. She asked Robicheaux if he heard from Evangelina since she left town.

"No," he answered.

"I bought a few of her paintings. I was so sorry to hear she moved back to Texas. She left us with a great idea, though. We're going to start having Art Walks once a month sometime in the future."

I thought she said aardvarks. She laughed.

"No, couyon. *Art. Walks*. One Saturday each month, downtown will get together to host local artists and display their work."

A few days later, an office email announced that with Christmas falling on a Thursday, all Thomas, Madison offices would close the Friday after. Employees who wished to be compensated for that day would simply input either vacation or sick time onto their timesheets. While everyone was joyful of the extended time off with pay, I was shit out of luck. Not only would I not be paid, but I would also lose three days of work, a major detriment to getting the reconciliations done by February. A fact not lost on Breaux. I was thus encouraged and given security clearance to come in and work during the long holiday break.

Christmas Eve morning, I showered, shaved, and headed to the office. Danny greeted me with a nod of the head. It would be only the two of us there, serving what purpose in the whole grand scheme of things I didn't understand. All I knew was I needed to complete the bank reconciliation for the month of October for Martin's Grocery before I left.

I had a difficult time staying focused. I made a pot of coffee, stared out the windows, took multiple smoke breaks, and got more despondent as the day wore on. Finally, it got to that point. No way would the reconciliations be completed in time. I only started in September for Christ's sakes. I gave up.

At the same time, a cold front plowed through outside. The temperature plummeted something like twenty-five degrees in a matter of minutes. I went down to the first floor, returned Danny's nod, and for reasons unknown made my way to Girard Park rather than my apartment. There I stood under the pavilion over the pond struggling to light a cigarette in thirty mile-per-hour winds with no coat on. I'd gone from a warm empty forty story office building to a cold desolate thirty-three-acre public park for no other reason than to suffer for some higher power's amusement I gathered.

I awoke Christmas morning face down on the kitchen floor in a puddle of my own vomit with no recollection of the walk back to the apartment. I struggled to my feet, stepped over a couple beer bottles, and tried to locate my phone. It was nowhere to be seen. I even checked the stove, which I never once used in the four years I'd been there. After relegating myself to the thought I lost it, I later found it in the refrigerator.

That afternoon, I got a text from Darby. She had a gift for me and wanted to come by if that was okay. I responded that it was and got to cleaning myself and the apartment. She called after it got dark and said to go downstairs. A huge white SUV with tinted windows sat parked out front. The passenger side window came down.

"Hey!" said Darby.

"Hey. What's this?"

"Herman totally surprised me. Hop in."

I climbed in and pulled the door shut. Darby handed me a box elegantly wrapped in shiny red paper. Inside was a journal with my name engraved on the Italian leather cover.

"Wow!"

"You like?"

"I do. Thanks."

I gave her a peck on the cheek. She blushed.

"Ruston," she said. "I'm sorry I'm a little crazy sometimes. Thank you for not taking advantage of me. I love Herman, I do, truly. You understand, right?"

I nodded my head.

"I better go," she said.

I returned to the office the following day. And the day after. All weekend for that matter. While everyone basked in five days of holiday festivities and cheer, I completed the October and November bank reconciliations for Martin's Grocery.

2015 rolled in just as I took a piss in the men's room at The Bistro. Harleigh pestered me for about a week to go to their New Year's Eve party and I was glad I did. We had our picture taken in front of a gold shower curtain decorated with purple and green Mardi Gras beads. Some girl named Jennifer even gave me half an hour of her time before she realized I was a lost cause. It was close to four when the place shut down.

I followed Harleigh outside. She tended to the bamboo plant behind the lattice fence.

"We survived another year, Rosceaux," I said.

She put her hand up to my face.

"I give you shit but you know I believe in you, don't you?"

I smiled.

Then she slapped me. Hard.

"So stop being a whiny little bitch and get back to writing. It's a whole new year, man. You need to catch your head."

I rubbed my face.

"That hurt."

"Good."

She unlocked her bike and pedaled away. I began making my way back to the apartment.

"Hey!" Harleigh shouted. "Look at me! Riding off into 2015!"

"Yeah," I yelled back, "but you're prepared! You got your helmet and pads on!"

"Dude! I swear! If you're still like this a year from now, I'm gonna kick your ass!"

She continued down Johnston with both middle fingers raised high.

CHAPTER 21

December 2010 – March 2011

SWLA Free Press
plunging headfirst
by ruston delahoussaye
Volume 5 Issue 8

The first round of layoffs occurred at the end of October. More followed the week after Thanksgiving with the final one slated for December 30th. Only maintenance would remain into the new year. When my time came, few remained to shed tears with. Instead, I looked ahead to my first sit down with Robicheaux in the morning. I submitted a couple stories to him. There was interest. We agreed to meet at the Lafayette Public Library on West Congress.

On the way, I happened to pass in front of the plant. I noticed my desk and chair outside near the garbage bins. That desk, hit countless times by various forklifts over the years, stood bent and broken, while my chair, thoroughly stained with body sweat and spilled coffee, had been comfortable enough. Though they served their purpose well, there they sat, discarded, no longer wanted, or needed. Don't I know the feeling. I steered the Cutlass ahead and didn't look back.

I recalled the night I left that voicemail on my sister's phone. I'd stumbled out of bed, pissed in the garbage, tripped over a beer can, and just about took my bookshelf down with me. All my books fell to the floor. I picked one up opened to a random page. The author complained too many books existed at that point and questioned what the world would want with more. In another, a fellow told of a check he received in the amount of $175 for a story he submitted. Intrigued, I flipped ahead. I found him at work on a manuscript. He described the days as both prosperous and marvelous, and went on to say with the rent paid, the only thing left for him to do was write.

Those books were from my father and grandfather's personal collections. There was Fante and the Los Angeles dust. Miller, who'd signed his name to the door of the art studio at The Shadows, and Burke, whose crime novels entertained my dad for years. A few, like Carver's short stories and Bukowski's poetry, made immediate impacts on me. After I exhausted those, I began making weekly trips to the public library in Jeanerette. By chance, I happened upon Robicheaux's magazine. He accepted submissions of all sorts.

I drove to my mom's place on Glover, located my grandfather's old typewriter up in the attic, and took it to an office supply store in New Iberia. A smile came to the face of the elderly gentleman behind the counter as he ran his hand along the old machine. He offered to fix it up on his own time, on his own dime. Turned out, he knew my grandfather. Small world.

My first story concerned a man in his late sixties forced into retirement. A can of warm beer in his hand, a Colt .45 by his side, his last days a race between the bottle and the bullet. The bottle often victorious because it was the more patient. I chose not to tie the end into a neat bow. Most people enjoy smooth round finishes. I preferred jagged edges.

I walked into the library New Year's Eve morning with my manila folder of short stories and poetry under my arm. The librarian, kind and gentle, said she'd direct Mr. Robicheaux to my whereabouts as soon as he arrived. In the meantime, there was coffee, and the restrooms were to the right.

The SWLA Free Press mostly made its money from advertising, with a modest circulation along the Gulf Coast. Besides fiction and poetry, it contained articles, columns, opinions, cartoons, and reviews of various sorts. Robicheaux believed he could reach a certain segment of society with my writings. Namely, those walking a thin line while an endless stream of negativity constantly scrolled about in their heads like the ticker at the bottom of a twenty-four-hour news channel. Their vulnerability, their sanity, their very souls hanging by the thinnest of threads. My words, sharp and biased, ready to slice through. I didn't know about all that, but he was willing to publish me at six cents a word.

Months later, I stood with him in front of a two-story building near the corner of Buchanan and Garfield. He gave me two sets of keys. We then walked the two blocks over to Parc International. It was opening night of the 27th anniversary of Downtown Alive, an outdoor live music event that happened early on Friday evenings during the spring and fall months. People gathered to eat, dance, and laissez les bons temps rouler.

Robicheaux was offering me a taste of what Lafayette had to offer. Not only were musicians scoring with festivals, fais do-dos, folk jams, and Sunday brunches, but writers were cashing in as well. He picked up on this, self-funded the magazine, and was beginning to see a return on his investment. He had been on me to move from my place in Jeanerette. Toward the end of the evening, he asked me to consider writing a screenplay for him.

I drove back to Jeanerette to collect my things. A letter in the mail indicated I was eligible for Trade Adjustment Assistance, meaning I would be able to take courses at the local community college with all tuition paid and job placement upon graduation. I tossed the letter in the garbage.

The next morning, I left the keys for the trailer in the mailbox and headed to Lafayette. I felt elated, as though a new life was opening before me. Robicheaux mentioned a food truck scheduled to be at the library that afternoon. I parked in front of the apartment, unloaded the Cutlass, put a pot of coffee brewing, sat before the typewriter, and got to work.

CHAPTER 22

The vibe of the office changed with the arrival of the New Year. The 2015 tax season was upon us. No longer would there be a mass exodus come five o'clock. Things got serious. Even the bullshit crew were not spending nearly as much time bullshitting near the breakroom. My concern though lay with the bank reconciliations. The February deadline fast approached. I was on edge.

On the morning of the twelfth, I received a forwarded email from Breaux. It contained a list of items to be discussed at the weekly CPA meeting currently ongoing in the conference room. As I glanced over the email, Bridgett walked into my cubicle.

"Let's go! What are you doing? We're waiting on you!"

Without a word, I stood and followed her into the conference room. Ten or so people were inside. Guillory and Breaux, Darby, the other CPAs, along with their respective secretaries. Bridgett took a seat. No other chairs were available.

Guillory brought up a subject, someone put their two cents in, the secretaries scribbled on yellow legal pads, Guillory brought up another subject, and the scene repeated. I recognized a few of the talking points from the email Breaux sent. Then, everyone turned their attention to me. Guillory asked where we stood on bank reconciliations. I was not sure how to respond.

He leaned back in his chair.

"You have a completion percentage?"

A what? I had no clue what he was talking about.

"No," I said.

"Well, see that you get one."

I stood ignored for the remainder of the meeting. Back at my cubicle, one of the secretaries poked her head in. I didn't know her name, but I had seen her before. She was the only black person who worked there.

"Russell, right?"

"Close enough."

"Do you know what Mr. Guillory meant by completion percentage?"

"No."

"It's a spreadsheet based off the Master List. We call it the CPS. I did bank reconciliations some time back. You check a box when you complete a month for a client and it will give you a percentage for each one, plus a total for the whole office. For instance, when you finish the year, it will say one hundred percent complete. Do you understand?"

"Yes."

"I'll email it to you. You have any trouble, let me know."

"Thanks. I appreciate it."

She gave a firm nod of the head and walked away. I still didn't know her name. Just as I stood to grab some coffee, Darby appeared.

"Uh, what was that about?"

"What?"

"Don't play dumb with me. What was that black bitch doing in your cubicle?"

I looked at her. She got in my face.

"I asked you a question. What was Beverly doing here?"

So, that was her name.

"She told me about the CPS."

"Why didn't you ask me?"

"Why didn't you tell me about it before?"

"What are you implying?"

"Nothing. I just…"

"Jesus! What is your problem?"

She burst into tears and ran off. The email Breaux sent was still up on my screen. It originally had been sent out Thursday afternoon. One of the subjects to be discussed was bank reconciliations. He must had forwarded it to me from his phone a minute or so before they sent Bridgett to fetch me. A dick move. I got up to find Darby. I found her crying at her desk. I apologized and consoled her as the others looked on. It was awkward as fuck.

Beverly emailed the CPS to me. It had months laid out left to right, a list of clients top to bottom, formulas applied, with totals on the far right. After I updated it, it showed 67% of the bookwork was complete. Darby told me not to concern myself with some companies as their returns always got extended further into the year. Without those, the total only rose to 74%. Martin's Grocery had fucked me royally. I would not make the February deadline, and still believed I would be let go at the end of the month. The whole point of this was to write. I had not moved to Lafayette to do bookwork. I stood that much closer to the edge.

Along with tax season, it was also time for Carnival. Barricades would soon be going up to make way for the multitude of parades that rolled through the city. Drivers found them to be a nuisance. So did I, back when I had a car.

Besides barricades, King Cakes also began to appear. One was in the breakroom every Friday. On one particular Friday, a few members of the bullshit crew stood around chowing down on one of those King Cakes when suddenly there was a loud crunch, I heard it from my cubicle, followed by silence, then roaring laughter. Someone had unexpectantly chomped down on the baby. I heard the person say they chipped a tooth. While the others died of laughter, the newly chipped king went into the breakroom and spit pieces of the purple plastic baby, along with their tooth, out into the sink where it sat for the remainder of the day. In addition to unplanned dental work, this individual was now on the hook for the purchase of the next cake. The following Friday, I walked in on someone attempting to re-hide the baby in that cake before anyone noticed they'd gotten it. I turned and walked out.

On the thirty-first, Harleigh, Theresa, and I headed to Henderson for some boiled crawfish. They were small, as the season was still early, but seasoned well and easy to peel. I put away almost eight pounds, plus potatoes and sausage, along with a few beers. I felt bloated and useless, much like I always did after a vigorous crawfish binge. As I summoned the energy to stand, Theresa and Harleigh speculated as to why Evangelina closed shop and took off like she did. Theresa said she would get to the bottom of it and sent Evangelina a friend request on Facebook. Meanwhile, I went piss and wash my hands. When I got back, Theresa had her arms folded tightly across her chest.

"That bitch blocked me! Can you believe that shit? After all the business I gave her. She's lucky I don't go over there and bust one of those paintings over her stuck-up head."

We were well lubricated by that point. Back at their place on Carl Street, Theresa and Harleigh sparked up while they continued to harp on Evangelina. Harleigh came up with the idea that maybe Evangelina was still in the area. I mentioned I knew where she lived. The next afternoon, Super Bowl Sunday, we headed for her house.

Theresa took a right at the roundabout on to Ridge Road.

"Turn left near that salvage yard," I said from the backseat.

As Theresa steered the car down the gravel alley, I began to feel uneasy.

"What will we tell her?" I asked.

"We'll ask her what her deal is," Harleigh said.

"What if someone else is there?"

"Then we'll just say we're looking for a friend who used to live there."

"What if…"

"Geez dude! For real?"

"Will you two chill out?" Theresa said. "Ya'll making me nervous."

She inched the car past fenced in yards filled with rusted engine parts.

"Why are you driving so slow?" asked Harleigh.

"Shh! You're gonna draw attention to us."

"Don't shush me!"

"Goddamn! Goody two shoes Flanders back there got me paranoid."

"You're driving too slow! We look suspicious."

"No, I'm not!"

"If we know her, and we're just coming by to see her, wouldn't we be driving at a normal speed because we've been here before?"

Theresa thought it over.

"Oh, yeah."

She punched the accelerator. I flew back into my seat.

We stopped in front of the house. It appeared to be vacant.

"Ya'll go knock," I said.

"You go," said Theresa.

"That's gonna look suspicious if only one of us…"

"Oh, for fuck's sake!" Harleigh screamed. "Come on."

We walked up to the door and knocked. I braced myself for the expression on Evangelina's face when she saw us. Turned out, she was long gone. We peeked in through the windows. I happened to look into the room with the piano. I could have gone without seeing that.

On the way back into town, I told Harleigh and Theresa about how I would be fired in the morning for not completing the bank reconciliations in time. Neither had interest in my pity party.

"They're not firing you," Harleigh said. "Stop worrying yourself."

Theresa was less sympathetic.

"Send us a postcard from J-Town."

We went to the pub. The place was packed for the Super Bowl, many in either Seahawk green or Patriot red. I chowed down on a Cuban sandwich while everyone cheered and jeered with the ebb and flow of the game. Julian told me it would be close, and the Patriots would win. He was correct on both accounts, as an interception at the one-yard line sealed a New England victory in the final seconds.

The three of us left sometime after midnight. Harleigh put her hand up to my face.

"You're not getting fired tomorrow. Okay?"

"I wish I could believe you."

"Say hi to Dorothy for me."

As they drove away, she stuck her head out the passenger side window of Theresa's car.

"They're an awful crowd, ole sport. You better 'den all 'dem couyons. All 'dem!"

Alone in my apartment, I got drunk, stared at the TV, and overthought what lie ahead in the morning. It was over. This bullshit of being a writer, it was all over. Time had run out. I imagined Bridgett on her high horse hoofing it to my cubicle, a verbal lasso around my neck, dragging me out to pasture, or in this case the conference room, the same place I stood five years ago at the plant when they took aim and fired us.

I wondered if Darby would take one last elevator ride with me. If so, a stop on the twenty-eighth floor might be in order. I'd take her inside the file room and give her what she'd been aching for all this time, then bid her adieu with a tip of the hat.

Wait. I don't own a hat. Where would I find one at this hour?

I reached over for my beer, and promptly knocked it off the coffee table. It fell to the floor and rolled underneath the sofa. I had an impressive collection of half empty beer bottles going on down there. I got up and stumbled for another.

A heavy rain began to fall. The time and temperature sign on the corner read 3:35.

With all the overtime I'd been working, there was enough money in my account to cover rent for a couple more months, although when Robicheaux gets wind I lost the job, back to Jeanerette I go. I would get on as a stock boy at the lone grocery store in town with my sister Rebecca, making minimum wage working part-time hours alongside disrespectful teenagers glued to their phones, pass the days waiting for the inevitable, like a heart attack, or a rogue can of peas, maybe three of them for ninety-nine cents, rolling off a top shelf, one by one, and taking me out on aisle nine, where I'd lay sprawled out, like the dude on those yellow wet floor caution signs, the exact ones the janitor would place around my body.

Cleanup on aisle nine.

By daylight, the rain stopped. I headed for the office. I reeked of beer and two-day old crawfish. When I get back, I should stop at Nancy's for one last breakfast. Maybe invite her upstairs if Dean's not there. Oh yeah, he won't mind. Last week, when I opened the laptop to search for Evangelina's Facebook page, I had to reenter their Wi-Fi password.

Swingerz!!69.

Jesus. Can't see things right in front of me, like the shit for brain decision I made to move here and think I could make it as a writer.

I took a seat in my cubicle and waited. It felt as though I forgot something, like a hat, but that made no sense. I heard the bullshit crew going on about Speaker John Boehner inviting the Israeli prime minister to speak to Congress. The phone rang. It was Darby. She called on her cell to say she would not be at work today. Little David had a doctor's appointment. She went on to tell me about the Mardi Gras Ball her and her husband attended Saturday night at the Key Club in McMillan Branch. Julian came by. He asked if I saw the game last night.

"Told ya," he said with a wink of the eye.

I continued to wait. Someone walked out of the men's room. I guess the reason no other cubicles sat back here with mine was on account of the occasional stench emanating from the restrooms. I logged on to my computer. There were no new emails. When the bullshit crew vacated the breakroom, I went for a coffee. I looked toward the conference room. The door was closed. I imagined what they schemed inside. The completion percentage stood at 79%. Would they fire me this morning, or allow me to suffer for a couple more hours?

The day ended up going by without anyone mentioning anything to me about the completion of the bank reconciliations. In fact, no one mentioned them for the remainder of tax season. I never even saw Guillory or Breaux that entire day. After all I put myself through, I would be back in my cubicle tomorrow morning.

…Reality. At times, far worse than the imagination…

CHAPTER 23

February 6-8, 2015

I arrived at the office to find a manila envelope sitting on my chair. Inside was six months of check stubs and bank statements for a client I was not familiar with. I placed a call to Darby. She walked into my cubicle heavy on perfume, and dressed to the hilt in tight faded jeans, a white silk blouse, and open toe heels. She reminded me of a young girl suddenly blossomed and drunk with attention.

Darby was seventeen when a man twice her age took an interest in her, along with her virginity and her hand in marriage, from the small town of Krotz Springs, Louisiana, over to Lafayette, where she first settled into the role of bored housewife, then stay at home mom, now career woman. That much I was able to piece together. Someday I'd get the whole story. Under what circumstances though I was not sure.

She leaned in close and breathed something into my ear about fiscal years and how the bookwork for this client would not be due for several months. I reached for my lighter and cigarettes.

"Then I have time for a smoke," I said. "You coming?"

Downstairs, I hurriedly smoked a cigarette while Darby, oblivious to the stink of what I gathered to be discarded crawfish emanating from the trash dumpsters nearby, caught me up on the latest gossip concerning the office and her neighborhood alike. We were about to make our way back up when Winslow walked by with his shirt pulled up over his nose. I made introductions.

"Pleased to meet you," he told Darby.

He placed a hand on her shoulder and motioned towards me.

"Watch out for this guy."

He began to laugh.

"How many you got like that?" he asked me before pulling his shirt back over his nose and walking away.

"What's he talking about?" asked Darby.

"I went listen to his band a couple months ago with a friend," I said without thinking.

"I see."

She folded her arms across her chest.

"And who is this friend?"

"Oh, just someone who…"

I stopped.

"What is it?" she asked.

"You live in McMillan Branch."

"Yes."

"You told me this one time about something happening in your neighborhood."

"There's always something happening in my neighborhood. I could write a novel. No offense."

"No, this particular time was around Halloween."

Darby thought for a moment.

"I'm not sure. Sorry."

"Do you know a Hunter Hilliard?"

She made a face.

"He and his two roommates live around the corner from us."

"It might have been something with him. Do you know an Evangelina Davis?"

She shook her head.

"Nope. That name's not familiar to me."

"She drives a light blue *Volkswagen*."

With that, Darby remembered she saw Hunter in his front yard the morning of Halloween screaming profanities at a girl with strawberry blonde hair.

"What happened?" I asked.

"One of his roommates walked her to her car, and she drove away. The two of them dragged Hunter inside the house after."

"Any idea what was going on?"

"I think they were filming porn."

"Filming porn?"

"Yes. I've seen at least a dozen half naked girls around their place over the years. You know, most of those porn sites on the internet are just sick individuals taking advantage of young girls."

I didn't know that, but I nodded anyway.

"One of them even worked here," she added.

Just as she said that someone from the bullshit crew walked by. It seemed to rattle her.

"So, what happened to your friend?" she asked.

I frowned. I truly did not want to share Evangelina's story with her but doing so might help me find out as to why she left the way she did. Jesus.

Inverted nipples, the audit, and now this. I was getting in too deep with this woman.

Darby leaned in close. I lit another cigarette and told her everything Evangelina had confided in me concerning Hunter. When I got to the part about the pictures on his phone, her eyes widened with vindication.

"I knew it! Didn't I just say that? I told you!"

"Hold up swole up. That's a big leap in speculation. Look, Darby. Please don't tell anyone I told you about this."

She shot me a defiant look.

"What are you gonna do to stop me?"

I stubbed out my cigarette, looked around, then took her by the hand to the elevator. Once the doors closed, I brushed the hair from her face, ran the backside of my fingers against her cheek, and placed a single finger to her lips. I then violently pushed her against the wall and kissed her with all the want, passion, and desire I could muster. She completely surrendered. I reached around and grabbed a handful of her ass. She clutched at the sleeves of my shirt and whimpered. The elevator came to a stop at some random floor. We quickly separated.

I carried the scent of her perfume on me for the remainder of the day. Expensive perfume with intent and purpose. I searched yet again for Evangelina's Facebook page. Still no luck. It was crazy to think Darby had seen her leaving Hunter's place the same day I met up with her in front of the gallery. It would be so easy to believe Hunter had something to do with her leaving town, but I didn't see it. She was no longer concerned with him, and she certainly made no mention of him posting the videos he took of her on the internet. If something had happened, I would believe him responsible but both Theresa and Nancy saw her that morning she left and neither mentioned anything out of the ordinary.

In some stories, this would be the part where I put together some clandestine operation and sneak into Hunter's house in search of the elusive clue that would break the mystery wide open. But this was no such thing. I continued with the bank reconciliations.

Darby called later that afternoon. The entire office was now putting in hours with me on Friday afternoons and Saturday mornings. She asked if I would meet her at the dog parade tomorrow after work. I said sure.

"Ruston," she said before hanging up.

"Yes?"

"I need you to understand I love my husband."

"Yes, I understand."

She quietly hung up.

The next day, we met at the courthouse about 1:30. She stood near one of the blind justice sculptures with a little boy and small white shaggy dog. I noticed the dog was decked out in some sort of a costume. There was a man nearby with his back facing me. Well, I thought to myself, time to meet the 2013 Lafayette Businessman of the Year. As soon as I walked up to them, the man, holding a clipboard, walked away. He turned out to be one of the parade organizers.

"I'm so glad you could come!" Darby said.

She looked down at the little boy.

"David, I want you to meet mommy's friend. This is Mr. Ruston. He works with mommy in the tall building."

I smiled. His face flushed and sweaty from the sun, David was maybe three years old with dirty blonde hair. He looked up at me with accusatory eyes, like he knew exactly what I had done to his mommy yesterday on the elevator in the tall building.

"Hello," I said to him.

"And this down here is Peyton."

Peyton wore a black Saint's visor on his head and a mock headset around his neck. I petted him as he curiously sniffed my right boot.

The man with the clipboard barked instructions. Darby said to meet them over at Parc Sans Souci where the after "pawty" would be held. I told little David I would see him later and reached down to pet Peyton. He had lost interest in my right boot and was now vigorously scratching at the black shirt he wore with the gold fleur-de-lis on the side.

The parade headed south on Lafayette Street then made a left on to Vermillion. After it concluded, I took hold of Peyton's leash while David kept Darby occupied. Some brown lab in a cowboy hat gave Peyton lip, so we went off, found some shade, and people and animal watched. I now understood why I was there. Darby needed someone to look after the dog while she ran after her hyper little boy.

The park was a blur of activity. Kids climbed up on the letters of the Lafayette sign, parents took pictures, dogs barked, and music played. Then, out of nowhere, came a high-pitched scream. Little David was having a fit. They made a scene. Darby tried to conceal her embarrassment as she went about corralling him. Party over.

The four of us made our way to her SUV. Before they drove off, she said she would appreciate if I made an appearance at her church in the morning.

An Uber dropped me in front of Holy Cathedral about ten minutes before the service was to begin. The place looked much the same as it did four months ago, even the same two individuals greeted me when I walked in. The plan was to enter inconspicuously and make my way up to the risers. To my horror, Darby stood inside waiting for me. She walked up and gave a hug rated G for everyone.

Instead of hiding up in the risers, we sat directly behind the pastor's wife and kids. Everyone had kind smiles and warm handshakes. The lights went down, and the music started. We rose to our feet. Someone asked Darby where Herman was. She told them out of town. The music was more thunderous than what I remembered. Darby clapped and sang along. The pastor came out on to the stage.

"We're going to continue to worship God by receiving communion together. Our ministry assistants are beginning to distribute those emblems that represent our union with God."

Silver aluminum trays began making their way around. Each insert contained two small cups stacked atop one another. Bread in the bottom, juice on top.

"This is not a way or a means to be saved or get right with God," the pastor said. "Communion doesn't save us. Communion doesn't provide salvation. It provides people who are saved by the grace of God, through faith, an opportunity to profess their faith in Christ. Somebody say thank God for grace."

Everyone said thank God for grace. I didn't understand a word of what he said. The last time I was there, all I did was raise my hand. Now it was more involved.

The pastor continued.

"I want to bring your attention to first Corinthians, chapter eleven, starting in verse twenty-three. The Lord Jesus, on the night he was betrayed, took bread, and when he had given thanks, he broke it and said, 'This is my body, which is for you, do this in remembrance of me.'"

A tray made its way down our aisle.

"In the same way, after supper he took the cup, saying, 'This cup is the new covenant in my blood; do this, whenever you drink it, in remembrance of me.'"

Darby handed the tray to me. I raised my eyebrows. She smiled and nodded her head. I took two small cups and passed the platter down.

"So then, whoever eats the bread or drinks the cup of the Lord in an unworthy manner will be guilty of sinning against the body and blood of the Lord."

Holy shit!

"Everyone ought to examine themselves before they eat of the bread and drink from the cup. For those who eat and drink without discerning the body of Christ, eat and drink judgment of themselves."

Say what now?

"Everyone bow your heads, close your eyes. Paul is speaking of unconfessed sin within our lives. So, let's take a moment now and let us confess our sinfulness to the Lord."

The place went quiet. Darby closed her eyes and lifted a hand. I could hear her silently asking for forgiveness. Where do I start? How do I even begin? My forehead began to sweat. I would hate to spontaneously combust into the gates of hell right behind the pastor's family. Darby would be so embarrassed. Okay, here goes something. Jesus…

"You may partake of the bread."

Time's up.

"And of the cup."

I chewed the bread and downed the juice and braced myself for the lightning strike or ceiling tile about to strike me down.

"You may be seated."

The pastor made it through his sermon without any weather calamities or structure failures taking place. His message concerned bringing others to the Lord. The theme was 'Be a Bringer.' That was why Darby asked me to come. She scored major points with the congregation. I thought of the fishermen at Cypremort Point Beach who posed for pictures with their catches. After service, would they do the same with me? Maybe they would crown me catch of the day.

When the service ended, I was more than ready for an Uber to take me back to my apartment. Unfortunately, Darby had other ideas. She fetched David from the children's ministry, then invited me to attend the Scott Mardi Gras Parade with them.

"You remember Mr. Ruston? Say hello Mr. Ruston."

David glared at me. He knew what his mom and I were up to. I could see it in his beady little eyes.

I climbed into the SUV while Darby strapped David into his car seat. The little boy kicked his feet and screamed he wanted nuggets.

Mortified, Darby glanced at me. I placed a hand on her thigh.

"It's okay," I said.

She grabbed my hand and didn't let go as precious little David continued to make a fuss in the backseat.

We found a fast-food place near the parade route. David got his nuggets. I got a small coffee. The parade began. Sweaty wide-eyed kids ran after beads that landed nearby. I picked up a few and surrendered them over. A plastic cup about caught me square between the eyes. I one handed a pink football and gave it to David. After the parade, Darby drove me back to Lafayette. With little David fast asleep in his car seat, she pulled in front of my apartment.

"Touch my face like you did in the elevator," she whispered.

As I did, she reached over and began to fondle me. I didn't get hard. I pictured the news brief.

Darby continued to fondle me.

"What's the matter? It's okay. I know what to do."

She reached into her purse and produced a tin of wintergreen mints. I about shit myself. She shook the container.

"For next time," she said.

I laughed a nervous high-pitched laugh. A few hours ago, she swallowed the emblems that represented her union with God. Now this. They left to pick up Herman from the airport. Upstairs, I fell face first on the bed. How much more of that woman could I take?

CHAPTER 24

February 13 – March 15, 2015

Carnival season in south Louisiana ran from the sixth of January up until Ash Wednesday. January sixth, the twelfth night of Christmas, or the Epiphany, was when the three wise men brought gifts to the baby Jesus. Ash Wednesday was always forty-six days before Easter. Easter occurred on the first Sunday after the first full moon on or after the March equinox. A good deal of math involved for an event sometimes associated with debauchery and exposed breasts, though Lafayette did offer a family friendly Mardi Gras environment as did most other celebrations in the area.

On Friday the 13th, I snuck out the office by putting on my fool proof sham of going down for a smoke break. Harleigh and Theresa awaited me in the parking lot. I opened the back door to Theresa's car and climbed in. Harleigh handed me a White Russian daiquiri. I removed the strip of tape from the lid and poked it with a straw. Theresa put her window down, sucked at the last of her Fuzzy Navel, then tossed the empty cup into the dumpster. Harleigh, the well chewed end of the straw from her Cherry Bomb daiquiri still in her mouth, made a face.

"The fuck is that stench, dude?"

"Our toilets broke, Rosceaux," I joked. "We have to use these dumpsters."

Theresa stared wide-eyed from the rear-view mirror.

"For real?"

We drove to their place on Carl Street then made our way over to Cajun Field for Le Festival de Mardi Gras a Lafayette. The festival, which ran till Fat Tuesday, offered parades, food, music, and a carnival midway. After the festivities ended, we cut through the University Hospital parking lot and made a death-defying dash across Bertrand. Theresa dropped the stuffed bear she won at one of the carnival games in the middle of the road. A car zoomed by and completely obliterated it. Theresa shook her fists.

"You son of a bitch! Damn you!"

After her meltdown was complete, the three of us went to the Cuban restaurant on the corner. Over the next couple hours, we went through two pitchers of Mojitos, a plate of Cuban style tacos, and three individual servings of tres leches cake.

I needed to piss. I walked to the back, took a wrong turn, and somehow ended up on a dance floor packed with people. The dizzying strobe lights got me disoriented. Suddenly, the music stopped, the lights came on, and before me stood this petite dark-haired beauty with piercing black eyes. I fell instantly in love. Then, the lights went out, the music cranked, and my Cuban angel was swallowed by the energetic crowd, forever scarred from her face-to-face encounter with the Louisiana rougarou. I never found the restroom.

Back at their place, Harleigh and Theresa sparked up and started in on me. They were both beyond wasted.

"So, how far have you gotten on your novel?" asked Theresa.

"I haven't started," I said.

"So what the hell you been doing all this time? You're just gonna keep working at that Hilfiger place?"

"Hilfiger? Thomas. Madison. It's accounting, not fashion."

They both laughed.

"He likes working there," Harleigh said. "Some married woman, his office wife, fondles him down in the basement."

Theresa exhaled a puff of smoke.

"No shit? Does she know you're married?"

"She's married. Not me. And it's the file room not the basement."

"Did you know she's married? Who she's married to?"

"Yes, he knew," said Harleigh. "She's married to my old boss."

"Who?"

"Herman Naquin."

"Yep," I said. "A thirty-something year old guy got it on with a teenager and sanctified it through the holy bonds of matrimony. God bless America."

"You sick fuck!" yelled Theresa. "You got a married teenager playing with your pecker down at the hospital?"

"She's not a teenager! Who said anything about a hospital?"

They both exploded into laughter then eventually dozed off. I smoked a couple cigarettes and played on my phone. When the sun came up, I had an Uber take me to the office. I was not in my cubicle long before Darby walked up.

"You're wearing the same clothes you had on yesterday," she said with a hint of repulsion.

She leaned in and took a sniff.

"You smell like weed."

I tried to change the subject.

"I didn't see your SUV outside."

"Herman dropped me off. We're taking David to the children's parade after work."

She leaned in again.

"You sure you're okay?"

"I'm fine."

Then, with a shrug of the shoulders, added, "Mardi Gras."

I was more than fine, I was elated. There would be no domestic duties for me to perform that afternoon. At twelve, I remained on thirty-nine long enough so as not to run into the Naquin family unit out in the parking lot. On my way back to the apartment, Vermillion was blocked off for the parade. I decided to blend in with the crowd and hope Darby would not spot me. I happened to catch a pair of beads. Two young kids stood nearby.

"Is that for your little boy?" one asked.

I handed the beads over.

"All you, little man," I said.

The taller boy was Matt, the younger one Michael. When the parade came to an end, I bid farewell to my young friends then made my way through the barricades back to my apartment. I took a long hot shower and watched the 6:30 parade from my window. I did the same for the Queen's Parade Monday night.

Mardi Gras morning, I went down to the coffee shop and walked in on a tense discussion concerning which member of the Robicheaux clan would stay and man the shop and who would go to what parade. An older woman in a glittery purple and gold shirt that read "What happens at Mardi Gras stays at Mardi Gras" glanced at me with a smirk on her face when Samantha dropped an f-bomb concerning the plans she made to attend the parade in Grand Marais.

Sheila put three drinks down on the counter. I prepared mine and headed for the office.

The following day, three members of the bullshit crew, each with ash on their forehead, stood near the breakroom. One had just returned from a weekend on Bourbon Street. He was showing the others pictures on his phone.

"Man, I hate that shit. Tits without tan lines are pointless."

"Check these out."

"Aw man, freckles! I fuckin' love freckles."

They made no attempt at being subtle.

"Those are deflated."

"Who let the air out!"

"HA!"

"Those look like saggy water balloons."

"Those will be down to her knees in twenty years."

The annual St. Patrick's Day celebration Patty in the Parc took place on March 14th. After carrying Harleigh's bike upstairs, we donned our green shirts and made our way to Parc International. Harleigh would color her hair for the occasion and always pressured me to do the same to my beard. I successfully denied her for another year.

We sampled all there was to offer food wise. Crawfish etouffee, red beans and rice, barbecue pork sliders, and bread pudding. An After-Patty Party was held at the sports bar across the street. Sometime after two that morning, Harleigh went to the restroom while I signed our receipt. I saw a familiar face. It was Hunter Hilliard in the flesh. Or specifically, in pink shirt, brown cargo pants, and beat up faded green cap. He sat a few tables over with two other guys. My mood soured. Harleigh returned. She noticed my discontent.

"What's wrong?"

"Remember I told you Evangelina was seeing a doctor?"

"And world traveler."

"Yeah. There he is."

She looked.

"Who? Needles?"

"Needles? Because he's a doctor?"

"Well, that. But mostly because of his dick."

"Excuse me."

She motioned with her hands.

"Long and thin," she said.

"And how would you be privy to that information?"

"He dated some girl Theresa knew. She described it as this long thin thing. He kept trying to stick it in her mouth and record it on his phone."

Harleigh hollered over to Hunter.

"Hey Needles! How's it stickin'?"

The others at his table got quiet. Hunter glared at her, then narrowed his eyes at me.

"Dude, if you don't shut your bitch up I will."

Harleigh pounced. She knocked Hunter to the floor and beat him about the head several times before I pulled her off him. Hunter's buddies picked him up and rushed him out a side door. Harleigh calmly examined her knuckles as I left an extra twenty on our table for the trouble we caused. Back at the apartment, she asked if I thought Hunter had anything to do with Evangelina leaving.

"I don't think so. She had a restraining order, along with a gun. She talked about wanting him to go after her just so she could kick his ass."

"That's what I'm talking about! Sounds like my kind of girl. Maybe I misjudged her. You didn't fuck her, did you?"

"No, I didn't."

"Obviously. You need the girl to make the first move, like that hurricane girl did."

"Ha! Hurricane girl."

"What was her name again? Sharon?"

"Lauren. And Evangelina did make the first move."

"Yeah, then she passed out. You think someone like Hunter would have stopped at that point?"

"I'd rather not think about that."

I paused and lit a cigarette.

"I never had someone like her show interest in me before."

"You were a good friend. She trusted you. She's from Houston, right?"

"Pasadena."

Harleigh took out her phone. She tapped on it for a minute or two.

"There she is."

She found an address in Pasadena near a playground fittingly called Strawberry Park. I noticed it was only thirty minutes from Discovery Green.

The sun rose about 6:30. I carried Harleigh's bike down the steps.

"How long are you going to be working those long hours?" she asked.

"No idea. I assume it'll calm down after tax season."

"How about we go take a ride after that?"

"Where?"

"Where? Where else? Pasadena, Texas, fool. If Theresa doesn't come, we can rent a car. You can stalk Evangelina from that park across the street. Maybe she'll swoon when she sees you."

"Maybe. She may also pull her gun."

"Indeed a possibility. How about I get you a bulletproof vest for your birthday?"

She climbed on her bike and headed home.

CHAPTER 25

March 23 – April 11, 2015

I finally neared completion of the 2014 bookwork. Darby became the liaison between me and the other CPAs in the office. Together we printed unadjusted trial balances, put folders in their proper order, and got the Completion Percentage Spreadsheet up to date. Soon, fiscal year bookwork was all that remained to be completed.

For the most part, my accuracy kept the powers that be out my beard. The one-two punch of Jim Guillory and John Breaux were vile reminders of past events that immensely altered the course of my life. Guillory, the model, medial, mediocre, middle-aged middle manager companies copied and pasted into positions such as his, along with Breaux, destined to fester in the bowels of lower management for decades to come, represented the sort that would lay off hard-working devoted individuals like my dad and grandfather in addition to sending jobs like my shipping clerk gig across the border without hesitation.

On the first of April, Guillory called me into his office, pointed a pink stubby finger in my direction, and thanked me for my hard work and dedication. I half expected him to shout April Fool. Instead, he asked if I had interest in becoming an official employee of Thomas, Madison, Smith and Associates, and the job security that went with it. Without waiting for an answer, he told me to leave the eighth of May open on my calendar, as that would be the day of the annual after-tax season crawfish boil. He then got to the matter at hand. Two weeks remained of tax season. Had I ever done a tax return before? He picked up the phone and called for Breaux to come immediately.

I cringed. It was painful to witness those two interact. Guillory showed no tact when he addressed Breaux. He ripped into him at times to the amusement of the bullshit crew. As we waited, Guillory explained the returns I was being asked to do were as simple as it got. He said most were individual returns CPAs brought with them from previous firms. He described them as somewhat of a nuisance as they could turn a mighty profit off a single thousand-dollar return compared to ten one-hundred-dollar returns.

When Breaux arrived, Guillory laid into him, questioning why he had me continuing with bookwork when tax returns needed to be done. Watching Breaux grovel and fellatio Guillory to make amends made me sick to my stomach. Back at my cubicle, Breaux gave me a crash course in tax preparation. He said to attack them with BFI: brute force and ignorance. A few weeks ago, I thought I might be terminated. Instead, Guillory entrusted me with more responsibility. Darby once talked of him as the ultimate salesman. To me that meant nothing more than conning a legless person into arch supports. Regardless, he did not allow me a chance to respond to anything he presented. He overwhelmed me with kindness and gratitude before blindsiding me with crawfish and job security.

Job security? That was a laugh. There was no such thing. My father and grandfather illustrated that for me perfectly. The chalk outlines in this office might need that illusionary job security so they could rot in perceived comfort. I understood it, but then again, I didn't. Why some chose to climb up on a chair and put their heads through a noose with four-digit monthly mortgage payments while raising kids who drank a six-dollar gallon of milk each day with the possibility of that chair being kicked out from underneath them at any moment without warning by a company or corporation who'd let them go at the drop of a hat or stock price was beyond me.

I took a deep breath. So, that was it? Take root in this cubicle and slowly rot the remainder of my existence away? What else was there to do?

Darby walked over. She seemed to be in some discomfort. She pointed to the stack of returns on my desk.

"What's going on?" she asked.

"Identity theft. Are you okay?"

"It's just my stomach. You're doing these returns?"

"Yes."

"Well, look at you. Mister Company Man. You're trying to make partner?"

"That's the plan. Hey, what's this about an office crawfish boil? Guillory told me to keep May eighth open on my calendar."

"He invited you?"

"It would appear so."

"I'm impressed. He's never invited a contract worker before."

Darby got with Barry in IT to install a second monitor on my desk. She said the use of two screens would greatly increase my productivity. She also wrangled me another calculator as mine possessed a font so ancient I believed it was chiseled into cave walls long ago.

I found the returns easier than bookkeeping. Darby showed me how to pull up a client's prior year return on one monitor as I entered the current year on the other. Most returns I did only consisted of a W-2. Others were more involved with various 1099 forms but no more difficult.

That night, Harleigh called to tell me she invited her mom over for Easter dinner. Mrs. Willie Domingue, the former Onelia Romero, was seated prim and proper on the sofa when I arrived there Sunday. She was a petite woman, more so than her daughter, with long grayish hair and black rim glasses. We had ourselves a fifteen-minute or so conversation where she asked questions about my life that showed genuine interest. She told me she would include me in her prayers. Her words felt sincere.

After Harleigh's husband killed himself, she went back to Winnfield to stay with her mom and dad. It was at that time she saw her parents' marriage with a new perspective. While not as far gone as Randall, her father's transgressions were well-known to her. He was also prone to violence when under the influence. Harleigh realized she'd been conditioned to accept her mother's fate as her own. She thus became disillusioned with the whole idea of marriage as well as religion. But rather than self-destruct, she self-expressed, channeling her discontent into different hair colors, multiple piercings, and conspicuous tattoos. She would never again allow herself to be a victim, much like Evangelina declared. Years later, after her dad got sick, some sort of reconciliation occurred before he passed. Even her sporadic relationship with her mom had been on slightly more stable ground.

We bowed our heads as Harleigh's mom said grace. Most of the usual crowd didn't show. Those that did quickly feigned excuses of other engagements. Easter Sunday at Harleigh and Theresa's usually resembled an R-rated sex comedy with Theresa and her web cam girlfriends putting on a live cam show while the entire house filled with pot smoke.

After dinner, Theresa and I cleaned up while Harleigh and her mom talked. Theresa ended up taking a nap. I sat in the kitchen by myself doing nothing more than being there for my friend if needed. After her mom left, Harleigh stretched her arms up over her head and exhaled a long satisfying sigh. Her wildly disheveled recently bleached blonde hair and red puffy eyes demonstrated she was mentally done. Theresa offered to drive me back to my apartment. The three of us stood silently in the kitchen for a moment. When I got to the door, Harleigh and I exchanged one last glance. No need for hugs or five dollar greeting cards with her. That last glance said it all.

Monday morning, I headed to the coffee shop. The only two in there were Nancy and a short overweight man with a sweaty upper lip. He worked his charm on her so intensely neither noticed when I walked in. Nancy made introductions. Gary from Indiana. They met on the cruise. Nancy placed my coffee on the counter. As she slid my debit card back to me, I told her thanks. At the same time Gary whispered something into her ear. Her face flushed red. She turned to me.

"Huh? What did you say?"

"Nothing. See ya'll later."

Friday afternoon, a torrential rain fell. I recently invested in a pair of Delcambre *Reeboks* along with a slicker suit but forgot to take them with me to the office. After arriving at the apartment completely drenched, I received a text from Harleigh. She was scheduled to work the afternoon and evening shifts the next day at The Bistro. I told her I would come spend the day with her after I got off work.

Thunder awoke me the following morning. I went to check the time on my phone but it was dead. I donned my boots and slicker and made my way to the office. I was halfway up to thirty-nine when I realized I left my phone charging back at the apartment.

The bullshit crew, already in non-tax season form, remained near the breakroom till well past nine.

"Liberal-in-Chief Obama wants a constitutional amendment to force Muslim prayer in schools."

"It's a sad day when our great nation is on the brink of becoming a third world country."

"Wake up, America!"

Darby came by. She said her husband drove her to work because many roads were flooded throughout the city. By noon, the rain had not let up. About two inches of water covered the floor of the smoking area. I sloshed over to The Bistro and took a seat at the bar near the cash register. Chris, one of the bartenders, came from the kitchen.

"Hey Ruston. Just put a pepperoni pizza going."

"Can I get two slices?"

"Sure."

"And a beer."

"You got it."

He set my beer down on the bar. As he went to swipe my debit card, I looked back toward the kitchen.

"Harleigh make it in yet?" I asked before taking a sip.

Chris looked at me.

"You haven't heard, have you?"

I shook my head. It took all I had to swallow that sip. It went down like sawdust.

"Closed up early last night. We weren't busy on account of the weather. There was a break in the rain. Harleigh got on her bike and took off. No one's seen her since."

He slid my card back to me.

"Let me go check on that pizza for you."

CHAPTER 26

April 20, 2015

I lay in bed clad only in a pair of boxers, one hand behind my head, the other resting on my stomach clutching a cigarette. I'd barely moved since leaving the office at five. I flicked the ash from my cigarette and checked the time on my phone.

11:45 p.m.

No one had seen or heard anything from Harleigh for over a week now. On the last day of tax season, my buddies with the Lafayette Police Department, Detectives Landry and Wilson, made their second appearance at the office through no fault of my own. Their only interest was when I last spoke to Harleigh. Detective Landry mentioned they'd learned of a previous disappearance and considered her latest vanishing act no cause for concern. First, the detectives had come by about a possible child abduction, now a missing woman. That night, I dreamed Harleigh stole Darby's SUV, traveled to Texas, kidnapped Evangelina, and showed up rattling the gate downstairs. I walked out to find Evangelina lying bound and gagged in the middle of Buchanan with Harleigh's foot across her chest like a big game hunter posing with its kill.

Harleigh wasn't home on the eleventh when Theresa got there that morning, which wasn't anything unusual. They did not keep tabs on one another. Chris tried calling her phone after she failed to show for work. When he got no response, he called Karen. After Karen couldn't get in touch with her, she called Theresa. Theresa then called me. At that time, I was at the office without my phone. Theresa drove to my apartment and called my phone a second time before she walked up to the gate and looked up the steps with the flashlight app on her phone. She did not see Harleigh's bike perched where it would normally be if she was there. She then drove to The Bistro. Chris suggested she drive the route Harleigh took on her way home but by that time many roads in the area were underwater. She called the police. They advised her to contact all local hospitals to make sure Harleigh hadn't been in some sort of accident. When I got back to the apartment that afternoon, I saw the two missed calls on my phone. By that time, Theresa had called the police again in addition to Harleigh's mom. There was an accusatory tone in her voice when she asked why I didn't answer my phone when she called.

Not long after moving back to Winnfield, Harleigh packed her bags and left without a word, just as I had done. She eventually made her way back to Lafayette where she legally changed her name from Sheryl Domingue, and worked several different jobs before she met Theresa through a mutual friend. They decided to get a place together and split the rent. Her family reported her missing but there wasn't much they could do once authorities located her.

During late night drinking bouts, she sometimes confided to me she wanted to see what else was out there. Returning to Lafayette just hadn't worked out like she planned. She no longer was the blonde, naive, virgin teacher's aide who aspired to work with kids and found the good in everyone. That existence was over. She made it clear to me if she ever vanished to not take it personally and not to go looking for her.

Early one morning on the longest day of the year, the sun just beginning to rise though it seemed it set only a short while ago, Harleigh and I sat at my kitchen table with a pint of whiskey and a pack of cigarettes between us. I put a pot of coffee on. Harleigh tossed two aspirin into her mouth before lighting yet another cigarette on an almost burnt out one. She told me about the night she went out with friends and met her husband, Randall.

"I wasn't planning on going but changed my mind at the last minute. I didn't see him until we were leaving the club. He offered to walk us home. When we got to the front door, I gave him a peck on the cheek. He blushed. One of my friends says to me, 'I bet you're glad you decided to come with us.'"

She stared at the cup of coffee I placed in front of her.

"But that's life, you know. Like a grenade. Each time a decision is made, a pin is pulled. Most have no life changing effect. But then one rolls right up under you…"

She stretched her arms wide and mouthed the word boom.

"Some explode in an instant. Others bide their time. Like when they decided to shut that plant down on you guys. How long did it take before it went off? Eight months? I decided to go out one night and three years later it almost cost me my life."

I rolled over and checked the time.

12:03 a.m.

The day had gone by without anyone wishing me happy birthday.

CHAPTER 27

I had not planned to attend Festival International de Louisiane 2015, but with the fais do-do stage right next to the office, I couldn't help but be drawn in. Wednesday at five, I smoked a cigarette in the smoking area with Danny, who lamented how miserable it was having to spend an entire festival weekend stuck in a guard booth only feet away from reveille, then walked over and got us both a bowl of chicken and sausage jambalaya from the food tent in front of the old federal courthouse building on Jefferson. It was a far cry from years past when Harleigh, Theresa, and I marked opening night by volunteering at the ticket booth followed by garbage detail before hitting up the twenty-four-hour diner on Johnston with other volunteers in the wee hours of Thursday morning.

Over the course of the weekend, I gorged myself on alligator balls, duck quesadillas, sweet potato beignets, boudin sliders, and White Russian daiquiris. Those were potent. I tried to keep to myself and wallow around in my somber mood but the atmosphere at festival would not allow such a thing. My co-workers in the office might shun and ignore me but on the streets of downtown Lafayette they treat me as one would a friend and neighbor. I met people from six of the seven continents, shook hands with a few musicians, and even spent time near the arts and crafts booths lined up along Vermillion with the hope Evangelina might be among those peddling their goods. I had no such luck.

Late Sunday afternoon, after polishing off my third daiquiri of the day, I stumbled and took a drunken tumble in Parc Sans Souci. I played it off by pulling out my cell phone, making it seem as though I simply tripped while accepting a call. I maintained my spot on the grass for the remainder of the day, the sun baking me alive. Mercifully, the shade from the Hunt Bank Tower slowly approached and eventually enveloped me. I stretched my legs out.

"Is anyone sitting here?"

Others were coming to share in the splendor of my shaded glory. I smiled and made room. Some sat in lawn chairs, others on the cool grass. A soccer ball appeared. Back and forth it went, while up on stage a trio from Belgium played an upbeat number in their native tongue. Festival International de Louisiane 2015 drew to a close. It was there that it all crashed in on me. There would be no novel. I was destined to follow in the footsteps of my father and grandfather. All that remained would be what I might get myself into without Harleigh around to look out for me. Drunk, sunburned, and with no feeling in either leg, I headed to the apartment.

The following morning, it was back to the office and quarterly payroll returns. Breaux had gotten me started on those the day after tax season ended. I found them difficult to latch on to. Darby took a few days off and without her help I struggled mightily. Breaux said one return should take no more than two hours to complete. They were taking me twice that long. In addition, I had to redo the ones I thought I'd completed. 941 deposits were made during the quarter. I had no idea what that meant. Breaux was livid. To top it off, I neglected to update the SUTA rates. Still more returns had to be corrected. I was getting my ass handed to me.

When Darby returned, she told me she took time off for a stomach issue. I didn't pry. Fortunately, she was eager to help when called upon. With her assistance, I was able to begin completing the payroll returns within the mandated two-hour time frame. Breaux rewarded me with the massive payroll folder for my buddies at Martin's Grocery. Included were several new employees who had not been previously entered into the system. Breaux gave me a phone number. I was to call and get personal information such as social security numbers and street addresses. That I did.

"Uh, who is this again?"

I guess I did not sound convincing enough.

"We'll get back to you."

Darby got the information for me. As she stood in my cubicle gingerly explaining to the good folks of Martin's Grocery that I meant no harm, I happened to notice the lack of impressions through her tight white blouse where her nipple piercings would be. She noticed my leering eyes and in turn folded her arm across her chest.

I made it through the remaining payroll returns unscathed. Friday morning, Breaux came by with three months of bookwork for Riley Automotive. I wasn't sure if I were to continue with the old bookkeeping program or start with the new one. I called Breaux's number. No answer. I walked over to his office. He was not there. Darby told me he stepped out. Was there anything I needed? Nope, I said, and went back to my cubicle. I felt my simple question would unleash too much of a shit storm for a Friday afternoon.

When she called Monday morning, I told her of my dilemma.

"Didn't they tell you at that seminar you went to?" she asked.

"No, they didn't."

She called Bridgett. Bridgett called Breaux. Breaux showed up at my cubicle and took a seat. He opened the new program and proceeded to hack away while I stood quietly off to the side. I assumed I was due another crash course, but after a few futile minutes, he threw both hands up exasperated.

"I don't have time for this!" he cried.

He then stood and walked away. Now what?

The phone rang. It was Bridgett.

"Why are you making this so difficult?"

"Excuse me?"

"All the clients have been imported. It's ready to go. I already showed you how the program works."

"No, you didn't."

"Yes, I did."

"Fine."

I hung up. Breaux had Riley Automotive opened on the screen. I scrolled around. The last check entered was 11620. The check stubs in my hand began with 11624. Close enough. Darby came by. With her help, we figured it out. It took thirty-five minutes to reconcile January, twenty minutes for February, and only ten for March. Darby went back to her desk. Breaux later came with instructions for the program he'd printed off the internet. More bookkeeping would follow in the morning. It was only 10:45.

Friday was the office crawfish boil. Darby showed me on Google Maps where it was to be held. The satellite picture only showed a sugarcane field off the Grande Pointe Highway. She said Guillory recently bought property out there. I agonized over whether I should go or not. I was concerned it would be nothing but me and the bullshit crew and felt it possible they might tie me to a fence post or drag me behind a car after accusing me of whatever flavor the conservative hate happened to be for that day. But I'd been personally invited and ultimately that made my mind up for me.

As my Uber driver slowly made his way down the dirt road, he questioned if anything actually existed out there. Finally, we came across numerous cars parked along a gravel driveway. Darby's white SUV was not among them. I saw people standing underneath a gazebo by a two-story cabin. I walked over and stood next to a man with the letters DD tattooed underneath his left eye. He was loudly yelling at two kids playing near a pond.

"Stay away from the water!"

"I said stay away from that goddamn water!"

"Matt! Matt!! Stay away from the fuckin' water!"

"Michael! I'm not gonna tell you guys again!"

A few people made their way inside the cabin. I fell in line behind them. Darby had not properly prepared me for what I was about to face. It was the bullshit crew, friends and family of the bullshit crew, in addition to those in the office who wished to be in the bullshit crew. Apparently, there was a pecking order when it came to such things and those not privileged to participate in the bullshit crew were relegated to far off corners of the office where they shared whispered B-movie type tales of office intrigue and gossip. I didn't see Breaux, or Beverly. I did see Glenn Richard and Mike Touchet sitting together unarmed having a laugh. Julian was there, as was Bridgett, and Carmen the receptionist, along with Guillory, who acknowledged me with a nod of the head.

Several long narrow folding tables had been set up in the middle of the room, each piled high with red steaming crawfish. At the end of each table sat a huge garbage can. Numerous ice chests full of beer were placed about. I grabbed a platter and went about serving myself before finding a corner to sit. The crawfish were spicy and easy to peel. I went back for more. In front of me was a blonde woman with green hair. She held a small baby in her arms. Two young boys ran havoc around her. Matt and Michael, the boys who were playing by the pond, were the same Matt and Michael I met at the Children's Parade in February.

"Mom! Mom! That's Mr. Ruston! He gave us his Mardi Gras beads!"

As they whooped and hollered, the woman gave me a look equal parts helplessness and hopelessness.

"Sorry," she said.

"No problem. Need a hand?"

She hurriedly shook her head no. I watched the three of them walk over to a table where the guy with the tattoo on his face sat. I couldn't help but notice the uncomfortable way in which he stared at them. Also at their table was a tall redhead. I wondered if she was Darby's connection to The Bistro audit. Which reminded me, Darby had said the audit was delayed till May. She should hear something soon. In the meantime, I refilled my platter and returned to my corner.

As the night went on, the bullshit crew began to let fly loud, intoxicated, unrestrained, and uncensored rants concerning everything from anchor babies to the second amendment. They even mentioned the upcoming hurricane season.

"The government controls the weather. That's why they predominantly hit red states."

Someone said they heard the Governor of Texas deployed the State Guard because President Obama was about to use special forces to put the state under martial law.

"That Muslim motherfucker put fuckin' Muslim prayer curtains up in the White House."

"He wants to open the borders to illegals who will vote Democrat."

It was as though I was back in my cubicle. I had no idea if anything said was true or not but sensing it wouldn't be long before the torches and pitchforks broke out, I decided I best get going. Just as I stood, the front door opened and in walked a skinny female wearing fishnet stockings, stiletto heels, and a black mini skirt. She walked straight up to Guillory and circled him seductively before taking a seat in his lap.

"Ooh daddy, daddy!" she cooed into his ear. "I missed you so. Did you miss me, daddy?"

Everyone sat in stunned silence. She kissed Guillory on the cheek. Her bright red lipstick barely left a mark on his bright red face. I went up to Julian.

"Stripper?" I asked.

"His youngest daughter," he whispered.

I grabbed another beer and went back to my corner. Now I was enjoying myself.

CHAPTER 28

Summer 2015

Part 1

Summer months at the plant were brutal. Warm stifling air filled the closed-up warehouse overnight and awaited us first thing in the morning. It felt like walking into a preheated oven. Or hell itself. When I got to the office Monday morning, my shirt already damp with perspiration, I noticed no air coming from the vent near my cubicle. It would not surprise me none if the duct work in the ceiling had been detached and rerouted somewhere else.

Darby came by. She wore a jacket and complained her hands were ice-cold from the air conditioning. She asked about the crawfish boil. I gave her a roll call of those in attendance.

"Plus," I added, "a surprise guest."

"Who?"

"Guillory's youngest daughter."

She made a face.

"Oh, God. Andrea showed up?"

"She put on quite a show."

"She's disgusting."

I wouldn't go that far. I rather enjoyed watching Andrea make a spectacle of herself. Others found the level of discomfort in the room unbearable and soon made their way to the door. I, myself, had a grand time. Proud people humiliated by one of their own was a sight to behold.

"So, what's her deal?" I asked.

Darby glanced around.

"Let's go for a smoke."

Down in the smoking area, the blowers struggled to cut a breeze through the thick muggy air. Darby told me about Andrea Guillory, the youngest of Guillory's three kids. Andrea got her Master's in accounting, passed the CPA exam, and came to work at Thomas, Madison, Smith and Associates.

"Then she started doing porn on the internet. She called herself Hollie Roux."

I burst out laughing.

"Hollie Roux?"

"Yes."

"Come on, Darby. Seriously?"

"I'm dead serious."

"And how did that come about?"

"How else? She met Hunter."

At first, it didn't click.

"Hunter?"

Then it hit me.

"Wait. Hunter Hilliard?"

"Yes."

"Hunter Hilliard, your neighbor?"

"Yes!"

"Hunter Hilliard got Jim Guillory's youngest daughter into porn?"

"Yes. That's what I believe happened."

"What you believe happened?"

"You should have seen it. She was so full of herself. Especially after everyone found out."

"How did they find out?"

"Someone shared a video of her. Word got around."

I thought of the Ash Wednesday breast judges.

"How did they find it?"

"Huh?"

"With all the porn available, how did they happen to find the one with the boss's daughter in it?"

"Well, maybe they just watch a lot of porn, Ruston," she said curtly.

Or maybe she advertised it. I didn't say that aloud. Obviously, Andrea was the bad person here. Not the married men watching porn on their phones on company time.

"Was she embarrassed?" I asked.

"Not at all. She was mighty proud of herself."

Too bad Andrea didn't cue up one of her videos at the crawfish boil. I kept that to myself as well. I don't think Darby would find the humor in it.

"So, what happened?"

"She only worked here a couple months. Mr. Guillory was oblivious. Poor thing. He gave her one of our bigger accounts. Someone there recognized her and called her Hollie."

I wanted to laugh. It sounded so absurd.

"Mr. Guillory took time off after that."

"A training seminar in Memphis?"

"A what?"

"Never mind."

The story sounded far-fetched. Yet, that afternoon, as I took a shit in the restroom next to someone in the next stall giving courtesy flushes every fifteen seconds or so, the thought hit. Could Andrea Guillory, CPA turned porn star, be the subject for a novel?

I sat before the laptop that night and searched for Andrea on Facebook. Incredibly, she had accounts under both names. The one under Andrea's name showcased her life through a series of mundane posts concerning her dog, her apartment, and her affinity for Japanese culture. Her double life must had exhausted her for she constantly wrote of how tired she was.

On the other hand, Hollie Roux wasn't tired, she was "hot and ready for it," at least according to her Facebook page. With a name like Hollie Roux, one might get the impression she was a thick girl with a dark complexion. On the contrary, she was as thin and white as white could get. Pale even. A Google search with the safe function turned off revealed a voracious sexual appetite. Threesomes, gang bangs, lesbian, interracial, oral, anal, even dental, as I found pictures of her in a makeshift dental chair with the supposedly board-certified oral surgeon examining the back of her throat with his massive dick.

Over the next few weeks, I jotted story ideas down in the journal Darby had given me. While she fabricated the link between Andrea and Hunter, she was spot on concerning the new bookkeeping program. What once took hours now took minutes. For some clients, I completed four months of bookwork in less than an hour's time.

Breaux could not provide enough work to keep me busy. I spent many afternoons doing nothing but waiting for five o'clock to roll around. Bridgett got involved. When both failed to keep me busy for an entire shift, Bridgett presented Guillory with the idea that since it was the off-season, and I merely a contract worker, there was no reason for someone in my position to log forty hours each week. Guillory agreed, or was indifferent, and Breaux soon informed me not to come in on Fridays till further notice.

That Thursday, on the eve of many long weekends to come, I headed for the pub. When I arrived, I observed a familiar face. Andrea Guillory, dressed sloppily in oversized gray sweatpants and a white t-shirt, had just risen from an outside table. Hoping she might recognize me from the crawfish boil, I walked over to say hello.

"Excuse me," I said.

She turned to face me.

"Aw, fuck. Really?"

I froze.

"What are you, like fifty or something? You know, it's always the highlight of my day when some old creep comes up and says how much he loves me. Tell me, how long have you been jerking off to me? Weeks? Months?"

She swung her purse over her shoulder.

"Let me give you some advice. Shave off that stupid bird's nest of a beard you got going on and you might find someone your own age to play with your little pee-pee for you."

She finished me with an exaggerated smile and walked away.

I went back to the apartment with my beard between my legs. I climbed up to the roof and tore everything out of the journal. After I smashed the beginnings of a novel about a CPA turned porn star into a bucket of discarded cigarette butts, I lit it ablaze then pissed in it.

The next three days were a blur. Monday morning at the office, it hit as soon as the elevator doors opened. Grief, as thick as the oppressive humidity outside. It hung so heavy in the air even the phones sounded muffled. Taken aback, I paused for a moment before I made my way to my cubicle. Members of the bullshit crew stood subdued over near the breakroom. I shook the computer awake. Darby rushed in.

"He killed them!" she cried out.

"What?"

"He shot them!"

Her knees buckled. I grabbed her and sat her down in my chair.

"Who?"

She took out her phone. Her hands trembled something fierce.

"Rhonda had the purest blonde hair," she said as she pressed and swiped at the screen. "She dyed it green. It just began to grow out. Matt and Michael, such sweethearts. And Taylor, oh my God!"

She covered her mouth.

"She's never gonna remember them," she sobbed.

She handed me her phone. A chill went down my spine. It was the family from the crawfish boil. Rhonda in a blue blouse, her hair so blonde it looked almost white in the light. Matt and Michael, my Mardi Gras buddies, decked out in matching blue ties, their damp hair perfectly combed, canaille looks in both their eyes. The infant Rhonda held at the crawfish boil was not in the picture, but the guy with the tattoo on his face was.

Devin Dugas, looking bored and uninterested in a long-sleeved black thermal t-shirt, murdered his family before he turned the gun on himself. Being nosey, I later searched Rhonda's Facebook page. I discovered her mom was Debbie, the tall redhead from payroll. She happened to be babysitting Taylor at the time of the incident. Someone commented that Rhonda dyed her hair green to disguise herself after she left and took the kids with her.

Another mentioned Devin's numerous arrests, everything from domestic abuse battery to possession of drug paraphernalia. All the while I could hear the bullshit crew over in the breakroom portraying this guy as a troubled individual who only wanted the best for his family. They deemed any mention of past offenses as inappropriate.

On Devin Dugas's Facebook page, I found a picture of him sitting next to Rhonda with newborn Taylor in her arms. The comments underneath numbered well into the hundreds. "Rot in hell you son of a bitch," read one. "He was a good guy," read another. Back and forth they went, the people who knew them best, putting Rhonda and Devin's business out on to the world wide web for everyone to see.

The next morning, I caught an elevator ride with Beverly. She asked if I heard what happened. She then asked if I had a gun. I shook my head no.

"Good," she said. "I don't see why people need guns anyway. No one should have one. The government should take them all away. All they do is cause harm. Don't you think?"

"If they only caused harm there'd be no one alive south of I-10," I said.

Beverly just looked at me. I mentioned this to Darby.

"You know, they only hired her because she's black," she said.

"Really?"

"Yes. Can you imagine if they hired me only because I'm white?"

Maybe they did, I thought to myself.

I attended a vigil for Rhonda and her boys that night in Parc Sans Souci. I saw Jay from Faith Haven Trust. He remembered me.

"337," he said with a somber grin.

I explained to him why I was there. He asked what impression Rhonda and Devin had given me that night at the crawfish boil. At first, I only shrugged my shoulders, but after Jay pressed me, I admitted the thought briefly crossed my mind he might harm them someday. But it was not my problem. Someone would step in if it ever got to that point. As it turned out, no one did, and there we were.

The vigil got underway.

"Everyone knows someone who has experienced domestic violence," the lady standing before the microphone began.

The solemn event lasted over an hour. No one else from the office went. Organizers handed out purple ribbons and white candles. Families and friends, some wearing shirts depicting photos underneath slogans such as "Gone but not Forgotten," spoke somberly of lost loved ones. Wiping away tears, they put on a brave face, though the reality of what they'd gone through was as real and raw as ever.

At the conclusion, Jay walked to the podium. He said some things that led me to believe he had been in contact with Rhonda at some point. I asked him about it afterwards. He told me he couldn't divulge that information.

The next morning, I completed four months of bookwork for one of the smaller mom and pop clients in just over an hour's time. I went downstairs for a smoke. Best buddies Detective Landry and Detective Wilson were down there. With the seats closest to the blowers occupied by those seeking relief from another brutal summer day, Detective Landry and I sat near the garbage bins. Detective Wilson stood menacingly nearby with his arms folded across his chest.

"You weren't forthcoming with us," Detective Landry said.

"Excuse me?"

"People who know Harleigh said you too were involved."

"Anyone who told you that doesn't know her."

"How about you give us a statement concerning your whereabouts the night she disappeared?"

He was well agitated. They thought she would resurface. Now, almost three months later, they scrambled to make up for lost time.

I recounted the entire Friday evening and Saturday morning to them.

"Can anyone vouch for you during non-work hours?" asked Detective Wilson.

"No, sir."

They informed me security cameras at The Bistro showed both Harleigh and Chris leaving the premises around two. A neighbor's camera captured Chris arriving home alone and on schedule. They were in the process of putting out an alert for those on Harleigh's route to check footage from the morning of April eleventh. Was there anything I wanted to tell them before they would learn of it later?

"Focus on Johnston, St. Mary, and Congress," I said. "She always went that way home."

Back up on thirty-nine, Bridgett awaited me near my cubicle. She asked what I was working on. I showed her what Breaux had given me. She rattled off the names of fifteen or so clients.

"What about those?"

"I put them aside."

"Why are they not completed?"

"I have only been working on what Mr. Breaux gave me."

"They need to be done by the end of the month."

"Okay."

She spun around and walked away. Ten minutes later, Guillory called. I went into his office and took a seat. Last time I sat there, he showered me with appreciation and goodwill. This time, I got a monologue concerning fiscal years. He asked about the clients Bridgett mentioned.

"I put them aside."

"Why are they not completed?"

"I have only been working on what Mr. Breaux gave me."

"They need to be done by the end of the month. Was that relayed to you?"

"No, sir."

Guillory called Breaux over. I sat there while Guillory railed on him for reducing my hours when bookwork for the clients he mentioned remained incomplete, even though Bridgett set it all in motion, and Guillory himself gave the final say so.

The verdict was as such. Fiscal year bookwork needed to be completed as soon as possible. Since I already entered six months into the old bookkeeping program, the remaining months would need to be as well. In addition, it was time to begin second quarter payrolls. Guillory then topped it off.

"The firm's conducting an audit on a local restaurant in the area. Receipts from the past year are coming next week. Make a spreadsheet detailing food and alcohol sales for me. See that you have everything completed before the end of the month. I realize I'm asking a lot from you, but I know you won't let me down. Put in all the hours you need."

The following day, after everyone left at noon, I remained in the office until six. Saturday, the Fourth of July, also Harleigh's birthday, I went in and stayed till eight that night. Monday was a paid holiday. I worked well past sunset and walked to the apartment in the dark.

Tuesday the box of receipts arrived from The Bistro. Most bared Harleigh's name. Progress was slow. I worked fourteen-hour days and went in on Sundays. The month trudged on.

Finally, on the twenty-eighth, light appeared at the end of the tunnel. Fiscal year bookwork was complete, the remainder of the audit receipts would be tallied up in the morning, and payroll returns were well in hand. For the first time in almost five weeks, I could breathe. I took a deep breath and looked at the time.

7:36 p.m.

My cell phone rang. It was Darby. When I answered, I only heard static coming from the other end. I figured she butt-dialed me and hung up. She called back. Same thing.

"Darby? Hello? Hey!"

I didn't know what to make of it. I turned my computer off and took the elevator down. Danny stood in the smoking area with a small radio held to his ear. He said a shooting occurred somewhere off Pinhook.

"I think it's bad," he said.

There were faint sirens in the distance. I made it one block down Buchanan before I took a right on Jefferson. As the wail grew louder, I began to jog. Ten minutes later, I stood winded at the intersection of Pinhook. Traffic was at a standstill. I crossed the railroad tracks and continued down a narrow street to my right void of vehicles.

Two blocks down, the road made a sharp left. I saw police in riot gear surrounding a building at the next corner. A lifeless body lay prone out front. Numerous cars, ambulances, and blacked-out SUV's parked about haphazardly displayed disorienting lights of various colors. The sirens were deafening. As I stood amid the chaos, I felt my phone vibrate in my pocket. It was Darby. Suddenly, I saw her. She stood not twenty feet from me. I hollered her name. She rushed over and threw her arms around me. She was so hysterical she left bruises on my neck that didn't go away for days.

At that moment, someone took our picture. The resulting image became a symbol of the latest mass shooting tragedy to grip the nation. Illuminated by the pulsing glow of dozens of emergency vehicles, the photo featured blurred people dashing about, the signage of the Cort Rickland Community Center, and two individuals locked in a frantic embrace.

The woman, her expression of anguish plain to see, held on to the man, his face obscured, with everything she had. Those who knew Darby would recognize her almost immediately. They would also know the man she clung to was not her husband.

CHAPTER 29

Summer 2015

Part 2

Darby sat shell-shocked on the curb clutching her stomach. A policewoman came by. She asked if I could contact a family member. As far as I knew, Herman and David were inside the community center with Darby when the shooting took place. Neither survived.

I scrolled through Darby's phone and located her parents' number. It rang three times then stopped. I tried on mine. An answering machine picked up. I said my name, what happened, and for someone to come as soon as possible. Her father arrived thirty minutes later in his robe and slippers. He looked to be a serene man who didn't understand the world today. Safe in her daddy's arms, the EMTs checked her as the police asked questions.

Back at the apartment, I turned on the television. It was surreal watching local news outlets report live at a scene I just walked away from. Over the course of the night, the extent of the tragedy would become known. Six dead, eight wounded, three critical. One of the critical would later succumb to their injuries.

By sunrise, the footage played nonstop. Angst had its net cast over the happiest city in America. Lafayette was reeling. The President spoke of the shooting. The media did their thing. Even the Governor came by. The bullshit crew, though, were not nearly as sympathetic. This tragedy would soon be overtaken by the next, if they chose to accept it happened in the first place. They once deemed a school shooting the creation of a Muslim President hell-bent on taking guns from law-abiding citizens.

A few of them came by my cubicle after I arrived at the office. Unbeknownst to me, the photo of me and Darby was making the rounds on social media. They peppered me with questions.

"What were ya'll doing at that place together?"

That place, The Cort Rickland Community Center, was in an area well-known for drug activity. Other shootings often occurred but nothing of this magnitude. Numerous calls to tear the building down would amplify over the coming months.

"What?" I said. "I wasn't with her. I only..."

"Yes, you were. Why you lying?"

"I'm not lying. I went after Darby tried to call me."

"Why would she call you and not her husband?"

"Because he was with her."

"No, he wasn't. Another lie."

"He wasn't? What about David?"

"Her mom had him."

A wave of relief washed over me. Eventually, they left me alone. I headed to the breakroom for a cup of coffee then spent the remainder of the morning tallying up the receipts from The Bistro. The outcome was not close. Alcohol sales tipped the scales at sixty-two percent. I felt I let Karen down and considered fudging the numbers. Who would know? Would they audit the audit? In the end, I left them as they were and emailed the spreadsheet to Guillory.

I searched Darby's Facebook that afternoon to find out how she was doing. When I couldn't locate it, I figured she blocked me, just as Evangelina had. What I did find though was the photo taken of us last night. Now I understood the line of questioning from the bullshit crew. I certainly had no idea why she was there. She never mentioned the place to me. The thing that got me though were the calls she made to Herman before she called me. I happened across them as I scrolled through her phone. At the time, I thought he was still inside, and she was frantic to reach him.

August came in sticky, stifling, and sorrowful. The city, still in mourning, would remain so for some time. The days were filled with remembrances for the seven who died. A special service would be held Wednesday at one of the churches in the area. Banners and decals popped up in front yards and storefronts across the Hub City with proceeds earmarked for shooting victims and their families. I went into the coffee shop and purchased some along with a coffee. Samantha took my order.

"Haven't seen you in a while," she said.

She waited on me yesterday. I prepared my coffee and took a seat. A short thin man with salt and pepper hair rose from a table and glided over.

"Hello, Ruston."

I stared in disbelief. It was Borel. The last time I saw him he traded me a bottle of pills for a guitar.

"May I join you?" he asked.

I nodded my head. He must had lost over a hundred pounds.

"How are you, Ruston?"

"I didn't recognize you."

"Ruston, the Lord has been so good to me. With His help, I got myself straightened out. He's lifted so many burdens off my shoulders. I can breathe now. What about you?"

"I took a straight job."

"Mike still hounding you?"

I made a face.

"Where are you living now?"

"Up in Vidalia. I'm here with some members of my church for the healing service."

"I heard about that."

"Lafayette has many issues, Ruston. I feel God is calling me back to the area."

He leaned forward.

"Look Ruston, God is helping me to make amends. I want to apologize for our last time together. I hope you can find it in your heart to one day forgive me. For if you forgive men their trespasses, your heavenly Father will also forgive you."

I smiled.

"It's all good," I said.

He smiled back. His transformation was stunning. He was hot for Jesus. Meanwhile, my coffee had gone cold.

Later that morning, authorities released the name of the community center shooter. Speculation was it would be yet another angry white male motivated by a sense of discontent. It turned out to be a homeless fifty-eight-year-old black man. His name was not familiar to me. Neither his face. The person lying in the road that night was missing most of his. The bullshit crew had a field day. While any mention of Devin Dugas's past had been considered inappropriate, they deemed the past actions of Warren Granger indicative of all black people in general.

"Just goes to show," one of them said, "we should have picked our own cotton."

The healing service, held at a church off I-10, took place the following day. News vans with colorful logos on their sides dotted the parking lot. I saw Borel out front with four other people wearing yellow reflective vests. I went in and took a seat up in the risers. The place filled. Metal folding chairs screeched on the floor as people parted to make way for still others to enter. The worship band came out. Those who could rose to their feet. Hands went to the heavens. The lead pastor appeared and spoke of healing and restoration. A person inside the community center at the time of the shooting came out. The room fell silent. She told of hiding in a restroom with three other people as the gunman paced the hallway. They held hands and prayed.

Then the shooter stopped. The knob began to turn. The woman became angry.

"Devil!" she screamed. "I reject you!"

The man ran from the building.

A thunderous response ensued. The band broke into the chorus of a song they played earlier. Hands went higher. Tears shed.

The service was thorough. Officials gave updates on the status of the investigation. They honored first responders. Friends and family spoke of the seven lost. All the while, black and white photos of the deceased stared at us from the stage.

The next morning, the bullshit crew were busy forcing a narrative of the shooting to fit their agenda. Previously, they claimed Granger was hunting whites. Another time he was anti-women. Today, he was Muslim, had traveled to Syria, and routinely posted on terrorist websites.

Granger was no Muslim. He was Baptist with no social media footprint. He didn't even own a cell phone. But he did carry an AR-15 semi-automatic style weapon when he walked into the Cort Rickland Community Center on July twenty-eighth. Officials at the healing service indicated the gun had been stolen. They had not determined a motive.

As someone in the bullshit crew made the argument about Granger being a soldier of the Islamic State, I received a text from Nancy.

>Hey thought u like to know police are up in your apartment.
>Have search warrant
>
>>Thanks. Is Mike with them?
>
>He's in hospital.

That evening, as I neared the matching rectangular acrylic block windows on the building where Buchanan nudges right and my apartment comes into view, I expected to find the whole Robicheaux clan, along with members of the Lafayette Police Department, anticipating my arrival. Instead, it was the same deserted stretch of road that greeted me each evening.

Up in the apartment, a discarded latex glove lay on the kitchen floor, and the laptop was gone. The following morning, I made my return trek to the office. An unmarked patrol car with darkened windows sat parked in front of the courthouse. Best buddies Detectives Landry and Wilson emerged.

"Morning," said Detective Landry.

"Morning, sir."

"We made a visit yesterday, but you weren't in. Mr. Robicheaux is under the weather. His son was gracious enough to let us in."

"Find what you were looking for?"

"We found blood."

"Bullshit," I said.

Detective Wilson wore a smirk on his face.

"Would you care to tell us who it belongs to, or should we wait for the test results to come back?"

I understood the inquisition, but his cocky demeanor irked me.

"Ah. See, I'm not from your world. When you say you found blood, I'm thinking you discovered someone bleeding out inside my apartment."

I reached for my cigarettes.

"New Year's Eve, three years ago. Harleigh attempted to open a champagne bottle with a sword. I'm sorry, a saber. She nicked her knuckle pretty good. Theresa has pictures of it somewhere with the date written in black marker."

They both looked at me. I cupped my hand over my mouth and lit my cigarette.

"FYI, you're supposed to use the blunt end, not the sharp in."

Neither one much cared for me at that moment. I decided not to inquire about the laptop.

Later that day, Breaux informed me of my new work schedule. Eight hours a day, Monday to Wednesday, till further notice. On an excursion to the supply room, I happened to see Guillory, Bridgett, and someone I didn't recognize over near Darby's still vacant desk. They raved over the efficiency of the new bookkeeping program, likening it to automatic car washes, self-serve gasoline, and ATMs. Reducing my hours from forty to twenty-four saved the company $192 each week. They made it sound as if that amount might break the company. I grabbed a box of paper clips and went back to my cubicle.

On the twentieth, I received a text from Robicheaux. He would be coming by the office to collect rent. I waited down in the smoking area. By the time he showed, I had smoked two cigarettes and sat drenched in sweat. His appearance caught me off guard. His mop of jet-black hair gone, he looked frail and unsteady on his feet. I handed him the cash. He did not count it out.

"The cops were at the apartment?" he asked faintly.

"Yes."

"Are you writing about it?"

"You'll have it next week."

"I better."

With that, he turned and shuffled away.

The remainder of August was brutal. The tortuous long hot summer afternoons were made worse by the fact I could no longer sit still inside my apartment. To fill the lengthy stretches of time that came from working only three days a week, I waited until the coffee shop closed so as not to run into

Nancy, who I knew would question why the police had come with a search warrant, then walked through the blazing heat and high humidity over to Girard Park where I took a seat and waited for it all to end. When that didn't occur, I stood, brushed off the seat of my jeans, and headed back to the apartment to spend another redundant night alone.

September started with the long Labor Day weekend. That week I only worked the Tuesday and Wednesday and received no holiday pay for the Monday. No matter. My paltry income still more than covered my meager expenses. With no end to the heat of the summer in sight, I splurged on an air conditioning window unit. I had it delivered, installed, and cranked till my nose ran and my toes went cold.

Early one morning, during another sleepless night, I got a friend request from Darby on Facebook. Curious to see how she was doing, I accepted it immediately. Something was off though. The page contained no pictures. When I checked back later, it was gone.

On the first day of fall, I stood with Winslow in the smoking area. He talked of heading to New Orleans next week with his band to play a few gigs. I made my way up to the office. Eight months of bookwork for Son's Insurance awaited me in my cubicle. I got started. I could hear the bullshit crew in the breakroom discussing death panels in the Affordable Care Act.

"People over fifty-nine in Canada and Great Britain are denied heart procedures because they are too expensive. People like me will die because Obamacare won't allow the funding. What compassion."

"Obama is establishing himself as a dictator, just like Hitler."

"May God save our beloved nation."

When I opened the old bookwork program to Son's Insurance, something horrific appeared on the screen. It was the timestamp for prior years general journal. A year to the day, I was doing the exact same thing with this exact same company. All the air went out of the room. I stared at the screen in disbelief. A year had passed and here I sat. I got up, took the elevator down, walked through the parking lot, went over to the South Buchanan Parking Garage, and ducked behind a stairwell.

Ruston Delahoussaye
9403 S Buchanan St
Lafayette, LA 70595

Company Man

No feeling
No emotion
Constant drudgery
Robotic

With gritted teeth and clenched fists, I gathered myself and returned to my cubicle. What else could I do? Besides, eight months of bookwork for Son's Insurance needed to be done.

Back up on thirty-nine, Bridgett rushed over.

"What are you doing here? Oh, wait. Today's Wednesday."

At five, I made my way to the apartment. As I put my key into the mailbox, I got a whiff of Evangelina's scent. I spun around, expecting to see her standing right behind me but no one was there. I walked over to the parking lot. No light blue colored *Volkswagen* could be seen.

Inside the mailbox, a hand delivered letter in a bright red envelope sported her name in the upper left corner. I took it up to the roof of the apartment. It began with an explanation of what transpired over the Thanksgiving holidays. Her parents informed her they were no longer footing the bill for the gallery. They had lined a job up for her. Receptionist at an oilfield company. Two moving trucks were to meet them at the gallery Monday morning. It made for a tumultuous weekend.

She mentioned she almost had to leave me behind in Texas. Her parents planned to make the trip back to Lafayette with her. She stormed out of the house that Sunday morning and drove off. Her phone, on silent, blowing up on the ride back. That was who she argued with when we stopped in Lake Charles. She said that ride was one of the hardest things she ever had to do in her life and apologized wholeheartedly. She didn't want to get me involved, and there was nothing more to it than that.

On a brighter note, she added, she now lived in Austin. She met someone. A writer. Like you, she said. Unlike me, though, he was successful, having published two novels. Also an accomplished musician, he was putting the finishing touches on his first album. She created the artwork for the cover. All very exciting.

She asked if I remembered the idea she had to paint portraits of local musicians inside various venues around the Acadiana area. Together with her new beau, Beau also his name, they had done something of the sort in Austin. It turned out to be highly successful. There were plans to move to Nashville and do the same. They were currently on their way to Florida. Beau wanted to invite me out to dinner with them, but they did not know my work schedule. For him to consider me like that, wasn't he the best, she gushed.

She concluded by thanking me for my friendship.

"Tell Rosceaux I said hello. Your friend forever, Evangelina."

The impulse came. I walked over to the edge of the building and climbed up on the ledge. Only I stood two stories up with bushes and soft ground below. A running start would be needed to make the hard-concrete parking lot. The impulse began to fade. I climbed down from the ledge, flicked my lighter, lit Evangelina's letter alight, and watched the pages curl and blacken.

Hours later, I was on the sofa staring at the walls when I heard a horn blow outside. I went downstairs and saw Darby's white SUV parked near the curb.

"Get in!" she yelled through the open passenger side window.

I barely got the door closed before she hit the pedal and roared off. She disregarded the stop sign at Third Street, turned right, sped through the thruway, went up on the sidewalk, clipped a white picket fence, screeched right on to Simcoe, got the green at Moss, another at Jefferson, and ignored the red at Louisiana Avenue while my ass ate the seat.

She turned on a narrow one lane road and stopped in front of a no parking sign. The ride had taken less than five minutes. She reached for her purse and took out a prescription pill bottle. After she shook a few into her hand, she produced a huge silver thermos from the driver's door and chased them down.

We climbed out of the SUV. I followed her past trees with private property signs nailed to them over to a rusty metal swing next to a pond. We sat.

"How did you know where to find me?" she asked.

"Where to find you?"

"That night. I tried calling but couldn't get through."

"Danny told me there'd been a shooting. I heard sirens."

"Something drew you to me."

"Well, I just happened…"

"Herman didn't come."

"I'm sorry, what?"

"I called him a dozen times. He didn't come."

A porch light came on at a house across the water. We watched a small dog run out into the backyard.

"He thought I butt-dialed him. He got aggravated and put his phone on silent."

She paused.

"It was only the second time I went there."

"What for?"

"Pills."

"Pills?"

"I was only going to be inside like two minutes. I had the bottle in my hand. We heard gunshots and ran into the restroom with two others. The door wouldn't lock. One of the girls shit herself. The other starts throwing up. It was so disgusting."

Someone whistled for the dog. It scampered back into the house.

"I was numb. I don't know how else to describe it. Just numb. If he had opened that door, he could have taken us all out. Then Linda screamed she didn't want to die, and he stops right outside the door at the same time the police show up. Someone yelled put your weapon down. Then more gunshots. The police came bang on the door. We had to walk out with our hands behind our heads."

She wiped under her nose.

"We passed a dead body in the hallway, and someone shot in the head by the door. He was still alive. He was lying on his side with his hand in the air grasping for help."

"Why were you going there for pills?" I asked.

She ignored my question and stretched out her legs.

"You saw our picture?"

I nodded my head.

"I keep getting harassed over that picture. I had to hide my Facebook page. I was getting messages about being a crisis actor. Then they started coming knock at our door. Herman told me to take David and go stay with my parents."

She gently placed her head on my shoulder as the aerator in the pond generated ripples that glistened in the dark.

When we climbed back into the SUV, the clock on the dashboard read 5:07. She drove me back to the apartment.

"You have to get ready for work?" she asked.

"I don't work today."

She said Guillory told her to take as much time as she needed before she came back to the office. She asked if she could come up for a few minutes. I put a pot of coffee on. She went use the bathroom and stayed in there for a while. She then came out and curled up on the sofa. I covered her with a blanket then went piss. When I walked back into the living room, her cell phone rang. She jumped up and answered it like a busted teenager out after curfew. I gathered it was her mom. Darby told her she'd run to the store for creamer then asked if David still slept.

"Okay," she said. "I'll be back in a bit."

I unlocked the gate. She gave a hug then drove off with the unopened creamer I gave her. I heard something behind me. It was Sheila. She stood out front of the coffee shop in her Catholic School uniform smoking a cigarette.

"You paid for that? Don't let Nancy find out."

With that, she mashed her cigarette into the ground, flipped the closed sign on the door to open, and went inside.

CHAPTER 30

When the calendar flipped to October, my thoughts turned to Festival Acadiens. The most wonderful time of the year, as far as I was concerned, and I resolved to pass a good time despite recent events. After not hearing from Darby in over two weeks, I received a text from her on the seventh. No revelations, only mundane back and forth that went well into the evening. I told her about Bach Lunch and the cutting of the boudin. She said she would bring little David and come spend the day with me.

Thursday afternoon, the first cool front of the season graced Acadiana with its presence. At long last, the suffocating heat and humidity had gone. Brisk north winds rustled the huge oak at the Lafayette South Bank while the time and temperature sign on the corner plummeted from an afternoon high of 92 to 68 by sunset. I took it all in from the rooftop of my apartment, much to the amusement of the people inside the twelve-story bank building I was sure.

Friday morning, I went down to the coffee shop.

"Look at you," Samantha said. "Prostitutes and search warrants. Maybe you're actually packing something in those dad jeans of yours."

I faked a smile. My phone rang. It was Darby. She was crying and having a fit. I thought there'd been another shooting. No. She was only arguing with Herman. He had forbidden her to leave the house.

"No problem," I told her.

"No!" she screamed. "I'm a grown woman! I can do whatever I want!"

I listened to them argue as I walked to Parc Sans Souci. Why she kept me on the line I was not sure. Possibly as a witness in case something happened. But nothing did. All they accomplished, besides scream at one another, was to spoil the entire morning for me.

Later that afternoon, I headed to Girard Park. I got a text from Darby. She said she would meet me there. I found her trying to squeeze the SUV into a tight spot near the intersection of Audubon and Girard Park Drive. She made it fit, sort of, and killed the engine. She emerged wearing huge black bug eye sunglasses, a floral headscarf, and pristine white pants.

I pulled a metal folding chair from the back seat, per her request, along with a beach bag. Together we headed to Scene Ma Louisiane. Darby struggled to walk through the grass in her heels. We found a spot and set up camp. I asked if she wanted something to eat. She shook her head no. I headed for the food booths. When I got back, Darby, looking like a fifty's movie starlet in her glasses and scarf, walked over to the porta potty. She clearly was not enjoying herself. Why even come then? Out of spite to Herman, I assumed. Did she break out of the house? I didn't pry, and she didn't offer.

After the last band finished, I walked her back to the SUV. She offered a ride to the apartment and asked if she could come up. I put the television on. A story ran about a drug arrest. I recognized the woman in the mugshot from the healing service. The one who said, "Devil, I reject you." Darby pointed at the screen.

"That's Linda. The one who screamed she didn't want to die in the restroom."

Definitely not the story Linda told before the Lord, but I didn't mention it. Darby had enough to deal with. She told me she would be back at the office Monday morning. After a visit to the bathroom, she announced she had to get going.

Later, my cell phone chimed with a text message, then another. Both were from Darby. I barely got through the first when yet another arrived. They were gibberish and hard to understand. She didn't use much in the way of punctuation. Herman apparently had jumped her case when she got home and demanded she tell him where she'd been. At first, I responded with one-word replies, then sad faced emojis. Finally, at 11:55, she texted goodnight. And that was that. My first day of festival completely shot to shit.

The next morning, I was up and out of the apartment as soon as the food booths opened. By two that afternoon, I sported a nice buzz. Theresa called. She asked if I could come by later. She was standing at the door when I arrived. Several of Evangelina's paintings hung from the walls inside the Carl Street residence.

"What should I do with Harleigh's stuff?" Theresa asked.

"Let her mom take it, or just put it in storage. At some point, Harleigh will come for it."

"You really think she's okay?"

"You know she talked about leaving."

"Then why can't they find her?"

"Because she knows they're looking for her. She didn't want to be found after that shit with Randall happened. She learned from that."

"Why would she just leave her stuff here?"

"It doesn't mean anything to her anymore. She wanted a fresh start."

"Why didn't you answer your phone that morning?"

"You know why I didn't answer my phone that morning."

"You know they can check that. Right?"

"And that's a good thing. Right?"

"Those detectives keep coming talk to me."

Theresa went on to say she had trouble making rent without Harleigh's input. She needed more paying viewers to her webcam. With that, she stood, pulled down her yoga pants, and revealed a full bush of pubic hair. She planned to shave it live in twenty minutes.

"I have to go," I said.

On Sunday, I got to festival early, watched French Mass, then went for beignets and coffee. The music cranked about 10:30. I spent time at the Salle de Danse tent, where they had a dance floor, restrooms, and their own bar before heading to the Atelier tent. Later, festival closed right where it began at Scene Ma Louisiane. I gave my grease-stained bag of cracklins a shake while dancers waltzed to Cajun dance favorites nearby.

The next morning, I arrived at the office a few minutes before eight. I noticed Darby's SUV in the parking lot. Upstairs, my cubicle sat in disarray with everything disturbed and pushed out of place. Guillory called me to his office. He laid into me the second I walked in. Where had I been? We take work at seven. Why was I not there Thursday and Friday? We had payrolls to get out. Did I even want the job? If not, he would find someone who did. He ripped me for almost ten minutes. He had reduced my hours till further notice. I guess this served as such.

Back at my cubicle, Barry called. He proceeded to go off on me as well. It seemed best buddies, Detectives Landry and Wilson, paid him a visit Friday. They kept him late into the evening as they searched my computer. For what, he didn't say. He did let it be known he had better things to do with his time then responding to questions he had no answers for.

Darby came by. She dressed plainly, like the day I first laid eyes on her in the breakroom. She seemed on edge. There had been a knock at the door Saturday. Herman thought it another conspiracy theorist and called 911. Turned out the person was a journalist. She began to sob. I didn't say anything. I was still miffed at her from Friday. She said she had been with HR most of the morning. They decided she would work only a couple days each week for the remainder of the year.

I happened to get a visit from HR myself the following week. I disliked the guy as soon as he stuck his head into my cubicle. He gave me this prepared and practiced statement concerning the state of the breakroom. There had been a complaint. He asked I do my part to help keep it clean. That afternoon, I emptied the coffee pot and wiped down the counter. I didn't bother with the trash on the floor or the splattered food inside the microwave in order so others could do their part as well.

Breaux, looking more frazzled than usual, showed up at my cubicle the next morning with five payroll returns in his hand. The payroll had all been entered. What he needed me to do was prepare the reports and get them back to him as soon as possible. That I did. By the end of October, all the returns had been completed, and I was back to bookwork and twenty-four-hour work weeks. The month ended without hearing anything from Robicheaux concerning rent.

The week before Thanksgiving, the HR dude made a return appearance at my cubicle. I still adhered to my five o'clock breakroom ritual though not much else had changed in there. He reiterated from his previous monologue.

"I told you to do your part. When you finish with the microwave, clean up after yourself. I'm not gonna tell you again."

"Wait a second," I said.

He walked out. I went after him.

"Hey!" I yelled.

He stopped, as did everyone else in the vicinity. I went up to him.

"I don't have anything to do with that microwave."

"That is not what I've been told."

"You don't know shit!"

I returned to my cubicle. An hour later, I received an email from Breaux. It said not to report back to work until the Monday after Thanksgiving.

On the twenty-third, I went down to the coffee shop. Dean's truck, now sporting two Trump 2016 bumper stickers sat parked out front. Nancy stood behind the counter. She had a package for me. It turned out to be the laptop.

"I found it sitting on top of your mailbox. I don't think the mailman put it there. See, there's no postage or return address. I didn't want someone to walk by and take it."

"Thanks."

"What was the deal with that search warrant?"

"A friend is missing. They're covering all bases."

"Who?

"Harleigh Hebert."

"I heard about that. Someone told me she was kidnapped. Is that true?"

"No. She just left town without telling anyone."

Nancy said Dean got laid off but found work up in North Dakota. There would be no Thanksgiving cruise this year. She mentioned Robicheaux. He was not doing good. She asked if his son got with me about the rent.

"Yes," I lied.

That night, I attended the last Downtown Alive of the season at Parc Sans Souci. A food truck served up fried catfish so tasty I went back three times. Santa and his elves hosted a toy collection for kids in need. One of the elves reminded me of Harleigh. Same mannerisms and body type. I wanted so hard to believe it was her. The woman happened to walk by on her way to a porta potty. It wasn't.

Thanksgiving Day, downtown was empty. I walked over to Girard Park. A few people were out there, mostly kids playing on playground equipment along with dedicated exercisers keeping on schedule. I hung around for a few hours then headed back to the apartment to place my frozen turkey TV dinner in the microwave.

Saturday made my tenth consecutive day off work. Bored and scrolling around on the laptop, I noticed Darby back on Facebook. She'd shared a meme.

Enjoy the little things in life.

Underneath, Linda from the healing service responded.

"Like your husbands tiny dick."

Darby shot back.

"Like you can talk with all the dicks you have in your mouth."

Linda replied.

"You jealous of all the dick in my mouth? How bout Ms Privileged McMillan Branch tell everyone the real reason she was at Rickland that night."

The real reason? Darby told me she went there for pills. Was that not true? Not long after, the meme and the comments underneath were gone.

Back at the office on the twenty-eighth, the breakroom looked worse than ever. While Darby didn't mention anything to me about the flare up on Facebook, she did talk about a birthday that passed. She hadn't felt much like celebrating and asked everyone to instead donate money to victims of the shooting. That they did, though she admonished Herman for doing so.

"He could have at least gotten me a card," she said.

That afternoon, rather than going into the breakroom at five to clean up, I headed for the elevator. Outside, I noticed orange-colored leaflets on the windshields of the cars in the parking lot. Curiosity got me. I went up to one. It told of a rally being held next week concerning the removal of the monument of Confederate General Allen Buford on the corner.

The next morning, the bullshit crew were up in arms.

"The Confederacy should have won."

"We'd be a lot better off."

"They just want to erase history."

Later that morning, Beverly appeared at my cubicle with a leaflet in her hand.

"You know that monument down there?"

"Yes."

"Do you know what it represents?"

"Allen Buford?"

"No. It represents white supremacy, racism, and slavery. It was put up during the era of Jim Crow to intimidate people."

"I didn't realize that."

"It's hateful. You understand how people could find it offensive?"

"Sure."

Darby came by later. She had a leaflet in her hand as well.

"Someone put this shit on my car. People are so stupid. You know that monument down there?"

"Yes."

"Do you know what it represents?"

"Allen Buford?"

"No. Well, yeah, it's him. But what I mean is it represents history. He's a hero. He fought for what he believed in, plus he donated land to the freed slaves. You didn't have anything to do with this, did you?"

"Me? No. Why?"

"Someone said they saw you in the parking lot with a stack of these in your hand."

Of course, they did.

The following day, Breaux came to my cubicle in full panic mode. He handed me three payroll returns. He needed me to make corrections and get them back to him as soon as possible. These were three of the five returns where payroll had already been entered and I was only to print the corresponding reports. Whoever entered the payroll had done a terrible job. They missed employees and entered incorrect amounts. I got the returns corrected and back to him in a timely manner.

Sweating profusely behind his desk with smudged reading glasses perched at the end of his nose, Breaux took them from me without a word. Back at my cubicle, the phone rang. It was Guillory, full of sunshine and puppy dog kisses, appreciative of my work, and questioning how the wife and kids were. In our last conversation, he did me raw. Now, he lubed me up before he rammed it in. He specifically asked about the three returns I just gave Breaux.

"Did you work on them?"

"Yes, sir."

"What did you do? Tell me exactly what happened."

So, I did.

"Let me make sure I understand. You did not enter the payroll for those returns?"

"Correct."

"And he told you to only run the reports?"

"Yes, sir."

"And why was that?"

"I don't know."

"Well, know this. That is not what I've been told. And now I'm dealing with a clusterfuck because of you."

He hung up. Breaux threw me under the bus. The bastard. Fuck him. Fuck both of them. I rose from my chair and stormed out of my cubicle. Darby walked up. She saw the fury in my eyes.

"Hey! Wait a minute."

She grabbed my arm.

"Jesus! What's the matter?"

I told her what happened.

"So? Next week, he'll probably jump your ass for something else you didn't do. Are you going to have a hissy fit each time it happens?"

I stared at her. It was as if she were channeling Harleigh.

"Don't worry. IT can go in and find out who did what."

She walked me back to my cubicle.

"I never saw you like that before."

"When I'm angry, I react. I don't reason."

"Promise you won't get like that again."

I promised.

The Buford Rally occurred on the ninth. I heard the bullshit crew say they would counterprotest. They didn't. The next day, Beverly again appeared at my cubicle. I assumed she would ask why I was not in attendance. Instead, she asked what I thought of transgender restrooms.

"I've never given any thought to transgender restrooms."

"That's very insensitive, Ruston. I'm offended you would even say such a thing."

I mentioned it to Darby.

"Her and her liberal bullshit. One transgender in this entire building and we're all supposed to cater to them."

"Here in the office?"

"I didn't say in the office, I said in the building. Jackie. First, it's Jack. Now it's Jackie. He works for the real estate firm on twenty-two."

Three weeks remained of 2015. The office was abuzz over the upcoming holiday schedule. With Christmas Eve and Christmas Day falling on a Thursday and Friday, everyone was guaranteed a long holiday weekend, ensuring a lengthy break before the looming tax season. On the sixteenth, Bridgett put out an email concerning an office Christmas party. Date and location to be named later. I also got an email from Guillory.

Ruston,

Please return to the office on January 4th, 2016.

Jim Guillory CPA/CGMA, CFE, CGFM

Heavy rain and strong winds battered the area the following day. I stayed inside the apartment and watched unappealing daytime talk shows with the volume turned off. The next day was overcast and damp with temperatures in the middle forties. At five, the local news came on. There was a story about The Bistro.

"Findings of independent accounting firm released."

I forgot all about Karen and the issues she was having. I couldn't hear what was being said, but the uncomfortable look on her face when she appeared on the screen told me all I needed to know. I bundled up and went downstairs. After walking around for a while, I took a seat near the water fountains in Parc Sans Souci. I noticed several light poles held missing person flyers with Harleigh's picture on them. Voices approached from behind.

"Homeless people are so pathetic."

"I ought to go kick his useless ass."

"Don't look at him. He's just gonna follow us and ask for money."

It was the bullshit crew. They headed for the seafood restaurant on the corner. Was tonight the office Christmas party? I considered busting up in there for my free meal but instead returned to the apartment.

The second to last week of 2015 began with a phone call from Darby. She was sobbing something awful. Turned out, it was not another mass casualty event. Instead, Jim Breaux, was no mo'. Darby said he had been let go and replaced. I wondered out loud if his termination was because of the payroll return debacle that occurred. Darby asked me to meet her for lunch at the poboy place. Sitting across from her a few hours later, she recounted the series of events as they occurred. Guillory, along with someone named Tony Landry, walked into Breaux's office first thing that morning and closed the door. Shouts could be heard. Someone threw something. Breaux walked out between his two executioners with his head down. All three got on the elevator. Only two returned. Guillory and Landry, patting each other on the back and laughing to beat the band. A moving company cleared out Breaux's belongings as we spoke.

Darby began to cry. She was sad to see him go. She talked of an email notifying every one of the change, and how this Tony Landry would personally go around to meet everyone, and for everyone to give him a warm welcome. Turned out, Darby knew the guy well. He and Herman were members of the Hub City Tea Party of South Louisiana.

Hub City Tea Party? Grown ass men sipping from dainty cups with extended pinkies?

Geez.

I asked again if this had anything to do with the three payroll returns I corrected. I didn't much care for the guy, but if I had checked those returns properly before I finalized them, maybe Breaux would still be employed with the company. Darby said talk around the office was this was more about the availability of Tony Landry then it was about John Breaux. They were looking for an opportunity to sack someone and bring this guy on board.

That Wednesday, I went down to the coffee shop. A sign out front indicated it would be closed tomorrow through the remainder of the year. I pulled open the door. Nancy stood near the counter with Gary from Indiana.

"Ruston!" he called out. "Nancy told me you're an accountant. I don't see why people waste money on you guys. I can do that stuff gagged and blind-folded."

Nancy let out a loud laugh and playfully slapped him on the arm.

"Shush, you. I said if you were good."

Gary looked at me and smiled.

Nancy said she was closing for two weeks to go to Indiana with Gary. Dean, still in North Dakota, would meet them when he got time off. Since they missed their yearly cruise, the three of them planned to spend the holidays together.

All I received for Christmas was a friend request from Borel on Facebook, in addition to an invitation to like a page called Borel Ministries. It had a Lafayette address. A small vacant building on Clinton with a For Lease sign in the window. The ministry page contained Bible verses and coming soon posts. Borel's Facebook page read like the bullshit crew, only opposite. He adored Obama and was all about Hillary. He bashed Republicans as 'conservaturds' and said they planned to take away social security and do away with the minimum wage. Some on his Facebook page didn't appreciate that all too much. Back and forth they went with insults and personal attacks.

I spent the final week of 2015 holed up inside my apartment. Cabin fever set in. Under a heavy overcast sky, I went for a walk in the Freetown neighborhood, one of Lafayette's oldest. It was to be added to the National

Register of Historic Places per the sign near the community garden on Garfield.

Walking amid shotgun houses of various colors, I met a few brave souls out there defying the elements. Kids on bicycles, families taking down Christmas decorations, an elderly gentleman dressed to the nines on his front porch, and a dedicated grill master flipping burgers in his driveway. I noticed another flyer with Harleigh's picture on it. This one had Theresa's cell number at the bottom. I didn't see the point. Harleigh was long gone. Maybe Theresa needed some sort of closure. One thing was for sure. Harleigh will be some pissed when she lays eyes on these.

I went into the superette for a plate lunch before I made my way back to the apartment. Standing at the corner of Stewart and Johnston, I took a long look at The Bistro over on the next corner. I thought back to all those lazy afternoons I spent there with Harleigh. She had been with me since my first day in Lafayette. She was the rational oftentimes blunt voice that talked me from the ledge on numerous occasions. What I wouldn't give to walk in and see her standing behind the bar once more. I just hoped she'd found a healthy environment to settle into.

2016 came in with me on the roof of my apartment listening to the revelry over on Jefferson while wondering what awaited me at the office Monday morning. When I got the job, the goal was to survive the eight hours that day. The problem was there was always another eight hours to endure.

This new guy, Tony Landry, maybe he would turn out to be one of the good ones. They do exist. Like Nolan Armentor, assistant shipping manager at the plant. When we lost our jobs, only salaried people were eligible to receive severance. He pulled some strings. I was sad to see his name in the obituary the following year.

It began to get light. I climbed down from the roof, gathered my laundry, and headed for the twenty-four-hour laundromat on Taft.

CHAPTER 31

January 4, 2016

On the first Monday of the new year, I stepped off the elevator and walked to my cubicle. It looked just the same as I left it two weeks ago. The bullshit crew gathered near the breakroom. The topic of conversation was President Obama's God given name, Barry Soetoro. So they said. Darby sprang into my cubicle. She was all done up with makeup, hair, nails, perfume, and jewelry. She made up not speaking to me in over two weeks in less than two minutes. She had big news. She and Herman had separated. She now lived with her parents along with little David and their dog Peyton. She told me about taking David to the New Year's Eve celebration at the children's museum. She also mentioned the classes she planned to take. Cooking classes, dance classes, painting classes, pottery classes, even a creative writing course. She then spun on a dime and walked away, leaving a heavy layer of perfume in my cubicle. Meanwhile, the bullshit crew moved on to the subject of Obama's birth certificate.

"I can prove I am a U.S. citizen. Can he do the same? We know he lived in Kenya."

"There is no record of him ever applying for US citizenship."

"This casts doubt about Barry's legitimacy and qualification to serve as president."

"When he got sworn into office, he used the Koran instead of the Holy Bible."

I leaned back in my chair.

Happy New Year.

I saw the email concerning Tony Landry. Another would come later that morning. That one mentioned full day Fridays and half day Saturdays. I continued with the bookwork I worked on before the holidays. With Breaux gone, I did not know who would assign work for me to do, though I was sure I would find out soon enough.

I went for a smoke. One person sat downstairs in the smoking area. Jackie, Winslow's coworker. She looked to be upset. She stood when she saw me and wiped tears from her eyes.

"Hey, Ruston. Happy New Year."

She gave me a hug.

"Happy New Year to you, too," I said.

"How were your holidays?"

"Fine. How were yours?"

"Good. Great, actually."

"Are you okay?"

"I was, till our HR rep came talk to me just now. Telling me I make people uncomfortable. I make people uncomfortable? He should hear what people say about me behind my back."

"I'm sorry to hear that."

"He told me there was a complaint. That some people were upset over me using the women's restroom. Someone even mentioned molesting a kid. A kid? There are no kids in this place."

She paused for a second.

"They should be more concerned about their priests molesting kids."

She stopped.

"I'm sorry. That was wrong. I shouldn't have said that. I'm just really upset."

I smiled.

"Hey, for Halloween I told my coworkers I was dressing up as Father John Bergeron."

She snickered.

"Oh my God! Ruston! That is so insensitive."

She put a hand on her hip and shook a finger at me in mock anger.

"You ought to be ashamed of yourself."

I finished my cigarette and headed for the elevator. The redhead from payroll, Debbie, Rhonda Dugas's mom, got on with me. The last time I saw her was at the crawfish boil. She looked at me, then raised her hand to press floor thirty-nine. When she saw it highlighted, she put her hand back down. Up we went. I wanted to say something. But what was there to say. I failed her. Everyone failed her. If she was anything like the bullshit crew, she'd been raised to live in fear of those different from her. Blacks, Muslims, Syrian refugees, illegal immigrants, transgenders. But not her son-in-law. Not David Dugas. After all, he wasn't a bad guy. He was "troubled". After we passed a few floors, I decided to keep my mouth shut and pretend she wasn't there.

Later, I got a coffee from the breakroom. Back at my cubicle, someone stood inside. They startled me. Hot coffee spilled onto my hand. It was Tony Landry. After I dried my hand on my pants, he gave me an overcompensating handshake.

Originally from New Orleans, Landry worked for a prestigious accounting firm near Slidell. His white teeth, blonde hair, and boyish good looks made him out to be some bad boy heartthrob from an eighty's teen comedy. Thomas, Madison chomped at the bit to hire someone of his caliber.

So he said. He talked about himself for a good ten minutes, even telling me about an inside the park home run he hit in high school. I half expected him to produce a signed 8x10 glossy of himself to display in my cubicle. I remembered I saw him before. Last summer, standing over near Darby's desk with Guillory and Bridgett.

"I heard some questionable things about you," he said. "Be that as it may, I understand you keep up with the bookwork. There's also a list of payroll returns you supposedly work on."

He glanced around my cubicle with a look of disgust.

"Ya'll have some issues in this building. I mean, they told me about this one guy who thinks he deserves his own restroom because he's transgender. What is that about? I mean, come on, he has a dick, right. What? He thinks wearing lipstick gives him the right to go in there and put his nose up some woman's snatch. Fucking liberals, I tell you. November eighth can't come soon enough. We're gonna take our country back."

With Breaux gone, Tony Landry was now my immediate supervisor.

Happy New Year indeed.

CHAPTER 32

January 9, 2016

Another tax season was on the horizon. Putting in sixty hours after being off for two weeks made for one long ass week. By Saturday, I was done for. Twelve noon couldn't come fast enough. I hadn't seen or heard anything from Guillory all week, though Landry made sure to stop by each morning with a condescending remark toward one minority group or another. Darby also kept up her appearances. She was in good spirits, or maybe it was denial.

The morning dragged on. At 11:53, Darby called.

"What are you doing tonight?"

"Tonight? Nothing."

"Mind if we come over?"

We? Sure, whatever.

About six, I got a text saying they were on the way. I went downstairs and waited on the bench outside. She drove up in her white SUV with David, Peyton, and her silver thermos. They'd picked up a pizza. I took Peyton's leash in one hand, the pizza in the other, and up the stairs we went. Darby and I sat in the kitchen while David jumped up and down on the sofa and Peyton barked his head off. Darby talked over the ruckus.

"Next week, everyone in the office is getting a dry erase board."

"What for?"

"So Tony can see what everyone has lined up in front of them."

She called Landry by his first name. I assumed because she knew him on a personal level.

"We're going to start grading clients from A to D. He only wants A and B clients."

I had no idea what that meant. I asked about Breaux. She took a sip from her thermos.

"Someone said he was going back to his old firm."

David jumped down from the sofa. He wanted nuggets. Darby tried to give him a bite of pizza but he resisted and ran back to the sofa. Darby brought a DVD for him to watch but I didn't own a DVD player. Undaunted, she pulled up a video game on her phone and shoved it in his face. The boy went from sixty to zero in less than a second. Meanwhile, Peyton took a shit on the floor. Darby went over and cleaned it up.

"Can we take him on a quick walk?" she asked.

We went downstairs. I held on to Peyton's leash as he pissed against the building. Darby walked over to the SUV and topped off her thermos. After a few minutes, we went back up. David, mesmerized by his game, never noticed we had gone.

Darby retook her seat in the kitchen and crossed her legs. She had on the same clothes she'd worn to the office that morning. Black pants, with knee-high tan boots and a gray blouse. She told me her plan was to move out of her parent's house as soon as tax season ended. She didn't go into detail about what caused Herman and her to split, but she did say it was long overdue.

As the night went on, the little boy grew cranky. Darby told him to play his game and be quiet. He in turn threw a fit and broke a piece off the coffee table. Darby was apologetic. I didn't care. I broke the same piece off the opposite end long ago. She wrangled everyone up and headed downstairs. Peyton went into his cage, precious David in his booster seat, and off they went.

Back upstairs, someone banged on the gate.

"Ruston! Hey Ruston!"

It was Borel. I invited him in. He helped himself to the leftover pizza on the table. He told me he had been working over at his ministry building on Clinton. Services would begin sometime in the summer. He would preach what people could not handle: Jesus.

"Not that religion bullshit," he said. "The rich took Jesus and made him into a high-class club. A gated community. Sitting high on their pedestals, looking down on everyone, condemning. Jesus came for those the religious stand against. If it weren't for religion, I'd have found Jesus long ago."

I couldn't care less. He continued.

"People have it backwards. Like that shooting. The ones who died, they're the blessed ones. They're with our father in heaven now. The pastor at the healing service didn't want to hear any of that and stuck us out in the parking lot. Once we get established, watch how fast his attendance dwindles."

He had to get going.

"Thanks for the pizza. I'll be in touch."

CHAPTER 33

Just as Darby said, dry erase boards were issued to everyone Monday morning. We were to list our top four "projects" on it. I currently had one. The bookwork for Donaldson Motors. Landry came by with four small payroll returns. He stood over me as I erased Donaldson Motors from the dry erase board and wrote the names of the four returns. After I completed those returns, I was to erase them and rewrite Donaldson Motors. Innovative stuff was afoot at Thomas, Madison, Smith and Associates.

When Landry left my cubicle, someone walked out of the men's room.

"Richardson," I heard him say. "How was Montana?"

Richardson, who I couldn't put a face to, apparently traveled to Montana with his family over the holidays. As they walked away, Landry asked if any black people lived there.

This would be my third go around with the payroll returns. More would come tomorrow. I knocked out what I had and went back to the bookwork. Darby came by after lunch. She noted the completed returns sitting on my desk.

"I hated doing fourth quarter payrolls," she said. "The 940s and the W-3s and L-3s."

"What are those?" I asked.

Darby freaked.

"Oh, my God. Ruston, you have to do the annual reports."

I had no clue. Darby stayed and helped me. She even created a cheat sheet to follow. The next morning, Landry came by with more. He stood over me as I once again erased Donaldson Motors from the dry erase board. He called later to say he checked the returns, and everything looked fine. Darby saved my ass yet again.

The following week, Landry was in a mood. He took great offense to it being Martin Luther King Day and complained about getting caught up in a parade that ran down Willow the day before.

"Plus," he screamed, "some bitch is crying about the monument on the corner. Mr. Buford was a fine man. What has she done? Besides collect a welfare check."

After another long week, I left the office at noon and headed for The Discount Mart on the thruway. I placed two twelve packs on the counter and asked for a carton of cigarettes. The cashier caught me eyeing a copy of the SWLA Free Press on the magazine rack behind him.

"Latest one," he said. "Want it?"

I had not laid eyes on one in forever. I heard nothing recently from Robicheaux concerning rent, or how he was doing health wise, but someone was still putting issues out.

"Sure," I said.

Back at the apartment, I discovered it wasn't Robicheaux's magazine he tossed into my bag but instead the porn mag sitting next to it. Served me right. I thumbed through it for a second then shoved it on my bookshelf.

That night, I read on Facebook about the effort to tear down the Cort Rickland Community Center. Most commentators spoke in favor. One even mentioned the Google Maps car caught a drug deal in the parking lot. I tried to see for myself, but darkened images dated 2008 showed no such thing. I plopped yellow Pegman in front of the apartment. The April 2013 images displayed For Lease signs in the downstairs spaces. I clicked near The Bistro. Harleigh's bike could be seen locked up along the yellow lattice fence. The arrowed backlit roadside sign read:

MON SERVICE INDUSTRY

TUES KARAOKE

TONIGHT HELMSELY ROMERO

I remembered exactly what day that was. I got there about two. Helmsley Romero drove up and asked the location of the nearest music store. I directed him a few blocks south on Johnston. I took a seat outside. Harleigh came out to join me. I zoomed in on the two individuals visible on the patio. One leaned back with their legs crossed, the other in the process of lighting a cigarette. I don't recall the conversation, but I well remember afternoons sitting out there listening to the traffic as shadows slowly stretched across the sidewalk.

That image captured just another day. What I wouldn't give to go back and live in it forever.

CHAPTER 34

Plans to attend the dog parade with Darby and her posse at the end of January fell through. The following weekend, she asked me to go to the children's parade with them. That Saturday morning, she told me Herman would take little David himself. Super Bowl Sunday, she called to come over. She arrived with David and Peyton, along with an eight-piece chicken with biscuits and sides and her thermos.

She was in a sour mood. Since Herman planned to take David, she told him she would spend time with her friend, who I gathered was me. He responded by demanding she come for the boy immediately. I guess he thought she would not be able to mess around with David on her hip. The boy ended up missing both parades. To make up for it, Darby got him a handheld game, which he occupied himself with on the sofa.

Darby was not so much interested in the football game as she was the commercials. At halftime, Herman called. She went out into the hallway and closed the door. Peyton ran up to it and whimpered. Precious David couldn't be bothered.

"It's none of your fuckin' business where I am or who I'm with?" I heard her scream.

"Yeah? Oh yeah? Really! Well, you'll never see your son again if you pull that shit!"

She came back into the apartment. David pried himself from his game and asked for a biscuit. Darby snapped at him.

"Look the mess you made! Play your game and shut up!"

The little boy climbed back on the sofa and sulked. Meanwhile, Peyton took a shit near the window.

Darby went into the bathroom while I cleaned it up. After a few minutes, she came back out and took a seat at the table.

"What was I thinking?" she said.

"I'm sorry. What?"

She proceeded to tell me how she came to marry one Herman Naquin, the 2013 Lafayette Businessman of the Year.

It all began when a major accident shut the Whiskey Bay Bridge down in both directions. Traffic detoured to Highway 190, which ran through her hometown of Krotz Springs. In addition to working at her father's fabrication shop, she also worked part-time at a convenience store in town. With the increased traffic, her boss asked her to come in and lend a hand.

Ten minutes after she arrived, a short professional looking guy walked in and took a liking to her. He told her he was twenty-two. She thought he looked at least thirty. He stayed in contact with her. A couple weeks later, he took her to a cheap two-star hotel over in Livonia.

"I was still a virgin," she said. "He gets on top of me, and he's kissing me and humping me but nothing's happening. Then he sits off to the side of the bed. When I sat up, he yells 'don't look!' He reached over and started fingering me. It hurt. His goddamn short fat porky fingers hurt!"

She grabbed her thermos, took a hit, and slammed it down on the table. Peyton, who had dozed off, woke up startled. David played his game and kept quiet.

"Then he got a little hard and after a minute he came inside me. Of course, just like that, I get pregnant. He couldn't give me an orgasm, but he could ejaculate. He tried to force me into getting an abortion. That is how I found out how old he was. He said he could lose everything. Then he decided we should get married immediately. My mom and dad didn't understand. I had to stand there and lie about how much I supposedly loved this man. But, because they loved me so much, they went along with it."

She began to cry.

"We didn't tell anyone about the baby. We were gonna say I got pregnant on the honeymoon. Then I lost it. I remember thinking, what have I done? I'm seventeen, I quit school, and I'm married to a stranger."

The room fell silent, save for the football game on television. Right at that moment, the Broncos recovered a fumble at the Panther four-yard line. A few plays later, they ran it in for a touchdown, essentially putting the game away.

By that time, Darby looked downright sloppy with her makeup smeared and shirt untucked. Not accustomed to seeing her in such a fashion, I gingerly offered to drive them home. She refused. They made it to her parent's house with no trouble.

The following morning, the bullshit crew were in an uproar concerning the halftime performance from the night before. They claimed it was nothing but a glorification of The Black Panthers. Someone mentioned red coffee cups. I guess I was not at work the day that went down.

Landry walked into my cubicle with a stack of W-2's in his hand. He asked if I saw the halftime show. He said that was the kind of shit that would lead to another civil war. After he left, I took the 1099-MISC he gave me and paper clipped it to the one I still had in my desk from the previous year.

◆ ◆ ◆

Mardi Gras morning, the weather app on my phone showed sixteen degrees outside. Authorities urged everyone to protect pets, plants, and pipes. Even with the brutal cold, the three parades ran downtown as scheduled. On the sixteenth, ice began to accumulate across the area. Most businesses in the building shut down so employees could make it home before things worsened. Ours soon followed suit.

The next morning, I got dressed, went downstairs, unlocked the gate, and about bust my ass. The entire sidewalk was covered in ice. I went back up, not knowing how I would make it to the office. I got a text from Darby. Thomas, Madison would remain closed till further notice. The following afternoon, most of downtown lost power, including the apartment. I bundled up on the sofa and dozed off. When I came to later, I thought I heard a utility crew working outside. Just as I reached for the curtain, a gunshot rang out from down below. I dropped to the floor and crawled away from the window. Police soon arrived. I cracked open the door.

"Put your weapon down!"

"What are you doing? He didn't do anything wrong!"

"He tried to kill me!"

"Drop your weapon!"

"What the fuck! He was only protecting his family!"

"Tase him!"

"Stop! He's not resisting!"

"Hit him again!"

One by one, I slowly made out the voices of who were down there. Nancy, Dean, Samantha, along with Gary from Indiana. From what I gathered, Samantha was inside the coffee shop when Gary knocked at the front door. She called her mom and dad. When they arrived, Dean pulled his gun. Gary insisted Dean tried to kill him. Nancy said he only fired a warning shot. Dean was popped for resisting arrest and illegal discharge of a weapon. Gary said it should be attempted first degree murder.

"You were trying to break in and go after my daughter!" said Nancy.

"Officer, I simply stopped to see if they were open."

"You're full of shit! How can we be open if there's no power?"

Nancy accused Gary of stealing money from the coffee shop. An officer asked Gary how he knew the Robicheaux family.

"We met on a swinger's cruise," he answered.

"Swinger's cruise?" Samantha said.

Gary proudly boasted how he'd been doing Nancy for over a year now.

"Oh, my God!" Samantha screamed. "That's disgusting!"

"You didn't know?" Gary asked her.

"No, I didn't know!"

"But you knew about your little sister being a mud shark."

"Oh, my God!" yelled Nancy.

I had to Google what that meant.

"That's right," Gary said. "Your little girl likes that colored dick."

"That is so disgusting!" said Nancy.

"No, mom, that's not disgusting," said Samantha. "You're disgusting. What were you thinking, cheating on dad like that?"

"Your father's in on it, too," said Gary. "Who do you think he does when he goes tan?"

"Miss Rachel?" Samantha cried. "He's fucking Miss Rachel?"

The drama continued for another hour. It called for popcorn, but I had no power.

A lot had just gone down. Dean tased and arrested, Samantha discovering her parents were swingers, and Nancy learning of her youngest daughter's affinity for black boys. Did I witness an already dysfunctional family disintegrate for good?

Later, with power restored, I put a pot of coffee on. I got a text from Darby. We'd be back at the office in the morning.

CHAPTER 35

March 2016

Even though Fat Tuesday was three weeks past, colorful Mardi Gras beads still dangled from tree branches, overhead power lines, and the occasional stop light. Sometimes a pair would fall to the street, and either be washed away by the rain or scooped up with the trash. Prized possessions a few weeks ago, they were now stepped over and ignored.

After I completed all the bookwork for the April fifteenth tax deadline, Landry began to hand me individual tax returns to do. He would then call me to his office a couple times a day to go over those returns. Though he spruced Breaux's former space up with reupholstered furniture and LED lighting, it still suffocated me. After he told me of the changes he made to a return, he would send me to fetch a reprinted copy off a printer near Darby's desk, then explain little nuances he expected me to remember for next tax season. It was on one of those occasions he pointed to a framed newspaper column on the wall.

"Bet you weren't aware I'm a writer," he boasted.

Darby pulled up some of his work on the laptop at the apartment that weekend. His writings were nothing more than letters to the editor of a New Orleans newspaper. One read as follows.

"I warned everyone about Obama and his objective to turn our country into a socialist state. Obama refuses to recite the Pledge of Allegiance. Rather than place his hand over his heart, Obama will turn his back and slouch. Why do Obama voters still take up for this Muslim Traitor? Obama wants to destroy America and be crowned King of the New World Order with one religion, Islam. The reason Obama gave away those one-hundred-dollar phones was to purchase votes from those liberal idiots. Hard working Americans are paying for those phones with added taxes to their bills."

The letter was signed Sovereign Citizen. Landry considered himself a Tea'd off Tea Party activist unrelentingly battling the Obama agenda. The letters, doused in fear, insecurity, and anger came off to me as limp dick.

On the first day of spring, I left the office at noon and headed for the apartment. Late that afternoon, right on schedule, I got a text from Darby asking if her and her cast could come over. I responded with my usual 'sure' and went downstairs to wait. I wasn't down there long before Borel turned the corner.

"Ruston. What's up?"

"Not much."

Darby's SUV drove up. I made introductions. Borel extended his hand.

"Borel Jeffery. Borel Ministries."

"You're a minister?" Darby asked.

"Yes, I am. What's that I smell?"

"Chinese take-out. Would you like to have dinner with us?"

"Of course."

Darby introduced David and Peyton to Minister Borel before the four of them headed upstairs. I got the Chinese takeout out of the SUV along with a box of twenty-count nuggets and followed. While Darby laid the food out on the table, little David retired to the sofa with his nuggets and handheld game. I grabbed a container of shrimp fried rice and leaned against the counter. Darby mentioned she'd seen some famous country singer in town and gotten a picture of him. Borel was unimpressed.

"That man is nothing but a common drunk. If he were a plumber, would you be gushing over him like that? I used to be a drunk. Wanna take my picture?"

I shook my head and dug into my fried rice. Borel's newfound sobriety hadn't cured him of acting the ass, which he was prone to do on occasion. They began to go at one another. Borel professed his Jesus. Darby countered with her own Jesus. Back and forth they went. If one of them had turned to me and said, "ain't that right, Ruston," I felt I might send them to their individual Jesus that night.

The subject of abortion arose. Darby said it should be illegal. Borel replied it should be made obsolete. Darby asked what he meant.

"You don't know what obsolete means? Out of date. No longer being used."

"I know what obsolete means. What I meant was how do you make it obsolete?"

"Simple. You find the reasons women get abortions and eliminate them. Soon, there will be no more abortions."

Darby asked Borel if he labeled himself a conservative or a liberal. He asked what she labeled herself as. Darby said she considered herself a Republican pro-life conservative. Borel laughed.

"I'll tell you what I am. I'm fulfilled. I'm fulfilled in my Lord and savior Jesus Christ. You see, you're unfulfilled. You have holes. That is why you label yourself, and others, to fill those holes. And it's still not enough. Labels mean limits, and one should never limit their thoughts or their beliefs. Your political affiliation is just another noose around your throat."

Borel climbed higher on his soapbox. He talked about a baker refusing to bake a cake for a gay couple.

"Not only would I bake those people their cake, but I would also love on them so hard they'd probably invite me to the wedding. All the while, the religious would ask why I was hanging around with such scum, like the Pharisees."

"If a man lies with another man, it is a detestable act," Darby responded.

Borel laughed.

"Cherry picked Leviticus. Leviticus also says you can't eat shellfish or get a tattoo."

I broke my fortune cookie open.

Winds of change are blowing your way.

Was a tornado about to strike the apartment? One could only wish.

Peyton got antsy. I excused myself and took him downstairs for a walk. When we returned, Darby and Borel stood face to face. Little David was oblivious.

"Okay, if you were there," Borel said to her, "what were you doing there?"

"What was I doing there? Sucking a black man's cock."

"You look like the kind that would."

Darby grabbed a plate off the table and fired it at Borel. It only hit the floor and shattered.

"I'm out of here," Borel said.

I followed him down and let him out. When I went back up, Darby was kneeling in front of David.

"Sweetie, mommy's sorry for all the yelling."

She looked at me.

"Just so you know, what I said is not true. Herman just thinks it is."

Darby turned her attention back to David. Brushing the hair from his forehead, she asked if he was ready to go.

"Bat man's clock!" the little boy yelled.

I walked them downstairs. Darby strapped David into his booster seat while I placed Peyton in his cage. She climbed in and put her seat belt on.

"I'm not coming back if that guy's here," she said.

"I understand."

"I told him I was at Rickland the night of the shooting. He went on about the people who survived not being blessed. That the blessed people died and went to heaven."

"Yeah, he mentioned that to me before."

"What kind of shit is that? And he's a minister?"

"Well, I haven't seen any paperwork that confirms it."

She gave a laugh. I waved to the boy in the back seat.

"See ya, David."

"Bat man's clock!"

The following week, Darby said nothing concerning the flare up she had with Borel. Meanwhile, I would return to the apartment each evening to find him sitting on the bench outside wanting another war of words with her. He told me the building on Clinton was taking shape and would be ready by midsummer. I didn't understand what his plans for the "ministry" might be, but I figured I would find out soon enough.

Easter weekend, I heard nothing from either of them. That Sunday, while lying on the sofa scrolling on my phone, I noticed Borel had shared an article on Facebook entitled, "Why we should vote Hillary Clinton for President." I opened it. At least I tried. My phone had a fit. The only remedy was to take the back cover off and remove the battery. The next morning, I put the battery back in and turned it on. After a minute or two, it chimed with a text from Darby.

Why are you voting for Hillary Clinton?

Puzzled, I responded.

Who said I was?

I stopped. I logged on to Facebook and saw I somehow shared Borel's article to my page. Underneath were thirty-nine comments, a combination of accusations and insults plus links to articles concerning Donald Trump that served to put me in my place. Someone even referred to me as a fag libtard.

My Facebook now contained two posts. My check-in at Darby's church and a link to an article about Hillary Clinton. Not one person who sent me a friend request made any previous attempt to engage with me before. Later at the office, Darby came by. I was in the process of explaining to her what happened when Landry appeared. He escorted her back to her desk.

Did he know? Of course, he did. How could he not?

Great.

CHAPTER 36

After a hell of a week, I left the office at noon and headed for the apartment. Landry never mentioned the Facebook post, but I gathered by his demeanor he somehow knew of it. Now under the impression I supported Hillary, a fallacy that clearly irked him, he made sure to acquaint me with how many abortions 'Killary' got, in addition to the number of people her and her husband set up to be murdered. Granted, I had no intention of voting for her, but that was none of his business. Besides, how pathetic for someone to allow something like that to get under their skin.

I explained to Darby over the phone what happened as she was no longer allowed in my cubicle. Landry told her Herman wouldn't appreciate her associating with the likes of me. The only time I now saw her was when he sent me to fetch a reprinted return near her desk.

She still kept me up to date with the latest going ons around the office. For instance, she called yesterday and let me in on what occurred at Mrs. Wilhelmina Aguillard's retirement party. The icon of the building, Mrs. Aguillard retired after forty-five years of service with The Yorkshire Investment Firm. Darby said Beverly previously made a complaint to whomever owns the property concerning Mrs. Aguillard's efforts to oppose the placement of transgender restrooms. Those complaints apparently fell on deaf ears. When Mrs. Aguillard made her grand farewell, Beverly had to be restrained by security.

"The black came out of her," Darby said.

"The what?"

"Listen what she said the other day. She told me about her pregnant niece. I asked if they were having a boy or a girl. She said they were going to raise it gender neutral. Have you ever heard of such a thing?"

I had not and said as much.

All the while, my Facebook was being lit up with comments concerning the article I inadvertently shared. The worse from an old high school classmate. Cody McNeese. He messaged me repeatedly to tell me he would make America great again by voting Trump 2016. I chose not to respond.

Borel never once came to my defense. He was too busy duking it out on his own page. He had choice words for Trump, but they came off to me just as Landry's words had for Obama. Flaccid. Each time he typed Republican, he spelled it RepubliKKKan. He was emphatic there was no way Trump would win the Presidential election come November. If that was the case, I thought, why bitch about it so much then?

Later that evening, I got a text from Darby. She asked if she could come over. She drove up alone.

"Mommy needs a stiff one tonight," she said.

Shit. Halfway up the stairs, she said she forgot something. She climbed back into the SUV and stepped out with a bottle of scotch.

"Oh yeah," she cooed, fondling the bottle in her hands. "Mommy needs a stiff one tonight."

I was relieved she meant the contents of the bottle and not me.

We started out in the kitchen before settling in on the sofa. With the kid and dog gone, so were her inhibitions. The more she drank, the more concern I had she'd be in no shape to drive herself back to her parent's house. I soon realized she planned on getting pie-eyed right there on my sofa.

I ordered a pizza. As we ate, she rambled mundane nonsense concerning nothing in particular. Then, she began exposing dark secrets of our fellow co-workers. Bankruptcy. Drugs. Domestic abuse. Gambling. Porn. I was aware of the last one, of course. She told me of Bridgett's husbands hand job fetish. How he made her tug one out at restaurants and darkened movie theaters. It struck me as humorous. I laughed. Darby scolded me.

"Ruston! That's not funny! One time, he made her do it in the breakroom while I stood guard."

I now had tears in my eyes. Darby giggled. Before long, both of us laughed uncontrollably, struggling to catch our breath. I had not laughed like that in a good long while. It felt cleansing. Darby stood and stumbled towards the bathroom. I laid my head back on the sofa and closed my eyes. After a brief respite, she returned. Standing glassy-eyed and unsteady, she looked about the room with both hands on the back of her hips.

"This building was once a dance club and bar," she said.

I nodded my head.

"Yes."

"It can never be a club again."

"How do you mean?"

"Because of the moratorium."

"The moratorium?"

"Yep. You see, some years back, Herman invested in a bar downtown. It did well, but whenever a new one opened, it took business away. He wanted to put a stop to that."

She sat back down, took a hit from her drink, and continued.

"He paid some people to go to the city council and say they didn't want Jefferson Street to become another Bourbon Street like in New Orleans. So, this moratorium passed that restricted the number of bars downtown. He even got Wilhelmina involved."

"Wilhelmina? Wilhelmina Aguillard?"

"You know her? So get this. She got it to where whenever a bar, or a club, closed, another one had exactly a year to open in the same spot. If the year passed, and a bar or a club did not open, that place could never be a bar again."

The moratorium was the reason Karen had been unable to secure a bar permit for The Bistro. I was about to mention that when Darby caught me completely off guard.

"But there was this one little place. Aw, what was the name of it? This little shithole off Johnston."

"The Bistro?"

She pointed at me.

"That's it! The Bistro! The! Be! Stro! Herman was so pissed. He said they bypassed the moratorium and stole money from him. So, an anonymous complaint got made."

She snorted and held a finger to her lips.

"It was Herman," she whispered.

She threw her head back and laughed. She could not be serious.

"Oh my God! Herman had such a vendetta against that woman. He and Tony would sit around and come up with all these lies they would say about her. They wanted to destroy her and turn the whole city against her. They did the same thing when Obama became President. Said he was a Muslim, and a Socialist, and that he would take everyone's gun. They were gonna tell everyone she allowed underage drinking and child trafficking in her place."

She folded her legs underneath her and closed her eyes.

"Herman ended up selling his share of the bar. He bought our house and invested in a couple franchises."

She dozed off. I didn't know what to make of it. Back when I asked her to help me with the audit, she specifically asked if I knew who made the complaint. At that moment, she slid off the sofa on to the floor. I picked her up and carried her over to my bed. Her phone rang. Mom and Dad. A few minutes later, it rang again. Hubby. I turned it off. The last thing I needed was for them to report her missing and for the police to trace it to my apartment.

When the sun came up, she was still asleep. I took a shower. As I stood in front of the sink shaving my head, she opened the door.

"I'm sorry," she said.

I wrapped a towel around me.

"You need to use the bathroom?"

"I'll wait."

I went back to my business. She stared at me.

"Herman doesn't like for me to see him naked."

"Okay."

"He's self-conscious."

"Okay."

"He has a tiny penis."

I changed the subject.

"Your phone rang last night."

"Where is it?"

"On the sofa."

"Are you going to be much longer?"

"Darby, if you have to pee, just come pee."

She shuffled over to the toilet and took a seat. I finished up and stepped out to give her some privacy. She passed gas something ferocious. In my bed, what had been left of her makeup was now smeared all over my pillow. I got dressed and went into the kitchen. She emerged, took a seat at the table, and put her head in her hands.

"How did I get in your bed?" she asked.

"You fell asleep on the sofa. I carried you."

"What did we do last night?"

"Eat pizza and talk."

"What did we talk about?"

I hesitated.

"Nothing in particular."

"I feel sick."

"Want some coffee?"

"Sure."

She took her phone into the bedroom. I could hear her as I put a pot of coffee on.

"Why was Herman calling my phone?"

"He doesn't need to know where I am."

"I'm at a friend's house."

"I've been here all night. I'm okay."

"I told you I'm okay."

"All right."

"Okay!"

"All right! Okay! I'll see you in a bit."

She walked back into the living room. I asked how she took her coffee. She didn't want any.

"I better go," she said.

With her shoes in one hand and bottle of scotch in the other, she climbed into the SUV and tore away from the curb. After taking a left on Garfield, the SUV screeched to a halt. I watched her open the driver's door and toss her cookies into the street. She then wiped her mouth and kept going.

CHAPTER 37

April 4-11, 2016

The following week, Darby made no mention of what she revealed concerning The Bistro. She did mention her doctor prescribing her antibiotics last year after diagnosing her with irritable bowel syndrome. When those failed to provide relief, she turned to Facebook. She got in touch with some shady characters over at The Cort Rickland Community Center who claimed opioids would do the trick. Herman was none the wiser, until she happened to go back the night of the shooting.

Why had she kept that from me? It didn't matter. I could no longer rely on her for help at the office, and she wasn't a friend. Simply put, I had no use for her anymore. Telling her though was out of the question. There needed to be a blowup, maybe an argument, something that would royally piss her off. Anything less, I might never get rid of her.

I was also about done with Facebook. The harassment over the Clinton post had not subsided, especially from Cody McNeese. In between posts about his two boys and their efforts on the baseball diamond, he constantly demeaned me for my love of Hillary Clinton. His favorite insult was liberal. Everyone was liberal, from the Pope to the media to the government. It just got to that point. I responded.

"Be sure and tell your boys besides being a liberal, I'm also a transgender Syrian refugee, and I work part-time cleaning restrooms for Maxine's Department Store. That way they'll grow up shit for brain just like you. Is that how things work in the McNeese family?"

I hit enter and logged off. The Department Store bit was something I picked up from the bullshit crew. They claimed President Obama forced Maxine's to allow transgenders to use the restroom they identified with, and children would be attacked in them by men disguised as women. Just the other day, they said over 250,000 Syrian refugees were to be accepted into the country. I had no idea if any of it was true, but if it rankled the bullshit crew, I assumed it would rankle Cody McNeese as well.

Saturday afternoon, on my way back from the laundromat, I spotted a local news crew near the corner of Jefferson and Vermillion. Not at all an unusual sight, as I saw them countless times around the area doing live shots and such. But on this occasion, they seemed to be expecting me.

"Mr. Delahoussaye, might we have a second of your time?"

The reporter, a beautiful brunette with an enticing scent, introduced herself and asked if she could talk to me about the disappearance of Harleigh Hebert. I politely declined. She continued asking questions as I walked away.

"No. Sorry, I can't. Sorry."

What the hell? No way would I talk to them about Harleigh. That would all but guarantee another visit from best buddies Detectives Landry and Wilson. I had not heard from them since last summer and wanted to keep it that way. That night, I tuned to the ten o'clock news and learned of a man who slit his girlfriend's throat, a drunk driver who took the life of a six-year-old, and two muggings that occurred in the area, but nothing concerning Harleigh.

Monday morning, I walked into the office to a blindingly bright floor along with the strong smell of disinfectant. It made my nostrils burn. Landry had a cleaning service come in over the weekend. When it got to be too much, I went down for a smoke break. On one of those breaks I logged on to Facebook. Cody McNeese had unleashed a tirade on my page. He designated me a liberal and Obama the anti-Christ. Trump 2016. Take our country back. Make America great again. So on and so forth. I chose to respond.

"Grow a pair of balls and next time you won't be intimidated by what I post."

A balloon with three dots appeared. Had he been waiting for me to respond all this time? Jesus.

"You Democrats are the ones without balls."

I quickly shot back.

"If you possessed a pair you wouldn't be on my page crying like a bitch."

He responded with one word, murderer, and followed that with a link to the local news channel. Apparently, the story about Harleigh I looked for Saturday ran on Sunday. And now it was on Facebook.

"A story you'll only see here."

Today made a year since Harleigh's disappearance. The reporter who approached me Saturday talked of the night in question. Security footage showed Harleigh and Chris locking up about two a.m. A neighbor's camera caught Chris arriving home, alone and on schedule, thirty minutes later. There were short interviews with various people. Friends, acquaintances, coworkers, her roommate, her manager, along with Detective Landry. Then there was me.

"We tried talking to Mr. Delahoussaye."

They played a video of me refusing comment and mentioned I was unable to account for my whereabouts that night. What I found interesting was how everyone, even Detective Landry himself, never mentioned or referred to me in any manner whatsoever.

Underneath the story were well over a hundred comments. Someone claimed they'd seen me drag a woman from The Bistro and place her in a light blue colored *Volkswagen*. Another posted that I tried to get her to leave a New Year's Eve party with me. The one with the most reactions claimed police found blood in my apartment. Then the lady from the New Iberia Park chimed in.

"OMG!!! This is the same guy that tried to abduct my son. The police didn't do a damn thing. I went to them but was a waist of time. Now look. He killed someone. How many others must loose their life? #justiceforharleigh."

The consensus among the commentators was that I was guilty. I made a move on Harleigh, she denied me, I killed her, case closed. I began receiving threats over Facebook messenger from people I didn't know.

"You're going to pay for what you've done."

"Better watch your back."

"Bubba's gonna rip you a new one when you go to jail."

These continued throughout the day. I went ahead and deleted my Facebook page.

CHAPTER 38

I dreaded what might be in store for me at the office the following day. I half expected to find a decapitated horse's head in my cubicle, or worse, day old discarded crawfish. Thankfully, I found nothing of the sort. The bullshit crew stood near the breakroom discussing baseball scores from the previous night. Landry came with six individual tax returns in his hand. He mentioned the news story.

"You got a raw deal. Ben clued me in. Good thing for the security footage."

Ben? Security footage?

"Be sure to complete these before you leave for the day."

He walked over to the bullshit crew and asked about a game on television last night.

"Did you see any black people in the stands?" he asked. "I sure didn't."

Darby called. She also watched the story and read the comments on Facebook. Unlike Landry though, she had a few concerns.

"They said you couldn't account for your whereabouts."

"Yes, I could. It's just no one can vouch for me."

"You dragged a woman down the street?"

"A friend drank too much."

"They found blood in your apartment?"

"That happened a long time ago."

"What about the one from the park who said you attempted to abduct her son?"

"Ben told you about that. Remember?"

She paused.

"Oh, yeah."

I succeeded in dousing her fear, though a part of me wanted to tell her it was all true so I could be done with her once and for all.

"By the way, do Ben and Tony know each other?"

"Duh! They're stepbrothers, Ruston."

Of course, they were.

She told me she was taking little David to the doctor after lunch, and she might come by the apartment later. After the bullshit crew cleared the breakroom, I got a coffee. All told, it geared up to be an ordinary day.

Bridgett called that afternoon. A couple boxes needed to go down to the file room. She called me because Julian, the office intern, passed the CPA exam and relocated to another office. Two boxes awaited me. I stacked them on the dolly and made my way down. I wasn't in there long before I heard the code being inputted and the door open. Bridgett walked in. She leaned against the wall with her arms folded across her chest.

"You're disgusting."

"Excuse me?"

"Darby told me about you. The things you make her do to you down here."

"Wait. What?"

She took a step towards me.

"I would never allow just any man to force me to my knees."

Aw, hell no! I left the boxes and hurried past her.

"Did you make that waitress do that to you before you killed her?"

I didn't respond. I got to the door and turned the knob.

"You are aware she's using you, right?"

"Who?"

She laughed.

"Who? Who do you think, dumbass? She's been trying to leave Herman. Once the divorce is final, she won't have anything to do with you."

"Divorce? She told me she wanted another kid."

"Another kid? God, you're pathetic. I'm telling you, you better get your rocks off while you can."

I hurried to the elevator. When it didn't open immediately, I went into the stairwell. Not a smart move. Eleven floors later, I arrived on thirty-nine out of breath and drenched in sweat. I went over to Darby's desk but she already left for the day. Everyone looked at me like I'd gone insane. I went into my cubicle but couldn't keep still. I got up and walked to the men's room and splashed cold water on my face. No luck. I was too anxious. What the hell was Darby thinking telling Bridgett something like that?

I shut my computer down and headed for the elevator. I had not completed the returns Landry had given me. Fuck it. Fifteen minutes later, I sat inside my apartment. I laid my head back on the sofa and waited for Darby. I kept telling myself no matter what she said or did, I had to hold firm. This was it. It was over. Even if she cried, got upset, and drank herself unconscious, which she ended up doing. I carried her to the bedroom and took off all her clothes. When I checked on her later, I found she'd shit all over herself. It was disgusting. My cell phone chimed. It was a text from Darby. She would be there in five minutes.

I unlocked the gate and told her to come up when she arrived. She responded with a smiley face emoji blowing a kiss.

After a few minutes, the sound of barking and footsteps echoed from down below. Darby pushed open the door. She carried a brown paper bag in one hand, and Peyton's leash in the other.

"Hey!"

"Hey."

"My dad took David fishing so it's just the two of us. Does your stove work?"

"No idea. I never use it."

"Well, I hope it does because I'm fixing dinner tonight."

The dog ran over to me. I rubbed his head.

"Anything interesting happened after I left?" she asked.

"I had to go down to the file room."

"Darn, sorry I missed that."

"I did have company."

"Who?"

"Bridgett."

She hesitated.

"I really hope this stove works."

"Look, Darby…"

She turned to face me.

"Ruston, I don't know what Bridgett told you, but you can't believe everything she says."

She removed a rotisserie chicken from the brown paper bag. As she struggled to take off the cover, I remembered our first encounter in the breakroom when she heard my name.

"Ooh," the blonde said, "sexy."

It was not a complement. She flat out mocked me. Was Bridgett correct? Had Darby played me all this time?

"Darby," I said. "I need for you to leave."

"Jesus! What is your problem?"

"Look! Get your shitty ass out of my apartment!"

I watched my words penetrate. At first, she was shocked. Then she became furious.

"Shitty ass?" she screamed. "You bastard!"

She dropped the cover for the rotisserie chicken into the sink and briskly brushed her hands together. The mask she hid behind all this time fell off completely.

"Okay! You want the truth? I'll tell you the truth. I'll tell you the whole fuck-ing truth."

She tore off a piece of chicken.

"See this? This is me."

She called Peyton over. The dog hurried to her and sat on its haunches.

"And that there is you."

Peyton focused on the piece of chicken as Darby moved it from side to side.

"I dangled myself in front of you like this, and this is how you reacted."

She threw the piece down on the floor. Peyton pounced on it in an instant.

"All I had to do was show you a little attention, along with my tits and I had you wrapped around my finger."

She tore off another piece. Peyton inhaled it and waited for more.

"I won't lie though; you are a good kisser. But when I shook that tin of mints in your face. Oh my God! I thought you would shit your pants! The expression on your face was hilarious!"

She scratched the back of Peyton's head. What followed was her inane attempt at reasoning.

"Everything was going fine till that shooting happened, but turned out, it was a Godsend."

"Godsend?"

"Herman was so jealous of that picture of us. Then Linda tells everyone, 'Wanna know the real reason Miss Privileged McMillan Branch went to Rickland that night?' She meant the pills."

Peyton licked her fingers.

"I told the cops I went to pick up a friend. Herman thought Linda meant a black guy. Cheating on him with you was one thing, but the second he thought I was messing around with a black man, he kicked me out of the house. I was like, 'Thank you, Jesus!'"

She folded her arms across her chest.

"Happy now?"

I looked at her.

"You and your husband deserve each other."

She picked up a glass from the counter and fired it at me. But just like the plate she threw at Borel, it only hit the floor and shattered. Her form was all wrong. She had no follow through.

"Fuck you! You fucking prick!"

She reached down and picked Peyton up with such force the little dog yelped in pain.

"You're so pathetic. Telling me you were working at the office for a story. You think this shitty looking typewriter makes you a writer? I found some of your stuff on the internet. Talk about stupid. You are nothing but a stupid pathetic loser."

She stormed out the door and down the steps. That went about as well as I imagined. Served me right. I used her, she used me. Hopefully, that was the end of that. A minute or so later though, the sound of footsteps came up the stairs followed by a light knock at the door.

"Yes," I said cautiously.

Nancy walked in. She stepped over the shattered glass on the floor.

"You alive? The way that woman ran out of here I thought she murdered you."

"What are you doing here?"

She held up a bank deposit bag.

"I forgot this."

She looked around.

"Is this where you have your sex orgies? Why did that woman leave like that?"

"It's a long story," I said.

"I saw you on the news."

"Okay."

"People were talking about you in the shop this morning."

"I bet they were."

"They said you were dragging someone down the street."

"It was Evangelina. She drank too much. I was only trying to get her home."

"You abducted a kid from a park?"

"It was a misunderstanding. The police already questioned me about it."

"You tried talking a woman into leaving a New Year's Eve party with you?"

I explained I mostly talked to that woman about the October and November bank reconciliations for Martin's Grocery, but I only confused her. I asked how the family was doing. She said Sheila was dating a black boy, and her and Dean would not pay for her to go to college if she continued to do so. She then told me they caught Gary from Indiana trying to rob the shop, but the police arrested Dean instead. Because of the arrest, he lost his job. They were struggling so much they might be forced to close the coffee shop. She then paused and looked at me with flirty eyes.

"Just so you know," she said. "Gary and I are no longer a thing. So, I'm available."

"Available? You're a married woman!"

"Ruston, I told you. Dean won't mind."

She crouched down before me and placed a hand on my knee. I pushed it off.

"Nancy, no."

"Aw, come on."

"I'm not interested."

"We'll have some fun."

"No."

"Don't be shy."

"Are you deaf? I said I'm not interested, you fat fuck!"

Nancy recoiled and leaned away from me.

"What did you call me? You little bitch!"

She stood and headed for the door.

"I'm gonna tell Dean you tried to rape me! No, I'm going to tell the cops you were the one who took the money! I don't know what I ever saw in you!"

After she stomped down the steps, I hurried behind her and locked the gate. I got back up, reheated the rotisserie chicken in the microwave, and swept up the glass from the floor. Later, I opened the laptop and attempted to get online. The password was incorrect. Nancy had wasted no time in kicking me off their Wi-Fi.

I lit a cigarette and looked around the apartment. It felt quieter than usual. Empty even. I turned the television on and stared at it all night.

CHAPTER 39

The last thing I wanted the following day was to bump into Darby. I had no idea how she would react. Would she jump all over me, or just ignore me? Worst case scenario would be her heels clicking over to my cubicle and for her to say she forgave me and carry on as if nothing happened. What would I do then? With the windows sealed shut, jumping out one wasn't an option. My plan was to simply stay in my cubicle and out of sight.

Guillory called. I ventured over to his office. He asked if I understood I worked for an accounting firm, and that we were currently in tax season.

"Well? Do you?"

"Yes, sir."

"I don't think you do."

He ripped me about the returns I failed to complete yesterday. They would need to be done as soon as possible. I returned to my cubicle. The phone rang. It was Landry. Back across the office floor I went.

Landry, with his immaculately pressed shirts and pleated pants, had recently grown a mustache worthy of early eighties porn. He mostly reiterated what Guillory told me. He also mentioned a get together at a downtown seafood restaurant after work tomorrow. I took the mention as an invitation.

Landry handed me a couple more individual returns. He said to get those done before I completed the ones from yesterday. Back at my cubicle, he walked up and took note of my dry erase board.

"Why is your board not up to date?" he asked.

He stood over me as I erased yesterday's returns and wrote in the ones he'd just given me. While Breaux had been sloppy and stressed, Landry was calm and calculating. He didn't rip you like Guillory did. He talked down to you. Case in point.

"Ruston," he said, "this world needs more people like you. People who understand their place and how things are supposed to work. There was a time when blacks knew their place. Women, too. You didn't have all these feminists running around sticking their tits in places they didn't belong. Gays neither. If two guys talked about having sword fights in the shower, they got their asses beat. Fucking liberals, I tell you."

He smoothed his thumb and index finger over his mustache.

"Oh, and we're not going to offer you full time employment. I've decided against it. In fact, we're going to work on getting your hours reduced as much as possible in the off-season. I anticipate it won't matter much. Your kind doesn't have much to begin with in the first place."

He turned and went over to the breakroom. I heard him ask the bullshit crew about a basketball game.

"They lost? Great. I hate Chicago. Know why? Obumma is from Chicago."

I logged on to my computer and got to work. Bridgett walked up. She told me Herman dragged Darby from her parent's house last night along with David and Peyton. The Naquin family unit were together once again.

"It's over for you," she added. "She told him everything."

Darby was a liar. Everything could mean anything.

"Better watch your back."

Clients streamed in and out of the office all day picking up tax returns. Each time one passed, I imagined it was Darby. It made for an agonizing day. At 6:30, after finishing all the returns I'd been given, I logged off my computer and headed for the elevator. Once I cleared the parking lot, I breathed a sigh of relief. I made the entire day without seeing Darby. Now, I only had to accomplish that feat each day from here on out. I walked over to the pub and got blitzed on two for one beer.

I staggered out sometime after nine. When I rounded the corner from Congress on to Buchanan, I saw Darby's white SUV parked in front of the apartment. I braced myself for what she would unleash on me. The driver's side door opened. Instead of Darby, out stepped Herman Naquin, the 2013 Lafayette Businessman of the Year. Up till then, I only saw him in pictures. Now, there he stood, with clenched fists and a puffed-out chest. A short stocky dude, he'd likely been clowned about his height at some point in his life. He dressed business casual in a gray button-down with black slacks and loafers.

"Look, pal," he said. "I know all about you, and what you been doing with my wife. It ends today. You hear me, pal?"

He looked up at me with jealous black eyes. His voice trembled with emotion.

"Are you deaf? Stop fucking around with other people's wives. Show some integrity for God's sake."

Integrity? Who was this guy to talk to me about integrity? With his brine shrimp dick.

"Let me give you some advice," he continued. "Stay away from Darby, if you know what's good for you."

Finally, something we both agreed on. He moved to the side and allowed me to pass. I walked over, unlocked the gate, then turned back to face him.

"Hey. Let me give you some advice."

I stepped in and pulled the gate shut.

"Grow a beard. She liked the way it tickled when I tongued her ass."

With that, I locked the gate and headed up.

CHAPTER 40

April 14-15, 2016

A stack of payroll returns awaited me in my cubicle the following morning. The bullshit crew were already gathered near the breakroom. The topic of conversation: A Baton Rouge schoolteacher busted for inappropriate relations with a student. After they left, I went for a coffee. Back in my cubicle, Bridgett came up from behind. I almost spilled coffee on her shoes.

"Hey!" she screamed. "Watch it!"

"Sorry. You startled me."

"Uh-huh, you scared now. Darby told me about last night. Some man you are, running your mouth behind a locked gate."

Was Darby in the SUV, or did Herman give her a play by play? Bridgett snapped her fingers in my face.

"Hello? Look, clients are going to be in and out of here all day. Make sure the coffee pot stays full. Put another pot brewing when one starts getting low. Try to do a better job than you did yesterday."

Better job than I did yesterday? What did that mean? This would be my new reality moving forward without Darby. Having no clue as to what was going on.

I spent the day ducking in and out of my cubicle as though avoiding enemy fire. I happened to catch a glimpse of Darby over near her desk. She dressed modestly, her bitter face without much sleep or makeup. I couldn't help but wonder what sort of deviant plan she now concocted in her head.

Later that afternoon, I overheard Bridgett talking with someone near the breakroom. It concerned the party at the restaurant that night.

"Get what's his name to do it," an unfamiliar voice said.

Bridgett walked over.

"Hey, we need you to…"

She stopped.

"Oh my God! You don't even have a car! Could you be anymore worthless!"

She turned and walked away. I continued working on the payroll returns.

After five, I noticed the office had gotten quiet. The door to the women's restroom opened. Beverly walked out.

"You still here? I don't blame you. I'm not going to that party either."

I finished the last return on my desk, logged off the computer, and headed for the apartment. I got to Vermillion, then figuring I did my share worthy of a free meal, turned in the direction of the restaurant. I told the hostess I was with Thomas, Madison. She directed me to a room off to the left.

Inside, the bullshit crew stood about carrying on. I got a beer from the bar then retreated to a far-off corner by myself. More people arrived, including Landry, later followed by Bridgette. I stayed in the shadows and out of sight. Food rolled out on carts with steam rising from multiple metallic trays consisted of fried catfish, stuffed crab, shrimp etouffee, seafood gumbo, sweet potato fries, corn maque choux, and fettuccine. I served myself multiple times. No one said a word to me. It felt as though I slipped in stealth like to feast upon their riches.

The night went on. Everyone, including me, got drunk off their ass. Someone talked of successfully getting a man kicked off a flight for wearing a turban. Another mentioned certain people having a case of the heavy hand. The story about the Baton Rouge school teacher became a hot topic. A phone went around showing her mugshot. Landry lamented how they didn't look like that when he was a kid. Another said it was the student himself who came forward.

"Must be a liberal," Landry said. "If that were me, I would have kept my mouth shut. But hers, let me tell you, hers would be wide open, if you know what I mean."

He put his hands behind his head and humped the air. The lemmings laughed. A full bottle of beer fell to the floor. Half its contents poured out before an obedient server cleaned it up. A toast followed. Someone got a promotion of some kind.

"Accolades and advancements fill empty holes in empty lives," I said aloud. No one heard me. I stumbled over for another beer. Two of the bullshit crew walked up. Both sported red bloodshot eyes.

"Ruston," one of them said. "Good. Old. Ruston."

A server handed him a beer. He tapped the other on the forearm with it.

"Look, it's Ruston."

"Ruston," the other said. "How you been?"

In my inebriated state, I thought he asked where I was from.

"Jeanerette."

"What about it?"

"That is where I'm from."

Another wandered over.

"What ya'll talking about?"

"Ruston just said he's from the J."

"J-Town? No shit."

A few more came by.

"What's J-Town?"

"Jeanerette. Ruston says he's from there."

"Where's Jeanerette?"

"South of New Iberia."

"Da Berry."

Landry walked up. Crumbs of something or other from the dessert menu dotted his mustache. The rest followed like sheep.

"I passed through Jeanerette not too long ago," he said. "Talk about a sad little town. The plant they had there closed. All the jobs went to Mexico."

"Yep. That's how I lost my job."

"Couldn't have been much of one if a Mexican took it from you."

At first, no one responded. Then he laughed. Everyone quickly followed suit.

Even with the state I was in, I knew the direction this was headed. The schoolyard bully set his sights on me. The others gathered to witness the carnage. I was the gay kid. The transgender kid. The poor kid. The black kid. The Muslim kid. The new kid. I was whatever was different from them. Thus, I was a threat. At that point, the smart thing to do was put my head down and walk out. But I didn't. Instead, I ran my mouth.

"Mexicans didn't take our jobs. Rich white Republican conservatives gave them our jobs. You know. Those people whose ass you kiss."

The bullshit crew released a collective gasp. Landry narrowed his eyes at me. My response had been nothing intelligent, nor politically accurate. All I did was step onto their playing field.

"I knew it!" Landry shouted.

He pointed a finger at me.

"He's a libtard! He's a fucking libtard!"

Landry proceeded to go off on me. I didn't catch much of what he said. I drank entirely way too much. He mentioned something about his grandfather. His grandfather retired from the oilfield. His grandfather had fired my grandfather. That was not true, but in my current state of mind it was. Now he talked about a wall.

"You support the wall, Ruston?" he asked.

"The wall?"

"Yeah, the wall. What's the matter? You deaf?"

"No, of course not."

"Of course, not? You want open borders? You want them illegals just coming across the border. See, I told ya'll. This faggot is a libtard."

My mouth began to move. My mind struggled to keep up.

"You know what your problem is? Your grandfather kissed ass. So, in turn, you were raised to kiss ass."

I pointed my bottle of beer at him.

"Fuck your fucking wall. Crying about people coming over the border. Where were you when my job went over the border? Oh yeah. You were down on your knees kissing ass like a bitch."

Landry took a swing at me and missed. Down he went. I went to give him a kick in the ass. I missed as well and fell on top of him. A chaotic mess of people scrambling and chairs scratching across the floor followed. I caught a knee in the face before being picked up and held from behind. Someone poured a beer over my head. I had a split lower lip, though I think I got that from tripping over a curb on the way back to the apartment. Somehow, I got out of there. Instead of getting out of my clothes and taking a shower though, I stayed up all night. I couldn't wait to return to the office in the morning. In my mind, I did a noble thing. I stood up for myself. No longer would they fuck with me. No longer would they scorn me. I earned some respect. I would now work in peace.

Hours later, with no sleep and still wearing the same beer-stained blood splattered clothes from the night before, I made my way to the office. The plan was to take the elevator up and head straight for the breakroom. Let one of them tell me something. I wouldn't be surprised if the guy from HR made an appearance on account of the feelings I hurt.

I walked through the parking lot. Danny stood at the gate.

"Ruston," he said. "I'm sorry, but I can't let you in."

With a shaky hand, he handed me an envelope. This man had a family and a mortgage. Whatever I did at this point could very well cost him his job. I turned and walked away. Danny called out to me.

"Hey Ruston!"

"Yeah?"

"You take care, man."

"You too, Danny."

"And thanks."

"Don't mention it."

If Landry had any balls whatsoever, he would have called me into his office and thrown me through a window. Instead, he had Danny give me what I gathered was a termination letter. I tore the envelope in two and tossed it into a blue trash receptacle. The impulse came. I stormed into the apartment, threw the laptop across the room, pulled down my bookshelf, and kicked over the coffee table. I dug around for any pills I could find. All I had were four expired aspirin along with three ten milligram tablets of melatonin. I swallowed them down, stuffed towels under the door, opened the jets on the stove, cranked up the window unit, stripped out of my clothes, and climbed on top of the bed. I had nothing left. I laid there and let it all go.

Sometime later, I awoke with my knees drawn up under me for warmth. Unless that climate change thing had some far-reaching effect, I hadn't winded up in hell. I sat up on my elbows and looked around. I was still in the apartment. Well, shit. Ending up as a ghost and remaining there for all eternity wasn't a possibility I considered.

I climbed out of bed, took a step, and hit my little toe on the dresser. It hurt like a motherfucker. Nope, not a ghost. I hobbled over to the stove, played with the knobs, opened and closed the door, then pulled it from the wall and discovered the shut off valve behind it in the off position.

Now what?

Sometimes, at this point in a story, a Bible found amidst the chaos and ruin sheds light upon the situation or happenstance. There were no such Bibles in my apartment. Instead, the porn magazine the clerk over at The Discount Mart mistakenly placed in my bag lay on the floor opened to a story. I sat down cross-legged and began to read.

The story, titled Working Stiff by Alex "Raffe" Ransonet, told of Bill and Bill's first day at his new job. Bill meets Rhonda. Bill gets the hots for Rhonda. Rhonda, of course, gets the hots for Bill. After work, they get it on in an alley outside a bar. The writer describes the sex as Bill's rod exploding white-hot sticky magma within the confines of Rhonda's love trench.

At the bottom of the page was an email address. They accepted submissions.

I put the magazine down and looked for the laptop. I found it on the floor near the window. After verifying it still worked, I discovered it was able to latch on to the library's Wi-Fi over on the next block. I took a seat and began pecking away. Two hours later, I had four thousand words concerning Darby's first visit to the apartment. I titled the piece Inverted. I set the laptop over on the windowsill and hit send. Half an hour later, I got a response.

If this is THE Ruston Delahoussaye, call me ASAP.

It was Alex "Raffe" Ransonet, author of Working Stiff, publisher of Cajun Coochie. He picked up on the second ring.

"Raffe."

"Raffe. This is the Ruston Delahoussaye."

"Ruston! Dude! What's going on? Man, when I got your email and saw your name, I about freaked. I don't know if you remember me. We never met but I wrote for Mike Robicheaux before I went out on my own. I'm sitting on a goldmine here. Printed pornography is making a comeback. People are getting back to physical things to buy and hold in their hands. Albums, books, magazines. I don't know if you read anything I wrote but I'm telling you man, it's horseshit. I'm no writer. I'm a publisher. You're the writer! I followed your shit. You're the shit, man! I'll print anything you send. Write whatever the fuck you want."

We agreed on five cents a word. And just like that, I was writing again.

CHAPTER 41

April 20-May 25, 2016

A new day had dawned. No longer would I sit confined to a cubicle on the thirty-ninth floor of a forty-story office building overlooking South Buchanan and West Convent in downtown Lafayette. I regained control, though Robicheaux's view of the matter might differ. While no novel had come out of the twenty months I put in at Thomas, Madison, Smith and Associates, I'd been more productive in the last few days than I been in years. With Robicheaux, it got to the point where he considered nothing I wrote good enough to publish. To remedy the situation, I would get hammered and sit before the typewriter digging up past traumas. But that cliched production did nothing but keep wounds fresh.

On the twentieth, I awoke at noon, snuck out of the apartment so as not to run into Nancy downstairs at the coffee shop, and headed over to the cafe on the corner where I got a fully dressed shrimp poboy with fries. The waitress, who'd served me before, observed a change in my demeanor.

"Something's different about you," she said.

"Today's a special day."

She thought for a moment.

"Ah, yeah. Four twenty. Gotcha."

"Oh no. It's my birthday."

"That too. What happened to your lip?"

"I didn't keep my mouth shut."

She nodded her head.

She later returned with my bill and a small piece of pecan pie.

"On the house. Happy Birthday."

I spent the day not in a cubicle, nor a coffin, but in a state of contentment. Opening ceremonies for Festival International 2016 began at 5:30. I unfolded the lightweight collapsible chair I recently purchased and placed it underneath the two shade trees across from the old federal courthouse building on Jefferson. From my vantage point, I happened to see Darby heading to her SUV in the office parking lot. I half expected to catch my former self over there walking slumped over and defeated. It had only been a few days, but my time at Thomas, Madison felt like a lifetime ago.

Festival weekend was a blast. I listened to music from all over the world, ate delicious food, and met people who were a delight to talk to. Gentle and gracious with goodness of heart, where did they all go on Sunday evening when it came to an end? I, myself, retreated to the quietness of my apartment. Feeling lonely, I googled a local online dating site. There was a monthly membership fee. No thanks.

The first weekend in May, I attended the Crawfish Festival in Breaux Bridge and watched Winslow's band play the Saturday evening. He didn't ask about work, and I didn't divulge anything.

After their set, I noticed a woman across the way. Cocky and confident in small dark round sunglasses, she sat with one leg crossed high at the knee. She stood and made a beeline straight for me.

"Hey," she said.

"Hey."

"That was you on that bad ass bike?"

"Bike?"

She revved an imaginary motorcycle.

"An Uber brought me here," I said.

She dismissed me with an open palm and headed back to her seat.

The week before the Memorial Day weekend, I received a call from Detective Landry. They wanted to meet. Both he and Detective Wilson waited out front of the Parish Courthouse the following day. They escorted me into an interrogation room. Detective Landry said he'd heard about the tussle between me and his stepbrother.

"I didn't think you had it in you," he said. "Tony's an ass. Always has been. We're not related by blood, just so you know."

They came clean. Detective Wilson told me of a camera at the ATM across from the apartment that verified everything I told them concerning the night of Harleigh's disappearance.

"Seriously? Then how come you guys kept hounding me?"

"Your name kept coming up. A number of people pointed a finger at you."

"Was it anyone who mattered?"

"In hindsight, no. We searched your apartment, your work computer. It all came up clean."

"We didn't find blood," Detective Landry said.

"You bastard."

"We're also aware you didn't take the money, either."

"Money? What money?"

"From that coffee shop. The owner fingered some guy from Indiana. Now she's singing your name. What can you tell us about her oldest daughter?"

"Samantha? She's given me a ride a few times."

Detective Landry leaned forward.

"Ruston, is there anything you can offer us concerning Harleigh's disappearance? Anything we may have overlooked?"

I noticed Detective Landry's wedding ring. He was a husband. Possibly a father. He looked at me as if his daughter were the one missing.

"Talk to us," he continued. "What does your gut tell you?"

I told them Harleigh left of her own accord and settled somewhere she didn't want to be found. They gave one another a look.

"Thank you for your time," Detective Landry said. "We appreciate you coming in."

I headed back to the apartment. A car was parked out front. As I pressed my hand up against the front window of the art gallery and peered inside, someone approached from behind. My feet came off the ground.

"Bloody hell!" I screamed.

It was Samantha.

"Asshole! What did you tell them?"

"What?"

"I saw you walk to the courthouse and go in with those guys. I know who they are. You son of a bitch! I didn't do nothing. You didn't see me do nothing."

"Samantha, I didn't tell them anything about you."

I pointed to the ATM across the street.

"There's a camera right there. They're probably watching us as we speak."

She turned white, jumped in the car, and drove off.

CHAPTER 42

The loneliness grew. It kept me awake at night. In my sleep deprived state, I imagined the camera at the ATM was able to see inside the apartment. To remedy the situation, I purchased blackout curtains for the windows and dressed in the corner of the bedroom. I also kept the bathroom door shut whenever I went in there to shower or shit.

When I did doze off, I dreamed Samantha confronted me about the missing money from the coffee shop. Nancy pretended to come to my rescue but instead took me out with a solid knee to the groin. She then hocked a mayonnaise and pickle flavored loogie on my face as I writhed on the ground.

My previous suicide attempt a distant memory, I felt I would keel over and die if I was not squeezing as much as I could from the laptop each day. The stories I sent **Alex "Raffe" Ransonet** were not dirty. Some were made up nonsense, others concerned particular incidents at work. Alex contacted me about flak he received concerning the political slant of one of my poems. Instead of asking me to tone it down, he suggested I ramp it up. So, I did.

Ruston Delahoussaye
9403 S Buchanan St
Lafayette, LA 70595

2000 Man

Imagine if Jesus were born not 2000 years ago but in the year 2000
He'd turn 16 this year
And what would he have to say?
Would he champion the gun?
The flag?
The monument?
The poor?
Illegals?
Refugees?
Transgenders?
And what would you say about him?
Would you shit on him?
The same way they did 2000 years ago.

Sunday afternoon, a commercial played for the dating site I visited. A free weekend was offered to anyone who downloaded their app. I named myself Ruston9403, snapped a selfie, and skipped the questionnaire. At first, no one appealed to me. Then I received a message from Ravenhair 5.0. Her face looked familiar.

Did u finish yur noval?
     Getting close. How you doing?
I'm gr8. U takin advan of free wknd
     Yes. I'm seeing what it's about.
Its boring lol
U gun send me dick pic
Lol

I didn't know what to say, so I typed LOL as well. I clicked on her profile. It was the woman who came up to Harleigh and me awhile back at the pub. I couldn't recall her name. She wrote back.

All these thirsty nigaz neeed 2 stay out ma inbox.

She then fired off one message after another. Her spelling horrible, I couldn't make out much of what she said.

R U DTF

I had no idea what that meant. Maybe this wasn't such a good idea.

Wanna cum ovr.
Luv 2 here more about yur noval.
Huge fan of yur wrk.

Twenty minutes later, I climbed the steps up to her trailer in Carencro. She lived on a spot of land behind her parent's house. The trailer sat some ten feet off the ground. She told me not to bother knocking as the front door didn't lock. A previous lover kicked it in. I did anyway.

She answered wearing a thin white V-neck tank top along with a pair of tight gray shorts. More beautiful than what I remembered, she drew me to her in a cordial embrace and gave me a peck on the cheek. She smelled of cigarettes and grape bubble gum. I still could not remember her name.

"Hey there handsome!"

"Hey! Nice to see you again!"

We took a seat on the sofa. Her mobile home was immaculate. The walls adorned with photos of Bible verses, naked women, and dead rock stars. A sliding glass door opened to a back patio. She offered a beer. I watched her walk barefoot over to the refrigerator. Her gray shorts enticingly snug in both front and back. She sat and folded her legs beneath her.

"How old are you?" she asked. "You look older than me."

"Forty-five."

"How old you think I am?"

I garnered early thirties a safe bet.

"Thirty-nine," she said. "Wanna know my secret?"

"Sure."

"Sex. Lots and lots of sex. Though I just had a hysterectomy. I'm aching for some action."

She'd never married, had two kids, lost custody, went through several meaningless jobs, fell off the deep end, and got heavy into drugs. Her parents recently found her living in an abandoned hotel near I-49 and I-10. They got her clean then got her the trailer.

She planned to take drafting courses in the fall. She reached for a green five subject spiral notebook of drawings. Page after page. All very detailed. A pair of end tables. A kitten. A lit matchstick. A sunflower. A large flaccid uncircumcised penis.

"That's Jonathan. Isn't he beautiful?"

"Close friend of yours?"

"Oh, definitely! Anthony, not so much. But for Jonathan to come out and play I had to keep inviting Anthony over."

Were Jonathan and Anthony a couple, or was Jonathan the name of Anthony's penis? Now I was looking at a vagina.

"That's mine," she said.

"Seriously?"

"Oh yeah. You know any other women who can draw their own cooter?"

"Cooter? Uh, no. You're the first."

I expected her to laugh. She didn't. She was mighty proud.

Her previous claim about having all the issues of the SWLA Free Press I was in turned out to be incorrect. She only had five. Maybe she thought that's all there was. I didn't question it. When she asked about the novel, I bullshitted her and said it was about a woman who lost her daughter to suicide after she discovered the father had molested her. That idea was to be the subject of my second screenplay, if the first ever did anything.

I needed to piss. I walked through her bedroom, stepped over a pair of recently peeled off red panties, and went into the bathroom. A small turd floated about in the toilet. After I was done, the turd only spun in circles. I had to hold the handle down to make it flush.

When I walked back into the living room, she was texting on her phone.

"Aw shit," she said.

"Something wrong?"

"One of my girlfriends. Baby momma drama on fleek."

"Fleek? Is that the name of the street she lives on?"

"That boy tried to play me."

"Yeah?"

"Yeah. I told him just because I'm white don't mean I can't go ghetto on his ass."

I thought she said gecko.

"Like a chameleon?" I asked.

She laughed.

"You cray cray."

"Cray cray?"

She put her phone down.

"Why you shave your head?"

"I had long hair and just got tired of it."

"How come you're not married? Do you have any kids?"

"Well, I…"

"I wanna get married. I need a cigarette. You smoke?"

We stepped out on to the patio and leaned over the railing. An ashtray overflowing with discarded cigarette butts sat between us. In the corner was a lawn chair dotted with white globs of dried bird shit. Nothing but trees and pasture as far as the eye could see.

"This is a flood zone," she said. "Anything built in the past few years had to be up off the ground."

Now she had to pee. I retook my seat on the sofa. I still couldn't recall her name. I found an envelope. It only said Resident.

She walked back into the room and began to dance.

"I used to be a stripper."

"How long ago?"

"Few years back."

She whipped her hair around and slowly bent over. I got hard. I reached for a pillow to cover myself with. She laughed.

"Such a gentleman, trying to hide his hard-on."

She took the pillow from me, climbed on my lap, and began to grind. We kissed. I put my hands on her ass as she worked her grape bubble gum flavored tongue around in my mouth. So help me if this turns out to be another figment of my imagination.

A noise came from down the hall. She jumped off and headed in that direction.

"Be right back," she hollered.

As I composed myself, the thought hit. We were not alone. Paranoia followed. Shit. Just as I stood to leave, she walked back into the room with a small boy by her side. His hair a mess, he looked like he'd just woken up.

"Bobby. This is Mr. Ruston. Say hello to Mr. Ruston."

Bobby held out his hand.

"Hello, Mr. Ruston."

She babysat the boy for someone in the neighborhood. She gave him a drink of water then went about putting him back to bed. That was the final straw. I came here thinking it might be possible to have sex with this woman. That possibility was indeed a reality. Harleigh was right. She was too fast for me. I was in over my head.

When she returned, I told her I had to get going.

"Aw, you have to leave so soon?"

"I'm meeting with my publisher in the morning."

"How exciting!"

We hugged.

"Baby," she said, "you're still hard. Here, let me fix that."

She squatted down and unzipped my pants. I barely lasted a minute. She knew exactly what she was doing. She swallowed it all down, then jumped up and giddily bounced into the bedroom. My head spun. I grabbed a kitchen towel, wiped off, and zipped up.

She came back with minty fresh breath and told me to be safe going home. I watched her go out on to the patio, lean over the rail, and light a cigarette. I closed the door behind me, walked to the end of her driveway, and waited for an Uber in the muggy late-night heat. I was disgusted with myself. I'd gotten blown by a woman whose name I didn't know, but damn it felt good.

Back at the apartment, I took a shower and climbed in bed. Next thing I knew, it was morning. Specks of dust drifted about in the sunlight. The smell of food emanated from the coffee shop below. I reached over for my phone and signed on to the dating app.

> Good morning.

gud mornin luver

> How did you sleep?

Back n bed

bobbys mom come 4 him

Cancel yur meeting n cum ovr

> Be there in 20.

CHAPTER 43

June 6-20, 2016

Jaime Mire was a nymph with an insatiable sexual appetite while I was a forty-five-year-old with a hair trigger dick. She couldn't get enough, and I struggled to keep up with her. When I couldn't rise to the occasion after we'd done it once or twice already, she turned to the various array of multi-colored and multi-faceted vibrators she kept in a bedside drawer. In the dark, I'd feel her reach over for one before settling on to her back. The vibrator would hum. She'd whimper. The first time I placed a hand on her thigh. She pushed it away. I laid there in silence as she unabashedly went about pleasing herself.

When I went back to her place Memorial Day weekend, she still had another week or so until she could begin to engage in sexual intercourse after her surgery. Two hours after I arrived though, she lit some candles, put incense burning, and came out of the bathroom completely naked. I sneezed.

She climbed on top of me, licked her fingers, and guided me inside of her. She shuddered, bit her lip, and moaned as she took it all in. Her body quivered. With her chin to her chest, she grimaced, threw her head back, gritted her teeth, and began to pound on me. She came hard and fast before collapsing on my chest. Her face wet with sweat, she looked me in the eyes.

"I'm so glad you're smaller than the guys I'm usually with."

She was able to finish me off before I lost my erection.

Besides the trailer, her parents had also gotten her a car. We split our time between her place and my apartment, living out of carry-ons and duffel bags, sleeping well past noon, spending afternoons drinking coffee and having sex in the comfort of the air conditioning. On warm summer evenings, we sat out on her back patio listening to the sound of cicadas in the distance. I scored major points with her for returning after the blow job. She sucked off many a guy only for them to never return. She fixed herself a Vodka Seven. I would down a couple beers. We looked up at the stars and smoked cigarettes to the nib. It was bearable but I knew it wouldn't last. The amount of sex needed to keep this woman's youthful vitality would be the death of me. Still, it beat doing bookwork in a cubicle.

She worked on her drawings while lying on the floor clad only in a pair of panties while furiously snapping her grape bubble gum. She was good at her work. She designed a few concert flyers along with accompanying t-shirts. Twitter and Instagram were her platforms. Facebook was blasé, she told me.

Everything she did recently she doused in clowns. They were all the rage, she claimed.

I poured a cup of coffee, sat before the laptop, and wrote a story about Ebola infected clowns coming for our guns. I sent it off to Alex then took a nap. Outside, the temperature rose to 94 with a heat index of 115. Sometime later, I awoke to Jaime standing in front of the bathroom mirror brushing her teeth. It was maybe three in the afternoon. I couldn't tell you the day. Her breasts swayed from side to side as she brushed. She spit, wiped her mouth, and stepped out of her panties.

I met her parents that evening. Neither one cared for me. I felt like a guy doing their teenage daughter when I was in their presence. Her dad, a personal injury attorney, had numerous billboards across the area with the slogan "Accident? Call Kent" plastered on them while her mom owned a local jewelry store.

One day after a visit from her mom, a bottle of pills appeared. At first, I didn't mind. They kept her off me for a few hours. In addition to the pills, Jaime got herself hooked on reality television shows. There seemed to be one on just about every night. She fancied the dating ones. In particular, the one where multiple men vied for one woman's hand in marriage. She longed to be a part of it.

"Can you imagine?" she'd say. "All that dick, just for me."

Each night, after we watched her shows and had sex, she would toss two pills into her mouth and be comatose in less than an hour. One night at the apartment, I put in my best performance thus far. She stared up at the ceiling afterward with moisture beaded across her lip. That should hold her for a while, I thought to myself. Ten minutes later though, she pawed at me for an encore. I couldn't get hard. She tried using her mouth.

"My God," she said. "It's like trying to blow up an inner tube."

She gave up, took her pills, and went into the bedroom. Only she forgot to pack a vibrator. She became enraged.

"You did this! You don't want me to have any pleasure! You want me to grow old! My God, I'm melting. Oh, what a world."

I suggested we head for her trailer. Her mood quickly brightened.

"Let me go pee first!"

We made a stop at The Supercenter. Into her basket went toothpaste, deodorant, and orange socks. We headed to the frozen food section for sugar-free popsicles then back across the store for blue toenail polish.

"Watch my purse," she said at the checkout. "I'm going talk to Andrea."

I paid for her stuff then waited in front of the eyewear place. Here she came with Andrea. Andrea Guillory aka Hollie Roux. Andrea squinted her eyes at me.

"You look familiar."

"I worked for your dad," I said. "We met at the after-tax season crawfish boil."

"Oh yeah, that's right," she said with disinterest.

She turned to Jaime.

"Bitch. What your mom gave you was weak! This shit will make you right."

Jaime put a small unlabeled pill bottle into her purse.

Weak? Jesus. What was I in for now?

Back in the car, we crossed under I-10, took the Gloria Switch exit, and made it to her trailer. She went into her bedroom and closed the door. I heard her vibrator start. It sounded as though she set it to jackhammer. I went out on the patio to smoke. I stayed out there a long while. When I came back in, the trailer was quiet. I put the television on, watched a replay of a baseball game from earlier that night, and dozed off. I awoke to Jaime kneeling before me unzipping my pants.

"Did you kill that girl?" she asked.

"What?"

"That waitress. She was with you the night I saw you. I won't tell anyone."

She took me into her mouth. I leaned my head back.

CHAPTER 44

If it weren't for the blowjobs and easy sex, I'd want nothing more to do with Jaime. Those pills from Andrea had her brain muddled. One minute, she sat on the sofa content with her dating show. The next, she paced the room gnawing at her fingernails. Each day was a delicate stroll through her minefield. One misstep and she would explode in anger. Especially if I failed to satisfy her. After one such occasion, she dug through my browser history.

"You son of a bitch! You couldn't get it up because you been jerking off to Andrea!"

"I was only doing research for the novel."

"Bullshit! You said your book was about a father molesting his daughter."

"It is. The daughter also does online porn."

That was not true, but enough to douse her rage.

Jaime continued to gulp down Andrea's pills. Cooking shows replaced the dating ones. She jotted down recipes and off to The Supercenter we'd go. It was terrible when they were out of a certain item she wanted. She would go off on stock boys, get in a manager's face, even accuse the cashiers of malicious intent. While she never cooked even one of those meals, our cabinets overflowed with items such as beef bouillon cubes, oyster sauce, and blanched almond flour.

She began to experience random bouts of depression. Overdramatic made for television movies replaced the cooking shows. In them, a husband would leave, a dog died, someone's kid got mono. Jaime would bawl out, zone out, completely miss the comeback, but be fully awake for the next sob story. One night it all came to a head.

"You're gonna leave me!" she cried. "I'm ugly. I don't excite you. Why don't you just leave?"

I was more than ready to, but we were at my apartment. Then my phone rang. The conversation already in progress, I struggled to catch up.

"… all the more because of how old you imagine him to be," a woman's voice said.

"Hello?"

"Yes, hello. Obviously, he'd been there awhile. Yes?"

"Yes?"

"Repeatedly breaking into the place, heartbreaking."

I remained silent.

"And the daughter. Oh my, the daughter."

Then it hit me. This woman was talking about my screenplay.

"The daughter?" she asked.

"When she calls him at the end, I thought that was potent."

"Potent? Sweetheart, that was explosive. I can't believe Mike's been sitting on this. Oh, I do hope he makes it. He's not doing well, you see. Look, your screenplay has come into my hands. Is there anything I should know beforehand?"

"I would love to have it filmed in my hometown."

"Perfect, darling. I'll be in your lovely area next week. My people will contact your people. Bye, bye now."

Her people sent an email. The woman's name was Julia Stansbury. According to Google, Julia Stansbury, a widowed woman of influence from New Orleans, owned a string of bed and breakfasts along the Gulf Coast. How she ended up with my screenplay I had no idea. We were to meet tomorrow evening at an event in McMillan Branch. Some hundred dollar a plate gala for something or other. My plate would be taken care of. The next afternoon, a summer thunderstorm raged outside. Jaime walked into the kitchen wearing only a robe. I pulled up the email and Google search.

"I have some business to tend to," I said. "If you want to head home, I'll catch up with you later."

Jaime glanced at the screen.

"Who the fuck is Julia Stansbury?"

I explained who she was and how she had interest in my screenplay.

"She's not interested in your screenplay! She's interested in you! You think I'm going to allow that botoxicated bitch to take you from me? You're crazy! I'll die before I let that happen!"

With that, Jaime grabbed the bottle of pills Andrea had given her and went to swallow a handful. I slapped them from her grasp. As the dozen or so tiny white pills flew across the room, Jaime balled her other hand into a fist and connected it with my jaw. I staggered backwards. She stormed out of the apartment and rattled the locked gate.

"Help!" she screamed. "I'm being held against my will!"

I hurried down and dragged her back up the stairs. We fell to the floor. I cupped my right hand over her mouth and pinned her arms down with my left. Now what? By the grace of God, I got hard. I unzipped my pants.

"Don't you dare! Don't put that thing in me!"

I stuck it in her. We both came hard and fast. Afterwards, she kissed me on the cheek and made a pot of coffee. She asked what the screenplay was about.

"The main character works at this manufacturing plant," I said. "After his wife passes, and he alienates his daughter, the plant closes. He doesn't know what to do with himself."

"Does he reconnect with his daughter?"

"Yes. She goes off on him. Then he breaks into the plant."

"Why?"

"He can't let it go. His job meant more to him than anything."

"What does he find in there?"

"Nothing. The place is empty."

"Like him."

"Yeah, like him. He walks around hearing echoes from the past. The assembly lines. The loading docks. He goes into his office and sits on the floor where his desk would be. The cops show up. He gets charged with breaking and entering. In the last scene, he's home alone with a gun in his hand. The phone rings. An answering machine picks up. You hear his daughter's voice then a click. Was it the gun or the phone? The end."

"Guns don't click."

"I know. It's supposed to be the sound of…"

"If she tries something with you, I'm gonna kick her in the nuts."

"Kick her in the nuts?"

"Julia Stansbury's a dude. I guarantee it. When you find out she's a dude, I'm gonna laugh so hard."

"I'm sure you will."

Jaime put on a skimpy new dress. I tucked in my shirt. On the way there, I tried to locate Darby's white SUV in McMillan Branch but never laid eyes on it. Inside the club, men wore tuxes and the ladies looked glamorous. Jaime and I did a few shots at an open bar. She began to dance around.

"Would you stop?" I said to her. "People can see your panties when you bend over."

"No, they can't. I'm not wearing any. I think I should play the part of the daughter. Don't you agree?"

Without waiting for an answer, she ran off to the restroom. Now that I had a moment to myself, I considered what lay before me. I truly believed my screenplay could be a success. Success meaning something that would make more of an impact than a profit. I wanted it filmed at the abandoned plant in Jeanerette, employing local actors and seasoned with local music. I felt hopeful, as though I were on the cusp of something special.

Finally, here came Julia. Her eyes lit up when she saw me.

"Ruston," she said. "How lovely."

Somehow she recognized me. Her people must had properly prepared her. Dressed all in red, she wore a smile that appeared recently injected. Jaime returned. She walked straight up to Julia and introduced herself.

"Such a pleasure," Julia said. "I was just about to tell your lovely boyfriend…"

"Oh, he's not my boyfriend. I just suck his lovely dick."

Julia looked at her.

"Tell me, Julia," Jaime continued. "It is Julia, right? When you do that, do you spit or do you swallow?"

Julia was aghast. Jaime laughed.

"Oh, come now, Julia. Don't tell me you don't do that. I mean, you can't tell me you got where you are because of your intelligence, or your looks."

I took Jaime by the arm.

"Will you excuse us?"

I began to lead her away.

"Take your time, Julia," Jaime called out. "I'll get back with you on that whole spit or swallow thing."

I led her out a side door.

"What are you doing?" I asked.

"What? I just asked a simple question."

The impulse came. I grabbed Jaime by the throat and slammed her against the wall. She reacted by lifting her dress and playing with herself.

"Squeeze harder lover," she said. "I'm gonna cum."

The impulse faded. I let her go and walked away. Jaime hollered after me.

"Where you going? You can't leave me! Where you gonna find another woman like me? I own you!"

Once I was out of earshot, I sat on a curb and lit a cigarette. Jaime was right. I was not going anywhere.

I never heard from Julia Stansbury again.

CHAPTER 45

A few days after the Julia Stansbury debacle, Jaime hounded me for a copy of the screenplay. I recited it to her from memory. There'd been only one copy. In the daughter's only scene, the father comes upon her in the courtyard of the university she attends. She goes off on him, releasing twenty plus years of frustration for all to see. Harleigh had smiled when I explained it to her. She understood the explosion of pent-up anger. She suggested the character brutally pound the father's chest with clenched fists before collapsing at his feet.

Meanwhile, Jaime played it for comedic effect, making goofy faces with exaggerated hand gestures. As much as I loathed her, I still found her irresistible. Check that, I still found her body irresistible. Parading around barefoot, clad only in a pair of panties, I was not going anywhere till she kicked me out or lost interest in me.

Come Monday evening, she lay passed out in my bed while I stretched out on the sofa. The local news came on.

"Fifteen months later and still no answers in the disappearance of a Lafayette woman."

I sat up. The anchorman stood before the camera with a grave expression on his face.

"Friends, co-workers, advocates for the missing, and amateur online web sleuths gathered today to celebrate missing Lafayette woman Harleigh Hebert's fortieth birthday. We have team coverage. Molly Lattimore is where Harleigh Hebert was last seen. Molly, what can you tell us?"

The reporter who questioned me back in April stood in front of The Bistro.

"Thanks, Jim. Harleigh Hebert was last seen leaving this establishment on the morning of April eleventh, 2015."

A small gathering of people was shown inside. Among them were Teresa, Karen, and Chris.

"Security footage from the night Harleigh Hebert went missing shows her walking out of The Bistro at 2:06 a.m. She unlocks her bike from this yellow lattice fence here, walks to that intersection, and begins riding south on Johnston."

A picture of a bike like Harleigh's appeared on the screen.

"Harleigh's bike ride to her residence on Carl Street covered three miles. It normally took her no more than twenty minutes. LPD put out an alert for anyone on her route to check security footage from the night in question but no images of her were found. The last ping from her phone showed her in the vicinity of St. Mary and Cherry Street, less than one mile from here. We now go to Vicky Avery with continuing team coverage."

Vicky Avery stood on a street corner near a parking lot.

"Thank you, Molly. This is the area where Lafayette Police last got a ping from Harleigh Hebert's cell phone. We talked to Detective Ben Landry with the Lafayette Police Department."

"The search is ongoing," Detective Landry said.

"Is it true her boyfriend might be a suspect?" the reporter pushed.

"An acquaintance is cooperating with the investigation."

The anchorman was back on the screen.

"We reached out to the mother of Harleigh Hebert. In an interview you'll only see here."

Mrs. Willie Domingue, the former Onelia Romero, sat on a couch next to Harleigh's high school graduation picture.

"I miss her," she said.

The camera cut to her hands fiddling with a wadded-up tissue.

"She's my only child. I don't see her much."

"When was the last time you saw your daughter?" asked Vicky Avery.

"She invited me to Easter dinner. We had a wonderful afternoon. She talked about coming visit. She hasn't been home in ages. I just want her home."

A missing person's flyer appeared on the screen, different from the ones I'd laid eyes on. This one, more detailed with Harleigh's date of birth, blonde hair color, height, and weight also sported Teresa's phone number at the bottom.

"Please call Lafayette Police if you have any information. In other news…"

I turned the television off. It had not occurred to me today was Harleigh's birthday. Though I appreciated them not having my name on blast, I assumed I was the boyfriend the reporter referred to. Just then, Jaime walked out of the bedroom completely naked. She went over to my record player and began placing my album collection in alphabetical order. She was doing the same to my bookshelf when she happened upon the issue of Cajun Coochie that I had.

"Why do you have a magazine of naked twelve-year-olds?"

"Those girls aren't twelve."

"Yes, they are! They got no hair on their cooters! You want to have sex with these kids?"

"No. That's the magazine I write for."

"Bullshit!"

She threw the magazine down and ran into the bathroom. A few minutes later, I heard an anguished scream. I went in there and found her covered in blood and shaving cream. Only it was not a suicide attempt. She was shaving the hair from her cooter, when in her manic state, she sliced the tip of her finger open. I told her I thought she had slit her wrists. She gave me a confused look.

"Why would I use shaving cream if I was doing that?"

I went lay back on the sofa. I got a terrible headache. Jaime, sans pubic hair, her finger wrapped in a bloody towel, sat beside me.

"Are you okay?" she asked.

"My head hurts."

"Want an aspirin?"

"Sure."

She handed me one.

"What was it like growing up in Jeanerette?"

"Jeanerette?"

"Yeah, you mention it several times in your stories."

"Oh. It was great. I knew everyone in my neighborhood. I'll still refer to a particular house by the name of the family that lived there when I was a kid. Things changed though as I got older. My grandfather and dad both passed away, my brother got into drugs, my sister went crazy, and my mom isolated herself. The plant I worked at closed, along with the sugar mill in town and the Catholic school across the bayou. The population dropped so much they can't even support a little league."

Jaime went piss. That aspirin she gave me had not done jack. When she came back into the room, she climbed on top of me.

"I know how to make you feel better," she said.

I was all for it, though to my astonishment, I got hard in an instant. I later found out it wasn't an aspirin she had given me, but an erectile dysfunction pill. She rode me for almost half an hour. I was aroused but too exhausted to cum. Jaime took full advantage, repeatedly slamming the full weight of her body down on me in a frenzy. I didn't dare try to stop her. It may had been akin to waking a sleepwalker.

After she got her fill, she jumped off and announced she wanted to go to her trailer. Still sporting a major hard-on, with blood smeared across my face and chest, I got dressed. Back at her place, her dad came over. He was beyond pissed. He had instructed Jaime to return an old cable box for the television.

Only she had forgotten. So had I. He'd been hit with another two-hundred-dollar charge.

"Look at everything we've done for you!" he yelled. "We got you this trailer, paid your bills, bought you a car! I asked you to do this one thing, this one goddamn thing, and you couldn't do it! They're going to keep charging me till they get the box back!"

He looked over at me. I lay sprawled out on the sofa with an ice pack on my balls and a Vodka Seven in my glass. It was only six a.m. and I'd already written off the day. Frustrated, he turned and walked out. Everything here had been bought on his dime. I sort of felt bad for him. Another Vodka Seven fixed that.

We didn't leave the trailer to return the cable box until the following day. Afterward, we got something to eat. Near the restaurant was a music store. I marveled at the beautiful guitars on display. We went inside. I picked up one made of Brazilian rosewood.

"Didn't you say you wrote songs?" Jaime asked.

"Yes. A long time ago."

"Play me one."

"All right."

I began to strum and sing.

"Time for another

Cajun Summer

Time for some fun in the Louisiana sun."

Jaime's jaw dropped. I continued.

"Ridin' 'round

With the top down

Streamin' Zydeco on the radio

Me and you

On the bayou

Capturing memories on an iPhone."

"Oh my God," Jaime interrupted. "That is so gay."

"Gay?"

"Yes, gay. And I know gay. I was a lesbian for seven months."

CHAPTER 46

July 19, 2016

Four a.m. on the morning of the nineteenth, I received a call from Alex "Raffe" Ransonet.

"Ruston! I'm going to be in Lake Charles in a few hours. Meet me there. We'll do a face to face. I'll text you the details."

He hung up. I shook Jaime awake.

"Get dressed. We have to go to Lake Charles."

"Lake Charles? The fuck is in Lake Charles?"

"An awesome poboy place. Come on, let's go."

We got in Jaime's car and headed west on I-10. Per Alex's instructions, we were to meet near an abandoned parking garage about 5:30. We took exit 30A and followed the service road past the convention and visitor's bureau to a parking lot near a live alligator pond. There was one car there when we arrived. A young woman wearing a fast-food uniform stepped out.

"Are you Alex?" she asked me.

"No," I said. "We're here to meet up with him."

"Well, where is he? I have my son with me. I still have to drop him off before I go to work."

A small economy car with Texas plates drove up. A man with an abnormally long neck got out. He clapped his hands.

"Okay people. Time is of the essence."

It was Alex "Raffe" Ransonet. I now understood the nickname.

"Don't use your phones or any light whatsoever," he said as he pulled a camera from the back seat. "The cops routinely pass this place. I want to make sure I have the pictures first before they catch us."

The best I can describe Alex "Raffe" Ransonet is that he oozed like an open sore. The thought of him taking pictures of naked twelve-year olds now seemed plausible.

"At one time, there was a riverboat casino here," he told us. "Hurricane Rita washed it away. This parking garage is all that's left."

He led us down a sidewalk lined with palm trees. We slithered through a chain link fence and onto a well-worn dirt path littered with debris. Near the back of the parking garage was a stairway partially hidden by overgrown shrubbery. Up we went. It was nearing six a.m. The eastern sky began to light up the darkened floors. I saw elaborate graffiti, a sleeping bag with dirty feet protruding from underneath, and a brand-new shopping cart. Alex turned to me as we neared the top.

"Ruston, ya'll wouldn't mind looking after the kid while we go take care of business, would you?"

I looked at the woman. She looked back at me with uncertainty.

"I guess not," I said.

"Great!"

Alex clapped his hands. Somewhere someone coughed. The woman knelt before the little boy.

"Justin, you stay here, okay."

"Can I come?" asked Jaime.

Alex looked her over.

"Of course! The more the hornier!"

The three of them continued up. Minutes dragged. The boy looked at me.

"Where's my mom?" he asked.

"She'll be right back."

He wasn't convinced. I noticed he wore a number nine Saint's jersey.

"Hey. Do you happen to know who the Saint's first quarterback was?"

The kid looked at me like I was an idiot.

Footsteps approached. It was the boy's mom. She looked none too happy. With her shirt unbuttoned, she scooped the boy up and hurried off. Alex and Jaime soon followed.

"I'll send the papers for you to sign as soon as I can," Alex told her. "You're a natural!"

He saw me.

"Ruston! You sly dog, you! Girl on girl action! I like the way you think!"

As we made our way down, he told me about the magazine's Twitter account. I was encouraged to go on there and stir up shit. He also gave me a raise. Six cents a word up from five.

Back in the parking lot, the woman and her kid were already gone. I climbed in Jaime's car. She reached over and stuck a finger in my face.

"Smell," she said.

I pushed her hand away in disgust.

"The hell?"

She gave a sniff before shifting the car into drive.

"Yeah, I told that girl she needs to see a doctor about that. Isn't it cool how we're both going to be in Raffe's magazine? What time does that poboy place open? I'm hungry."

CHAPTER 47

August 2016

Part 1

Alex forwarded complaints he got about my work to me. It read like a transcript of a bullshit crew's bullshit session. Readers complained the politics didn't mix with the pornography. Alex said to pour it on. So, I did.

Ruston Delahoussaye
9403 S Buchanan St
Lafayette, LA 70595

Fits the party to a T

Some men possess the worst luck
Born cowards
Raised by cowards
Destined to become cowards
The worst luck
Everything wounds them
That 24-hour news channel wounds them
That opinion wounds them
They fight back
They hang flags upside down
They write letters to editors
They put signs in yards
They debate on social media
As the world decays
A peaceful man stands tall
Reminds us all
The end is near
Love everyone as God loved you
Yeah?
What about Muslims
What about illegals
What about abortion loving liberals
As the first trumpet sounds.

I located the magazines Twitter page. The first tweet concerned an anorexic looking blonde with black boxes superimposed over her naughty bits. The second one showed a red-headed beauty with overly inflated breasts. Comments underneath ranged from admiration to longing. The discerning and distinguished readers of Cajun Coochie appeared to believe they were talking to the ladies themselves.

"Love your curves! What is your name?"

"Hello my future wife."

"You are so beautiful! Please share more pictures of yourself."

I scrolled until I came across a tweet concerning a short story I'd written about the bullshit crew's deeming of a school shooting as fake. The story's portrayal of legally responsible gun owners as being more concerned for their guns over other people's children did not go over well.

"You just lost a subscriber."

"Another liberal promoting his gun control agenda."

"Liberalism is a mental disease."

I did not know what to say in response. I also did not see the point. It was mostly a fictional story, a little truth blown out of proportion. In no way, shape or form did the story characterize my own opinion on the matter. I continued to scroll.

"Just post the girls. Nobody reads these stories anyway."

Such was the case with social media. Everyone had a soapbox. I remembered what Darby said about people referring to her as a crisis actor. I entered a reply.

"U ignorant redneck conservative bitch asses should become crisis actors before next false flag operation."

I had no idea if these people were redneck, conservative, or in possession of a bitch ass. But what did it matter? I hit post and logged off.

The next day, Jaime and I stopped at The Supercenter. Down the coffee aisle, Borel shouted my name and ran over to us.

"Ruston. Where you been? I been coming by the apartment. You're not on Facebook anymore."

He turned his attention to Jaime.

"How do you do? Borel Jeffery. Borel Ministries."

"You're a minister?" Jaime asked. "That is so awesome. I'm Jaime. I just told Ruston we needed to start going to church more."

She told me no such thing. Borel produced a flyer.

"Our first service is this coming Sunday. I would love it if you both could attend."

"We'll definitely be there. I've been praying for direction. What religion is your ministry?"

"Oh, this isn't a religion. Religion is like a hymen. Break through and you'll feel God."

Jaime's eyes went wide.

"Oh wow! That is so prophetic."

That evening, Jaime gave me a blowjob then opened a Bible app she downloaded on her phone. She read aloud from the World English version. There was a knock at the door. It was her mom. She came to see how the orientation had gone at the community college. Apparently, that had been today.

"You didn't go?"

Not only had Jaime not gone, but she also failed to sign up for the semester. Her mom was incredulous.

"You better not let your father find out."

She turned to me.

"What are you even doing here? What are you doing to my daughter? She's confused and you're not helping."

I zipped up and lit a cigarette.

"My dick does her a lot better than those pills you gave her."

"Don't tell me what's best for my daughter, you bastard."

Jaime screamed.

"Will you two stop trying to control my life?"

She ran into the bedroom and slammed the door. Her mom opened a drawer, rummaged around in it for a bit, and produced a knife.

"Let me tell you something," she whispered. "You stay away from my daughter, or I'll cut that dick of yours right off."

She put the knife down.

"And don't think I won't. Ask Jaime what I did to that guy Mitch."

I didn't bother asking Jaime what she did to that guy Mitch.

To avoid a confrontation with her dad, we went back to my apartment. Jaime took out her pills and retired to the bedroom while I took out my ladle and stirred the shit on Twitter. The guy who said the magazine lost a subscriber had responded to me. He posted pictures of a school shooting that supposedly proved the event was nothing but an active shooter drill. I responded.

"close your mouth and get off your knees and U won't be in position 2 swallow everything jerked off down your throat."

Come Sunday, Jaime and I made the five-minute walk from the apartment to Borel's ministry over on Clinton, a nondescript brick building with a glass double door. Inside was dark and quiet. Only a handful of people occupied the twenty or so folding chairs available. Jaime and I took a seat. This was a far cry from the pomp and circumstance of Darby's church.

Suddenly, from out of the darkness, came the sound of boots clomping on the hardwood floor. Borel appeared before us dressed as though he were about to offer a great deal on a used car.

"Understand this," he began. "In the last days, grievous times will come. For men will be lovers of self, lovers of money, boastful, arrogant, blasphemers, disobedient to parents, unthankful, unholy, without natural affection, unforgiving, slanderers, without self-control, fierce, not lovers of good, traitors, headstrong, conceited, lovers of pleasure rather than lovers of God."

With a brown Bible in his right hand, he furiously gestured with his left.

"Avoid such people! Avoid them! The day of the Lord cometh like a thief in the night. We will not be in the dark, brothers and sisters. We are children of light."

He paused and studied the faces in the room.

"Each of you will give an account of himself to God."

He then loudly slapped the Bible in his right hand into the palm of his left.

"When we stand before God and answer for the sins in our lives, crying 'what about Hillary' won't suffice!"

Things quickly deteriorated from there.

"We're told not to store treasures on this earth. Where moth and vermin destroy. Where thieves break in and steal. We're told to store up treasures in heaven. One Thessalonians four seventeen. Then, we who are alive, will be caught up in the clouds to meet the Lord in the air."

He pointed a finger at us.

"Hear me good. These people with their guns, and their statues, and their flags, heavy with their burdens, are not going anywhere. They've received their reward in full."

This wasn't a sermon; it was a liberal bent Facebook rant. Borel went on to tell how the affluent conservative folk took the wholesomeness of Jesus and refined him into a palatable white guy with blue eyes. He made the comparison of brown sugar to white.

"Natural sugar is brown and rich in nutrients but loses its color and purity after it is refined. It is the leading cause of illness. Obesity, diabetes, heart disease, cancer, you name it. It is all linked to the white man's gold. Jesus was a dark-skinned guy from the middle east. That won't fly with the white folk. Present him as a blonde hair blue-eyed white guy who hates dark skinned people and there's your business model. They did the same with blues music back in the day. Look how much money they made. Now, we're all going to go out and fish for people."

We, the members of the Borel Ministries congregation, looked at one another.

"I know what you're thinking. You're thinking of a million reasons why you can't go out and follow me. Let me remind you of Matthew four eighteen through twenty. Walking by the Sea of Galilee, Jesus saw two brothers, Simon, who is called Peter, and Andrew, his brother, casting a net into the sea, for they were fishermen. Jesus said to them, 'come after me, and I will make you fishers for men.' They immediately left their nets and followed him."

With that, Borel walked past us and out the front door. For a moment, no one moved. One by one, a slow exodus began.

We followed him outside and down the streets of downtown Lafayette. After we failed to come across any souls in need, Borel climbed atop a metal electrical box adorned with colorful dancing crawfish at the corner of Jefferson and Garfield and continued to preach.

"Yahweh saw that the wickedness of man was great on the earth, and that every imagination of the thoughts of man's heart was continually only evil. Yahweh was sorry that he had made man on the earth. He said, I will wipe humans from the face of the earth for I regret I have made them. Seven days from now I will send rain on the earth for forty days and forty nights, and I will destroy every living thing that I have made from the surface of the ground."

People at the cafe across the street watched from the windows. Others stopped and stared. Borel climbed down and that was that. The ten or so of us left dispersed in different directions. Jamie and I went into the cafe.

"His sugar analogy was spot on," she said as she stirred some into her coffee.

"Well, there's actually not much of a difference between…"

"It's about time someone in this town told it like it was."

I kept quiet. Enamored, she couldn't wait to go back. By midweek, we had returned to Carencro. When we got there, it began to rain. We waited until her parents left then parked the car behind the trailer so they wouldn't see it. The next morning, the rain continued to fall. It made for a lazy day. I wrote a short story about priests running a sugar plantation then decided to check Twitter. My shit show must not had stunk all that bad as it was only the one guy who kept responding to me. There had been another mass shooting. He tweeted a link to the story, and added, "Another event staged to push martial law." He then said he was done with me, yet an hour later, he fired off a series of tweets.

"Democraps are planning to take our guns away."

"Already planning for their next staged massacre."

"Another school. Maybe a concert. Or a shopping mall."

I responded.

"u wanna suk devil off your business but don't come spit his semen on our twitter page."

The following day, the rain still fell. After Jaime's parents left for a trip to Las Vegas, we ventured out to The Supercenter. If a Biblical flood was coming, I wanted to be prepared. We stocked up on beer, cigarettes, vodka, lemon-lime soda, and coffee. I went to the restroom while Jaime checked out. Winslow walked up.

"Thirty-nine Ruston," he said. "Where you been, bruh? I went up there looking for you and your people looked at me like I was coming for their white women."

"I moved on, man. How you been?"

"Same. I'm movin' back to New Orleans."

"No shit?"

"Yeah, bruh. Gave my notice. Been planning this for a while. I'll be just down I-10. Come look me up when you get a chance."

"I'll do that, man."

We hugged. Jaime rolled her basket up to us.

"Damn, bruh," Winslow said. "You got a different one every time I see you."

He laughed and walked away.

"Who was that?" Jaime asked.

"My real estate agent."

That night, we put a chicken stuffed with rice dressing into the oven, had sex on the sofa, then took a shower together. After we ate, Jaime asked about my mom.

"When was the last time you talked to her?"

"Six years ago."

"How does she feel about that?"

"She's probably fine with it. She went into seclusion after my dad passed. My sister and her daughter moved in with her."

"Your sister has a kid? So, you're an uncle."

"I guess. She doesn't claim me."

"How did your dad die?"

"Cancer."

"I'm sorry."

"After the bank he worked at all his life closed, he got on at another and took a physical. He died two months later. I was with him when he passed. Everyone had left the room. I pulled up a chair and put a game on. He was breathing in and out and then he stopped."

Outside, the rain came down in buckets. We climbed in bed. Jaime took her pills and was out in no time. I placed a hand on her warm bare ass. The steady rhythm of the overhead ceiling fan blended in with the rain falling outside. My phone buzzed, as did hers. Flood alerts. I turned them both off. In the morning when I awoke, the rain still poured. I put a pot of coffee on then opened the front door.

And about shit myself.

There was water. Everywhere. At first, I thought we were floating away. I went down the steps to look at Jaime's car. The water was up over the hood.

Oh damn.

I went into the bedroom and shook her awake. She lazily rolled over in naked splendor.

"I want you inside of me," she moaned.

"We have to get out of here!"

"What? Why?"

"We're flooding!"

"Flooding?"

"The water's up to the fourth step."

"It's okay."

"Okay? Your car is almost underwater."

"We live in a flood zone. This happens. We're fine."

"But…"

"Ruston, it's fine."

"What about your car?"

"Is there anything I can do about it right this instant?"

"No. I guess not."

"I want you inside of me."

I thought it over. The coffee still brewed, and I had nowhere to go. Even if I did, there was no way I could get there now. So, I obliged her.

CHAPTER 48

The rain fell for five days. More than twenty inches in spots. We were lucky it didn't pound us as hard as other areas. It seemed Borel's biblical prophecy had come to fruition, only if one hadn't paid attention to local weather forecasts. Come Sunday, Jaime saw a picture posted on the ministry's Facebook page. Attendance about doubled. They came to listen to the one who foretold of the deluge in the days before. If only they listened to the local weatherman, as Borel had, they themselves could foresee what was to occur.

The water around the trailer did not rise any higher. After the power went out, I waded over to Jaime's parent's house, saved from the floodwaters by being situated on a slight hill, and dragged their generator out from the garage. We were able to charge our phones and make coffee. Good Samaritans in boats came by to check on us.

"Ya'll okay?" they asked.

"Yes, sir," I told them. "We're fine."

And we were. Others were far worse off than us. Another boat came by. The driver, a huge mound of a man in full camouflage, cut the engine and placed a foot up on the side of the boat. He spit a wad of tobacco into the water and nodded his head.

"Jaime," he said with a gruff voice.

Jaime smirked and put her hand on her hip.

"Mitchey Mitch. How's it hanging?"

An urgent call came over the radio.

"Okay, boys," the driver of the other boat said. "Saddle up."

Later, Jaime pulled out a photo album. She and Mitchey Mitch hooked up months back. He'd done two tours in Afghanistan, had shrapnel in his leg, and drove a crew boat. He was the sort of man who would sacrifice life and limb for his country so sorry asses like myself could get paid to write stories and sleep till noon.

As Jaime showed me photos of her and Mitch, she told me how they came to part.

"He had me bent over that table there, doing me from behind. The entire trailer was rocking. My mom walks in and freaks. She runs to the counter and grabs a knife. When Mitch pulls out, mom sees his huge tentpole. It stuns her. He grabs his clothes and hightails it out of here with his big boner slapping against his stomach."

In a few pictures, Mitch sported what looked to be a woman's garter around his bicep. Jaime corrected me. It wasn't a garter; it was her panties. A reminder he nailed her sometime over the course of that day. She lovingly ran a finger over his face.

"Damn," she said. "I sure could use that in my life again."

While we waited for the water to recede, Jaime fielded nervous calls from her parents concerning the state of the house while I kept abreast of the local news and weather. I didn't want to be caught off guard again by any unknown news events or weather-related calamities. Sure enough, I learned of a recent spate of muggings in the downtown Lafayette area. A total of eight had occurred so far during the calendar year.

Not once in my six years in Lafayette had I felt any sort of fear walking the streets of downtown. I'd seen my share of shady characters, but they never bothered me even once. Perhaps my demeanor indicated I wouldn't offer much and pummeling me for fun would just draw unnecessary attention to them.

By the end of the week power was restored, and the water had gone down to the point where we were able to navigate the roads safely, though Jaime's water-logged car still sat in the mud behind the trailer. No problem. We sloshed over to her parent's house, due back from Vegas later that day, and borrowed her mom's SUV.

When we got to the apartment, there was a black wreath on the door to the coffee shop. A Google search confirmed my suspicion. Robicheaux had passed. Services were pending.

That Sunday, Borel preached before a rag tag congregation of outcasts and misfits who came to hear one of their own give voice to their plight.

"Why isn't the media here talking to him?" I heard someone wonder aloud.

Because he did nothing but announce it would rain after hearing the weatherman say so himself, I thought to myself.

Borel unfurled a pull-down screen on the wall and switched on an overhead projector. A crude hand drawn image of a Trump 2016 election sign appeared. The congregation booed.

"People are arguing back and forth on the internet over who is going to come visit our area first. Trump or Mr. Obama. You see these election signs? Here's what you do to them."

With a pen, he marked an X over Trump 2016 and wrote John 3:16.

"For God so loved the world he gave his only born son. Nowhere does the Book of Revelation claim God would appoint Donald John Trump to be President of the United States to save America from its sins."

He began a social media-esque rant on the rich.

"Elect a rich businessman for President?" he cried. "How about we elect a peace-loving man of God. You know what the Bible says about the rich?"

Up on the screen was a list of Bible verses that told us what the Bible said about the rich.

"Luke eighteen twenty-five. For it is easier for a camel to enter in through a needle's eye than for a rich man to enter God's kingdom. Luke six twenty-four. Woe to you who are rich, for you have received your consolation."

From there, he spoke exclusively to the socially excluded.

"God uses imperfect people in an imperfect world. Look at us! What does the world do with us? They throw us away. Cast us aside. There was a story I came across the other day. This young girl from a religious family came out as gay and her family disowned her. She tried to make it on her own out on the streets. One day, while she was walking on the side of the road, she came to the end of her rope. All she had to do was cry out to Jesus. Instead, she stepped out in front of a Mack truck."

A shudder went through the crowd.

"God could have used her to make this world a better place. Now the world thinks it's a better place with the likes of her gone."

A loud and angry murmur arose through the congregation. Jaime raised a hand to her mouth.

"That could have been me," she said.

Borel yelled above the crowd.

"They say welcome to God's family, until your son comes out of the closet. Or your daughter brings home a black boyfriend, or you announce who you're voting for."

He stood on a chair and posed like the missing Y in the Lafayette sign.

"The rich control this country. How do they control it? By playing to its hate and fear. Let me tell you what God said. Isaiah forty-one ten. Don't be afraid, for I am with you. Two Timothy one seven. For God didn't give us a spirit of fear, but of power, love, and self-control. Psalm fifty-six. I have put my faith in God. I will not be afraid. What can man do to me? You know what they try to do? They corral us. Pen us in poor neighborhoods. When they can't do that, they build new ones and put up walls. They say, oh, do not go into those poor neighborhoods at night. It's not safe. Meanwhile, in their neighborhoods, they slaughter their wives and their kids. How many times the headline screams of a white woman gone missing? How often is it the husband who is responsible? Now they're shooting infants in the head before taking their own lives. But we're the bad ones. Imagine if we walked into another church around here looking like we do. Imagine the hate and the fear that would be directed at us."

He climbed down from the chair.

"In 2008, they told us Mr. Obama was Muslim. In 2012, they told us a school shooting was fake. Now, it's all about martial law and the postponement of the election. Who knows what they'll cry about four years from now? They may claim some global pandemic is nothing but a hoax. The end is coming my friends, sure and quick. Therefore, you must be ready, for the Son of Man is coming at an hour you do not expect."

When he was done, there was no sense of peace and love in the room, but more like we just won the Super Bowl, so let's celebrate by turning over cop cars, breaking windows, and setting trash cans on fire.

That night, Jaime swallowed her pills and blacked out. Sitting in the kitchen by myself, I got a text from Darby.

Hey. How's it going?

I deleted it and blocked her number.

Over the next few days, it was becoming abundantly clear the end was near. Not of the world but of my time with Jaime. Back at her trailer, she would stay out on her patio talking on her phone for all hours of the day and night. One afternoon, I looked out the window and saw her standing with Mitchey Mitch. Was that a pair of panties around his arm? Did it matter?

Instead of parading around in them all day, she now wore pajama bottoms covered in cartoon characters. One day, after we went a full forty-eight hours without sex, she announced she wanted to go back to the apartment. She was adamant I pack everything, while she didn't take a single thing with her. We climbed into her mom's SUV and rode in silence. She stopped in front of the apartment.

"I gotta go do something," she said. "I'll be back later."

I stepped out with my duffel bag.

"Okay," I said. "See ya."

"Uh-huh."

The tires screeched and off she went. I checked the mail, unlocked the gate, and climbed the steps. Later, I unpacked and took a shower. It had been almost three months to the day I was last there by myself. I lit a cigarette and went over to the window. The Lafayette South Bank time and temperature sign informed me personal loans were available to cover unexpected expenses.

"Rest easier," it said, "with less burden."

That I will, I thought to myself. That I will.

CHAPTER 49

Services for Robicheaux occurred on the ninth in Breaux Bridge. I got an Uber and staked out the funeral home from across the street. When I deemed it safe to enter, I hurried straight to his casket and paid my respects. I barely recognized him. I placed a hand on his shoulder and told him thanks for giving me a chance.

Meanwhile, life returned to what it was before the Memorial Day weekend. Before the BJ. Before Jaime. She never did come back to the apartment. I was sure Mitchey Mitch was giving her her fill in more ways than one.

I still attended Borel's ministry on Sundays. His tirades slash sermons continued going off the deep end. His most recent ire was The Catholic Church. He claimed more rapists, murderers, illegals, Muslims, and transgenders resided in heaven than Catholic Republican conservatives. He even provided statistics to supposedly back up his claim. Near the conclusion of his "sermon," a tithe basket appeared.

"Let me assure you," he said. "Any money collected will not go towards defending pedophiles. You don't need a child molester in a robe to save you from your sins. Do they at least make them wash their hands before they put a communion wafer in someone's mouth?"

During the last week of September, another mugging occurred in the downtown area. That made nine for the year. The assailants didn't discriminate. The victims ranged from a well-to-do businesswoman closing shop for the night to a down on his luck homeless man robbed of the sixty dollars he collected over the course of a weekend. Each assault transpired in the same manner. Two muscle attackers approaching from behind, the victim knocked to the ground, a third appearing for a pat down and grab. All pit crew quick and stealth like. Still, there wasn't much apprehension to be found in the area.

On the first of October, a news van sat in front of the apartment. The reporter who approached me back in April talked out there with Nancy. I could about imagine what Nancy told her about me. The news that night did not mention yours truly. Instead, they focused on the devastating effect falling oil prices were having on the local economy. Nancy stood before the camera looking irate and pissed as she told of having to close the coffee shop on account of a drop in business. She said her and her husband were putting their home up for sale and hightailing it out of the state.

The following day, authorities released the results of the community center shooting investigation. It found the incident stemmed from an ongoing territory dispute between Warren Grainger and another homeless man named Buck Champagne. When Grainger arrived that night with a gun stolen from an unlocked vehicle in upper Lafayette concealed under a trench coat in ninety-degree heat, he could not locate Champagne. For reasons never to be known, Grainger opened fire. The first officer on scene took him out with one shot.

In a sad twist, Champagne's body was later found face down in a coulee with no traces of foul play. An autopsy showed no drugs or alcohol in Grainger's system. The outcome of the investigation did nothing but add more heartbreak to an already terrible situation.

The Monday after Festival Acadiens, I bumped into Sheila outside of the apartment. She stood with a stack of mail in her hand.

"Hey fat fuck," she said. "Someone just drove up looking for you."

"Who?"

"Some skank with long black hair. I hope you got your shots before you messed around with that."

"I thought ya'll moved?"

"Mom moved, not me. Dad got hurt real bad. She closed the shop and sold the house to go be with him. He's not getting out of the hospital anytime soon."

"What happened?"

"Something fell on him at his job in Texas."

"But on the news, she said the economy…"

"She's so full of shit. She told that reporter she planned to sue the police because instead of arresting patriots like my dad they need to be arresting black people because they commit all the crime. She's such a fucking racist."

I played dumb.

"Your dad got arrested?"

"Oh yeah. Talk about a shit show. But the truth is with dad hurt and Samantha gone, mom didn't have any other choice but to close up and sell the house."

"Where Samantha went?"

"She's locked up."

"Locked up?"

"Yep. She stole money from the shop and from the cab company she worked for to pay off her credit card debt. Little here, little there. She came by here after hours. Sometimes there wouldn't be enough left to pay Uncle Mike."

"What happened to him?"

"Spinal cancer. Ate him up pretty bad. Brent has the building now."

She began to laugh.

"Dude, I never saw mom so pissed before. I heard her tell Gary what you called her."

"Gary? I thought they were no longer a thing."

"They were off and on. He was the only one who showed any interest in her. I don't see why she went on those cruises to begin with. Anorexic blondes with fake boobs get all the attention."

"Where is Gary now?"

"No idea. He caught a stroke. Paralyzed his whole left side, along with his pecker. Mom had no use for him after that."

A car with tinted windows drove up.

"I told my mom I was moving in with you, just to mess with her. I got me a real man. An old fart like yourself probably can't last five seconds, much less get it up."

She climbed into the car and off it went. I went over to the Discount Mart and picked up the latest issue of Cajun Coochie. It contained three stories Alex had yet to pay me for plus the pictorial Jaime participated in.

Alex worked photoshop magic on her photos. It was impossible to tell they'd been shot atop a smelly abandoned parking garage all staged and captured in less than fifteen minutes. He portrayed Jaime as the aggressor. The other girl, sans fast-food uniform, as timid. The caption underneath read, "Sasha is so hot! I couldn't wait till we got home. I had to have her now!"

I hoped the discerning and distinguished subscribers of Cajun Coochie appreciated Raffe's efforts while they sat atop porcelain thrones furiously fapping while mouthing the words, "she so wet."

Upstairs in the apartment, glass crunched underneath my feet. One of the windowpanes was broken. How in the world did that happen? Did someone throw something? I cut a piece of cardboard to cover the glass but had no duct tape to hold it in place. I walked the twenty minutes over to The Supercenter, picked up the tape along with a few other items, then waited outside for an Uber. It came just as Jaime walked up.

"There you are!" she shouted. "I went to your place and hollered for you. Threw rocks and everything. One of the little girls you play with told me you weren't there. Where's Raffe? The bastard hasn't paid me yet. He's got my cooter all over that magazine and I still haven't received a dime."

"I'll tell him you're looking for him."

"Yeah, you do that. Sorry I didn't come back. I couldn't walk right after Mitchey Mitch finished with me. I meant to call, but I deleted your number by accident."

"That's no problem."

"I'm glad you understand. Mitchey Mitch is so awesome. He has a six-figure income and a ten-inch dick. Meanwhile, you have, what? Ten dollars and six inches?"

The young female Uber driver looked at us. Jaime crouched down beside the open passenger window.

"Okay, it might be seven. You should let him take it out and judge for yourself."

I almost put the girl out of her misery and said never mind but I had two bags of groceries to get back to the apartment. She went down the thruway and took a right on Second. When she got near the Lafayette South Bank time and temperature sign, the police had the road closed.

"I'll get out here," I told her.

Yellow crime scene tape surrounded the corner of Buchanan and Garfield. A cop stood next to the ATM.

"Can I help you?" he asked.

I pointed across the street.

"I live there."

"Mike Robicheaux's place? Let me see some identification."

I showed him my driver's license. He looked it over.

"Your license is expired."

"May I ask what happened?"

"A couple got mugged last night. The culprits headed in this direction. We're doing a canvas of the area."

He lifted the yellow tape and allowed me through.

"You see anything, you let us know. Okay?"

"Yes, sir."

I went upstairs, taped up the window, then emailed Alex about Jaime. After an hour passed with no response, I decided to give him a call. It had been a month since we'd last spoke. Plus, he had not responded to any of the stories I recently sent him. His phone went straight to voicemail. On a whim, I turned to Google.

Man Arrested for Child Porn Production.

Multiple articles indicated Alex had been arrested on several sex crimes, including child porn. He was being held on a million-dollar bond. One also mentioned he was in possession of a pair of dueling pistols he apparently chipped off the I-10 bridge in Lake Charles. I gathered sooner or later the authorities would come calling questioning my role in Alex's enterprise. My stomach got queasy. The more immediate worry though was that I was out of work again. My phone rang. It was the office. I let it go to voicemail. What could that be about? Do they want me back? Want too strong a word. More like need. Maybe they had no other choice. At least I showed up and got the job done.

Did I really want to put myself back in that situation though? It was already October, and I knew damn well what that would entail. Twelve-hour days, plus weekends and holidays. I could make some stipulations. Namely, leave me alone and let me do my work. Keep Darby twenty feet from me and disband the bullshit crew. Maybe Landry had moved on. Maybe they'd offer vacation and holiday pay. I decided I would take whatever they offered.

I played the voicemail.

"Russell. This is Beverly. How far you got on the 2016 bookwork? There's nothing on the CPS. Call me as soon as you get this message."

Was she serious? I chose not to call her back, though that now meant I had zero prospects. Then a thought occurred. Robicheaux was the one who lined me up with that job. Maybe Brent might do the same. I decided I would ask whenever he happened to come by for the rent.

Weeks went by. I passed listless days over at Girard Park walking along the paths, sitting by the duck pond, and dozing off in the grass. It was there I decided I needed some sort of direction in my life. I turned to Google. The first result was a Bible verse.

Yahweh is my shepherd; I shall lack nothing. He makes me lie down in green pastures. He leads me beside still waters. He restores my soul. He guides me in the paths of righteousness for His name's sake.

Okay then. I would turn to the Lord. First thing He did was guide me back to the apartment. On the way there, a commotion at the university caught my attention. A five-foot-long alligator had escaped the lake located in the middle of the campus. A man with K-9 Unit written in yellow on the back of his shirt attempted to coax it back into the water with a red noose pole. The agitated gator resisted by hissing and twisting around in circles. Finally, after a few minutes, the man was able to successfully guide it back to where it belonged.

That Sunday, we set our clocks back one hour. The coming Tuesday was Election Day. As voters anticipated a new direction for the country, I wondered what new path awaited me. I decided I would ask Borel for help. I was not sure if he'd anoint me, baptize me, or make me clean the restrooms but I would do as told. Before heading out, I made a final visit to Cajun Coochie's Twitter page. That one guy continued to go off on me.

"Your an idiot," he wrote.

I apologized and deleted my account.

Over at the ministry, something was afoot. A moderate rain fell outside, but inside, no one bothered to take off their hats and jackets. I sat in a corner until Borel came out. He began by bashing Trump supporters.

"Make America great again?" he asked. "Who are they kidding? America was never great. Only God is great. It's the religious racists with their Jim Crow monuments that champion the man. The Bible is clear. We are to worship our Lord and savior, be subject to kings and rulers, and to defend the weak and powerless. It is not worship kings and rulers, be subject to kings and rulers, and defend kings and rulers. His supporters are not followers. They're swallowers. They can suck on him all they want. It won't wash away their sins!"

That was my cue. This was not a good idea. I got up to leave but noticed a small contingent of men near the door. I got an uncomfortable feeling. If someone were to begin to distribute the emblems that represented our union with God, I was not swallowing a damn thing in that place.

At that point, all who sat stood. There'd been a call to arms. The congregation of Borel Ministries was set to march to a Catholic Church a few blocks away, though storm it seemed a more accurate description.

"Brothers and sisters," Borel said. "They're boycotting football because our brothers are kneeling against police brutality and racism, yet they still attend Catholic mass. Where's the boycott for the rape allegations by their priests? These hypocrites need to be taught a lesson."

Everyone made their way to the door. Social media from a pulpit. I could no longer handle it. I didn't relate to social media, and I was having an even harder time relating to this. I came here looking for direction, so when they went east, I went west.

On the way back to the apartment, I saw a flyer for a "foodraiser" being held at The Bistro that evening. It appeared to be an effort to increase food sales before the end of the year. A couple hours later, I stood outside the double red doors waiting my turn in line. After paying a cover charge, I took a seat near the cash register. Chris handed me a beer. I happened to notice the metal display stand for The SWLA Free Press was empty. A breaking news alert on the television behind the bar caught my attention. There'd been some trouble at a Catholic Church downtown. Someone a few stools over spoke up.

"I heard he led those people from an abandoned building on Clinton where he lived and made them spread out among the pews and take out their guns."

"Actually," Chris said, "they took a knee, though I did hear they confiscated three stolen guns from them. The guy claimed he was a minister. The tithes he collected went to his heroin habit."

"A minister? Seriously? How stupid you gotta be to believe that shit?"

I saw Karen. She rushed over and threw her arms around me.

"Where the hell have you been?" she asked.

"I felt I let you down. I was ashamed to show my face."

"Let me down?"

"You asked for my help and I didn't do a damn thing."

"Ruston, I'm sorry if I put that kind of expectation on you. Harleigh had told me what it's like for you working at that place."

"She's the other reason I never came back."

"I sure do miss her."

"So do I."

"We had a birthday party for her back in July. Teresa told me she invited you, but you were out of town."

I just looked at her

"We should do a remembrance for her," Karen said.

"Why? She's fine."

Karen's eyes lit up.

"Really? You've talked to her?"

"No. But I know she's okay."

"How do you know?"

"I just know. Nobody could hurt her."

Karen breathed a sigh of relief.

"God, I just assumed the worst, you know."

"She's fine," I assured her.

Karen confided she still faced resistance in keeping the business open, thus the purpose for the foodraiser, though a compromise was around the corner. In less than a month's time, the moratorium on new bars in the area would be lifted, as those responsible for its implementation were no longer vested in downtown businesses.

I decided not to tell Karen what Darby said about Herman's vendetta. With all that she'd gone through, she weathered the storm with her spirit intact. It gave me hope, though sitting there for the first time since learning of Harleigh's disappearance was surreal. I walked in that day looking forward to spending a rainy afternoon with my good friend. I had just put in four hours at a meaningless job whose sole purpose was to cover rent while I wrote a novel I would one day hand to Robicheaux that would lead to bigger and better things. Little did I know that was as good as it got. But dammit, wasn't it great?

Chris, Karen, and I did a shot for Harleigh, followed by one for The Bistro. Others joined in. A man's wife was expecting. Shot. A lady hit five hundred bucks on a scratch off. Shot. Someone's cat had a litter of kittens. Shot. Come midnight, I was drunk off my ass. I went piss. On the wall of the restroom was Harleigh's missing persons flyer. When I stumbled out, I came face to face with an equally inebriated Hunter Hilliard. He looked at me with pause. Right there I remembered a story Evangelina had once told me about him. I was no actor, but I went for it.

"Hunter! Hunter Hilliard!"

"What's up bro? You look familiar."

"Dude! Bourbon Street bachelor party! You had these two skanks taking turns servicing the groom to be!"

The memory came sloshing its way back. He doubled over with laughter.

"Dude! Oh my God! You were there?"

He gave me a fist bump.

"I hardly remember that night," he said. "Pics or it didn't happen, am I right?"

"Dude! My bros had a bachelor party going on as well. It paled in comparison to what you guys had going on. Dude! I still tell people about that night!"

"Dude, you know they ended up not getting married."

"Dude, no way!"

"Yeah. The bitch found out and got all upset. I mean, what the shit? They were not even married yet. Women, man. I tell ya, that's why I stay single."

"What about that girl you had? The one with the art gallery."

Damn. I fucked up. Hunter was not with Evangelina at that time. But he was so far gone he didn't catch my blunder.

"Aw dude, she took off. I was only using her anyhow. She was one of those libtard Sander's whores. Like America would ever have a socialist for President. Though that dumb bitch would be the kind to vote for one."

"Come Tuesday, we take our country back!"

"Damn straight, bro!"

He gave me another fist bump.

"Stick around. We'll do some shots."

As soon as Hunter entered the restroom, I made for the door. Thick fog had rolled in outside. Behind the yellow lattice fence where Harleigh would lock her bike up to sat the bamboo plant she once cared for. Long dead from neglect, its stalk resembled a dirty and weathered human bone. The sight sent an unsettled chill down my spine.

As I made my way to the apartment, wet dew gathered in my beard. At Main, I took a left. I crossed Jefferson. That much I remember.

CHAPTER 50

November 8, 2016

When I came to, I knew I lay in a hospital bed though I couldn't understand why. My vision was blurry, and my head hurt. At some point, a policeman came in to talk to me. I had no ID on me, yet he was aware of my expired driver's license. He asked an array of questions I struggled to provide answers for.

"Do you remember where you were last night?"

"Bourbon Street."

"And where were you headed?"

"My apartment."

"And where's that again?"

"Behind the gas station on Pellerin."

"You work?"

"At the plant."

"What plant?"

"The bamboo behind the yellow lattice fence."

He told me Detective Landry would be by later. Shit. I still hadn't completed the 2016 bookwork. He would fire me this time for sure. I stabbed at some goulash on my plate then laid my head back down to rest. A doctor with a salt and pepper goatee entered the room. The name embroidered on his coat read Rabalais. Doctor Rabalais informed me I suffered a concussion, plus fourteen stitches to the side of the head. I would be released shortly.

After he left the room, I went look for a vending machine. The fact I had no money on me not a deterrent. Inside a waiting area, I passed a table covered with various newspapers. A bold black headline on one caught my attention.

BODY OF MISSING WOMAN LOCATED

Underneath the headline was a picture of Harleigh I took with Theresa's phone at Festival Acadien in 2010.

Authorities located the body of a missing Lafayette woman off Interstate 10 near exit 127 in Iberville Parish. Harleigh Hebert, the former Sheryl Domingue, had been missing since April 2015.

I tore the room apart. A middle linebacker posing as a security guard rushed in and took me down. He dragged me back to my room and strapped me to the bed. An elderly gray-haired nurse with serene eyes claimed I threatened to slit her throat. I don't recall saying that, but I was in no position to dispute her version of events.

Detective Landry appeared dressed in street clothes and a baseball cap. He pulled a chair up beside the bed and told me about a search warrant executed Saturday on a storage facility in Welsh. The process of inventorying the stolen merchandise inside routine until they discovered a bike registered to a missing person. The owner of the facility, who faced a mere misdemeanor charge, about blacked out when confronted with an additional charge of murder one. Cory Rollins, a married thirty-eight-year-old registered nurse from Lacassine, agreed to plead guilty to second degree murder before he led authorities to Harleigh's body.

On the morning of April eleventh, 2015, Rollins sat in a car at the corner of Johnston and St. Mary when Harleigh happened by. They exchanged words. I could about imagine what Harleigh told him. She despised getting cat called while she rode her bike. When he caught up to her, she flipped him off. He drew his gun and fired one shot. Just to scare her, he claimed. The bullet ripped through Harleigh's neck. Landry said she was dead before she hit the ground.

Rollins placed both Harleigh and her bike into the trunk of his car and stopped at The Supercenter for a suitcase before hitting I-10 east. For whatever reason, he hung on to the bike. The rains from that morning washed away all evidence from the scene of the murder. I was not familiar with Rollins' name nor his face. Detective Landry drove to Winfield yesterday to give Harleigh's mom the news. She did not take it well.

Detective Landry took out his phone. He showed me a grainy black and white video of a white brick building with four floor to ceiling windows near the corner of Main and Jefferson. I emerged through the fog walking left to right across the screen. As I reached the fourth window, two individuals come up from behind and take me out with one blow to the head. Another person appeared and rifled through my pockets. The three run off with my debit card, driver's license, phone, and keys. I laid there motionless for the next seventeen minutes, which Landry mercifully fast forwarded through, before a police car happened by.

Landry replayed the video. He hit pause when the third person came into view and pointed out a speck, which turned out to be a gold tooth, emanating from the person's mouth. Police identified two brothers, one with a gold tooth, the other in possession of a laptop, at The Discount Mart on the thruway as suspects. The other person, a cousin out on parole, denied any involvement. When Landry called my cell phone, it rang inside the cousin's pocket. Police arrested all three, putting an end to the string of muggings that occurred over the last eight months in the downtown area.

Landry unstrapped me from the bed and allowed me to take a piss. I looked at myself in the bathroom mirror. My entire head was black and blue. A bandage covered the stitches above my right ear. When I finished, Landry continued to sit with me. He told me the last activity on Harleigh's debit card occurred the day prior to her going missing. Rollins admitted to smashing her cell phone and throwing it and the murder weapon into the Atchafalaya Basin. They found her fully clothed. Her mom requested all her piercings.

"Ruston," Landry said, "the first time we talked to you, one of your managers, Mr. John Breaux, told us he wouldn't have been all that surprised if what the mother from the New Iberia Park claimed was true."

He folded one leg over the other.

"Jake didn't care for you from the get-go."

I made a face.

"Detective Wilson," Landry clarified.

Someone walked into the room. They looked at us with confusion then walked out.

"Your name was on a list of regulars given to us by the proprietor of The Bistro, Miss Karen Migues. After we next spoke to you, Miss Theresa Elias, Harleigh's roommate, claimed you and Miss Hebert were in a relationship."

Another person stepped into the room. They did a quick look around and left.

"Once we became aware that Miss Elias could not reach you on the morning in question, we obtained footage from the ATM across from your apartment. It matched the statement you ultimately gave us."

Landry took a deep breath.

"After that, we received a call from Mr. Brent Robicheaux, who led us to believe that maybe you had an accomplice. A search of your apartment turned up empty. We happened to be out there the following morning when we saw you walking down Buchanan. Jake told me to tell you we found blood."

The two individuals who came into the room earlier returned.

"Is there a problem?" Detective Landry asked.

"Why is this patient no longer restrained?"

Landry produced his badge.

"Because I'm here."

Both apologized and walked out.

"We were then contacted by one of your co-workers, Mrs. Bridgett Laviolette. She claimed your work computer had been used to conduct internet searches on how to properly dispose of a body. That IT guy was not happy to see us. The next day, Miss Elias called back to say you'd just left her place, and she'd recorded your conversation. All we heard was the two of you discussing what to do with Miss Hebert's belongings."

Detective Landry rose from his chair. He walked over to the window and pushed open the blinds.

"We continued to get calls about you. Cody McNeese. Herman Naquin, who I know personally. Mrs. Nancy Robicheaux. Even my stepbrother. Twice. That's how I learned of the scuffle you two had."

Landry took off his cap and brushed back his hair.

"The purpose of our last meeting had been to inform you of our suspicions that Harleigh was no longer alive. Since you were in obvious denial, I chose not to destroy the illusion you were under."

He stood next to the bed.

"I'll see to it you get your belongings back. Is there anything I can do for you in the meanwhile?" he asked.

I looked away from him.

"Just get me out of here."

A nurse gave me a prescription to fill along with a plastic bag containing my clothes. Landry's phone rang. He said he'd return later to give me a ride back to my apartment. As soon as I dressed though, I made a break for it. Outside, I hooded my eyes from the bright sunlight as I attempted to get a bearing on where I was. A man doing landscape work in the shadow of a skywalk saw me struggling.

"Need some help buddy?"

When I went to answer, I felt my dry lips crack and split. The man wiped sweat from his forehead.

"What's that?" he said.

"Where's the park?"

"Girard Park?"

He pointed.

"Take a left at that corner."

I took a left at that corner and trudged through the park. I passed the enclosed playground filled with kids while parents sat close by preoccupied with their cell phones. How many of us reminisce about these carefree childlike days of youth and wished to go back? But then who would buy the houses? Who would soak up the oil? Who would stoke the economy? And whose remains would be found stuffed into a suitcase and left to rot underneath the third longest bridge in the country?

At the intersection of University and Johnston, I got lightheaded. I considered letting go and letting gravity take me but that wasn't one of the options on the pedestrian crosswalk button. I turned left at The Bistro, passed behind the Buford Monument, and went right on Jefferson. Near the old Federal Courthouse Building, Danny hollered my name. He gave a friendly wave.

Downtown was busy with many parking spots marked off for those coming to vote in today's election. Along the side of the white brick building at the corner of Main and Jefferson was a stain on the sidewalk. That stain was to be the mark I left on the world. I looked up at big brother mounted to the building and thought about how everyone wanted something. Evangelina wanted her own gallery. Harleigh wanted a new start. Robicheaux wanted luxury lofts. Darby wanted a divorce. Nancy wanted a coffee shop. Jaime wanted to draw. I once wanted to be a writer. Now, all I wanted was to have bled out at this very spot.

I dug around in the dirt outside of the apartment for the extra set of keys I buried there years ago. After I located them, I went upstairs and found the door to the apartment unlocked. I listened for a moment, then drew a breath and slowly pushed it open. Everything appeared normal, except for a piece of paper on the floor, and the laptop was gone. In the bathroom, a soggy cigarette butt floated about in the toilet along with my debit card and expired driver's license. I found my keys under the bed. The paper near the door turned out to be an eviction notice signed by Brent Robicheaux. I'd been given thirty days.

I fished my cards out of the toilet and ran a bath. Laying back in the tub, I pictured the ones who'd mugged me over at the ATM with my pin number slash address conveniently displayed out front, though the disappointment felt when they accessed the apartment with my keys must had been astounding. Robicheaux's son would have found the downstairs gate unlocked. Did he attempt to reach me by phone, or had he just slid the eviction notice under the door before locking the gate on his way out? That was one possible scenario.

I peeled the bandage from my head. The stitches underneath reminded me of laces on a tiny football. I got dressed and went into the kitchen. The rent money I'd been socking away over the last fourteen months inside a thirty-two-ounce bag of New Orleans blend coffee came out to over four thousand dollars. That money meant I had time.

I grabbed a beer and took a seat before the typewriter. My pin long ago pulled yet there I sat. Had my grenade been a dud or was it biding its time. Nothing ever goes as it should. My first night here now so distant. The final one stamped December fifth. What remained? I still owed Robicheaux a novel, though what would I write about? As I placed my fingers on the keys, it was decided.

I would write about it all.